She was a vision. His great-great-grandmother had been a beauty in her day, but nothing to compare with Ginny Thornton. The first thing he noticed was the way the gown accented the whiteness of her shoulders and neck. The second was that she moved as if she had been dressing in corsets and ballgowns all of her life.

"You look lovely," he said and held out his hand to her.

She laid hers delicately on top of his. She was wearing soft kid gloves that reached almost to her shoulders. There was something very erotic about those gloves. Perhaps it was the way they exposed only an inch of skin between the top of the glove and the wide shoulder straps of her gown. Perhaps it was the thought that came to him unexpectedly of what it might be like to peel the glove slowly down the length of her arm.

"I think our guests have arrived," she said. "Shall we greet them?"

He offered his arm, felt her hesitation before she placed her hand in the crook of his elbow, and together they walked the length of the room to greet their first guests.

Praise for *Coming Home*

"Five stars."

—*Heartland Critiques*

"Ms. Hix provides us with an entertaining tale with ghosts, lost loves, found loves, young love, and an enjoyable plot line."

—*Rendezvous*

THEN AND NOW
COMING HOME
CEDAR CREEK
RASPBERRY ISLAND

THEN
and
Now

Willa Hix

JOVE BOOKS, NEW YORK

TIME PASSAGES is a registered trademark of Penguin Putnam Inc.

THEN AND NOW

A Jove Book / published by arrangement with
the author

PRINTING HISTORY
Jove edition / April 2000

The Penguin Putnam Inc. World Wide Web site address is
http://www.penguinputnam.com

ISBN: 0-515-12836-8

A JOVE BOOK®
Jove Books are published by The Berkley Publishing Group,
a division of Penguin Putnam Inc.,
375 Hudson Street, New York, New York 10014.
JOVE and the "J" design
are trademarks belonging to Penguin Putnam Inc.

PRINTED IN THE UNITED STATES OF AMERICA

10 9 8 7 6 5 4 3 2 1

To Larry
The best yet for the best ever

"In the middle of the road of my life
I awoke in a dark wood
Where the true way was wholly lost."
—Dante Alighieri

Prologue

"FIFTY DOLLARS," THE pawnbroker growled as he squinted through his loupe to examine the set of the ruby in one of a pair of earrings.

Ginny Thornton's breath caught. *Only fifty?* She had thought they would bring more. "The stones are quite large," she said softly.

"Fifty," the man repeated as he laid the jewels back on the counter and pushed them toward her as if they were of no more interest to him.

Ginny dug to the bottom of her purse and presented her last offering. She did not miss the widening of his eyes as she placed a matching choker and bracelet on the counter next to the earrings. The pawnbroker straightened, and Ginny took a moment's pleasure in having caught him off guard. "One thousand, or I shall take the entire set to someone else," she bluffed, willing to settle for five hundred.

"Seven fifty," the man muttered as he caressed the

perfect alignment of the rubies and diamonds in the bracelet.

Ginny held out her hand for the money, but the pawn-broker mistook her gesture and thought that she was going to withdraw the jewels. His hand locked on her wrist. "One thousand," he agreed, "and you redeem them in thirty days, or I sell them."

Ginny almost laughed. The man might as well have asked her to bring him the repayment the following day—a month would not be long enough. She nodded, knowing she would never see the set again. At least by coming to the city, she had lessened the chance that the distinctive jewels would be spotted by one of her friends, or worse, purchased and worn by someone she knew.

How had she come to this moment? How was it possible that in order to save face, she found it necessary to pawn the very jewels that Thomas had taken such pleasure in giving her? How was it possible that she, the daughter of one of the wealthiest men in the State of New York, found herself on this grimy side street on a winter's afternoon when she should have been at home in the beautiful mansion left to her by her parents?

The pawnbroker scooped up the jewels and turned to open a large, battered safe. "I might be interested in additional pieces," he commented as he worked the combination and swung open the heavy lead door. "What else have you got?" He counted out ten hundred-dollar bills and handed them to her.

"I won't be back except to reclaim my property," she told him firmly. There would be no repeat of this travesty, she told herself. She would speak to Thomas and make him tell her what was wrong—why bills had gone unpaid for months and why he had failed to tell her. "I shall not be back," she repeated, more to herself than to the pawnbroker.

He smiled for the first time since she had entered the cramped, shadowy shop. In that smile she saw that he knew exactly what would happen. If he saw her again, it would not be to reclaim the rubies. It would be to sell him something else. "I'll need a receipt," she said through clenched teeth, meeting his gaze steadily.

He wrote out the document and pushed it across the counter.

"Good day," she said politely as she turned.

"I wish you well, ma'am," he said softly, and she heard the pity in his tone.

Ginny pulled her bonnet lower on her forehead, taking no chance that she might accidentally meet someone she knew on the street. She felt like a common criminal, skulking about, glancing nervously over her shoulder, and pawning jewelry in a pathetic attempt to raise cash to pay bills that should never have been in question.

Before making the trip into the city, she'd sorted through the ropes of pearls, the garnet pendant, the diamond and sapphire earrings, trying to decide. Each piece was a declaration of her husband's love. In those early years of their marriage, each piece had represented a time in her life when her days had been filled with laughter and celebration and dreams. In those years she had dismissed her father's concerns about Thomas's extravagances as simply being overprotective of his only child. She and Thomas were young and rich and had their entire lives ahead of them. Why shouldn't Thomas enjoy that?

More recently, she had begun to appreciate her father's concerns and to suspect that the baubles were given out of guilt—for what, she did not know. She feared it might be another woman. How many times had she told Thomas that she didn't need such expensive baubles? How many times had he replied that he needed to give them to her, that they were his indulgence, not hers?

The door of the shop closed behind her, and, blinded by tears, Ginny almost stumbled into a couple on the sidewalk. *What had she done? What choice had there been?* Tomorrow guests would begin arriving for the

annual fortnight of parties and entertainments leading up
to the celebration of the New Year. Those guests would
expect to be fed and pampered as they had always been
when visiting the estate. The holiday fortnight was a
tradition her parents had begun when the house was first
completed. It was one she had continued when the estate
had passed to her, and to Thomas, of course.

She gathered her skirts and hurried back to the train
station. Thomas would be expecting her. He would want
to see the gown for their annual New Year's Eve ball
she had told him she would be shopping for in the city
today. She would tell him it was being altered. She
would not tell him that she had gone to the city to raise
the money they needed to pay for the ball because that
morning the cook had reported with regret that none of
the merchants in town would extend them any more
credit.

It was dusk when the carriage pulled under the portico
and Ginny stepped out. She dismissed the driver, then
stood for a long moment in the softly falling snow and
considered the house. Its limestone central tower soared
to four stories, the leaded and stained-glass windows lit
from within. Nestled in between the tower and the east
wing of the house was the glass-roofed winter garden,
its palms and ferns a welcome respite on a snowy winter
evening.

She rarely saw the house from this vantage point,
coming and going as she did by the back entrance that
led from the main house through the gardens to the conservatory or out to the yard next to the stables. But, for
one brief moment as she stood there on the drive looking
at the house, it was as if she had stepped back in time.
For the moment she was a girl again, coming home from
some party or visit to share the details of her day with
her parents. A staff of seventy served the house, and the
stables could house twenty carriages and three dozen
horses. Yet there was a sense of welcome about the
place. Her father had designed it that way.

In her youth there had been so many evenings like this, when she had come home from shopping or visiting with friends, knowing that her parents were eagerly waiting to hear all about her day. When she had married, Thomas did not like her going off on her own, even to meet with friends. She did everything with him, but he did not always share everything with her, especially of late.

A light flickered on in the fourth-floor sewing room. Addy MacDougall, the estate's laundress and seamstress, must be working late. Ginny knew every room, every nook and cranny of the 150-room mansion that was spread over two acres of floor space on four floors. It featured seventeen bedroom suites, twenty-eight bathrooms, forty fireplaces, three kitchens, a complete gymnasium, and a ballroom. It had taken a virtual army of architects, engineers, and craftsmen over a decade to construct the place. It had all the modern conveniences—central heating and plumbing, and even an elevator. The encompassing forty acres of grounds ran the gamut from woodlands to marshes to formal gardens that created a parklike atmosphere surrounding the house. In addition to all that, there was a working dairy farm and winery, and her beloved formal gardens and conservatory. Her father had seen to every detail, for this was the house where he would bring his bride, raise his family, coddle his grandchildren.

Ginny felt the sting of tears of regret. She had been the only child and she had been unable to provide her parents with a grandchild before their untimely death in a train accident on a trip to visit the western frontier. Yet, in spite of her grief over the tragic loss of her parents and the fact that she had been unable to conceive, she took comfort in coming back to this house—her home. Whatever had happened, she would always have Malmaison.

On her way from the pawnbroker's to the train station,

she had passed a sign that read, Prepare Now for the Dawning of the New Century. Ginny didn't really care about the new century. She only hoped that 1900 would be a better year than 1899 had been.

Chapter 1

"Samuel, please get your nose out of that book and pay attention." Emily Sutter's tone was a clear reprimand, and Sam understood that she was obviously having serious doubts about the wisdom of leaving him in charge of the estate while she was gone. In fact, he shared those doubts. What did he know about throwing a major party? Yet Emily Sutter needed reassurance, not more worries.

"Mom, I'm running nine international botanical projects. I'm pretty sure I can handle a simple party."

Emily sighed. "It is so much more than a 'simple party,' and you know it. We need this event to go particularly well, Sam. I know that your only interest in the estate is as a laboratory for your scientific research, but there is more to Malmaison than that." She took the book from his hand and replaced it with a sheaf of notes. "Now then, *Dr.* Sutter, try to concentrate on *these* research notes. Your plants will just have to wait, I'm afraid."

"Mom, I promise that it'll all work out, but I do have deadlines of my own to meet as well. The article on the Malmaison project is due by the end of next month, and we have nothing to report to date. I appreciate your devotion to the estate and all its history, but please try to understand that my work is in many ways its future. If I'm successful in my research on this particular project—"

"You will no doubt win yet another award and use the prize money to commence yet another research study," Emily said. "Samuel, I fully appreciate that you are among the nation's leading biomedical research scientists. I further appreciate that the gardens and botanical collections your great-great-grandfather launched here have formed the basis for much of your success. All I ask is that for the next couple of days you try to focus on the fact that by maintaining the historical past of the estate, your father and I make it possible for you to concentrate on the future."

Sam grinned. It was a discussion they had had many times over the years. It usually ended with his mother throwing her arms around him with an exasperated sigh and wondering aloud how someone so devoted to the history and romance of the estate could possibly have spawned a son who looked only to the future.

"In spite of your undisputed brilliance and talent for organization, my darling, the question still remains: Are you capable of making sure this year's gala is an unqualified success?"

Sam picked his book up again and quickly turned pages until he found the data he wanted. He began scribbling notes on the papers that his mother had handed him. "I thought you hired a new curator to take charge."

"I did, but she hasn't arrived yet and she should have been here hours ago. I'm beginning to be seriously concerned. If she isn't here within the hour, I'm going to have no choice but to cancel the trip your father has planned for us."

This got Sam's instant attention. "You can't," he protested. "Mom, you've been longing for this trip for years. Now it's finally going to happen, and you would chuck it all just to oversee a—"

"Samuel, if you refer to this event as a 'simple little party' once more, I will have no choice but to box your ears."

Sam laughed and held up his hands as if protecting himself from the diminutive woman. "All right, relax, Mom. I heard every word—honest." He repeated her instructions without the benefit of notes. "The string quartet in the winter garden at eight, followed by dinner at nine, with dancing to commence no later than ten-thirty. At eleven-fifty-three we pop the cork on the champagne. At eleven-fifty-five, I make the toast. At midnight we watch the fireworks from the balcony. Have I missed anything?" He closed the book in his hand and crossed the room, climbing the library's spiral staircase to the gallery for another volume he needed. "After that, it's more dancing and making merry, and with any luck at all, I'll be home in bed by dawn, right?"

Emily Sutter sighed audibly. "You are the most exasperating child," she announced.

"I'm thirty-two, Mother," he reminded her with his customary logic. "You're always worried that something will go wrong. Yet in the twenty years since you first discovered that my great-great-grandparents held these New Year's Eve shindigs and decided to recreate them, everything has always gone off without a hitch. I think worrying over the details is part of your pleasure."

"This particular gala is extraordinarily important, Sam. You know that. It is one hundred years of history all rolled up in the dawning of not only a new century but also a new millennium. What will people think about Malmaison in another hundred years?"

"We really don't need to concern ourselves with that,"

Sam replied. "After all, we will all be long gone." He placed his finger to mark a page in the dusty old book and came back down the metal stairs. "Perhaps the estate itself will have been subdivided into condominiums by then."

"Don't even joke about that." Emily gasped. She consulted pages of lists for the tenth time. "You're right. I can't disappoint your father by calling off the trip. He's so proud of himself for arranging everything." She added some additional items to her list. "You'll have to watch for the new curator. I just hope she's as good in person as she is on paper. Remember, she must try on her costume as soon as possible after she arrives in case it needs altering. Oh, and Spooner's Fish Market is supposed to deliver the shrimp this afternoon. I have no idea what we will do if the weather turns out to be as terrible as they are predicting. How will people get here?"

Sam looked at his mother over the tops of his reading glasses. He closed his book and set it aside. It didn't matter what he thought of the New Year's Eve gala. The idea that it might be anything less than an unqualified success was upsetting to his mother. In bygone days, former generations of Sutters had given the ball to celebrate the coming of a new year, and the event had involved a week of parties and festivities. Sam's parents had opened the property to the public, allowing hordes of tourists and schoolchildren to traipse through the house and grounds and to tour the working dairy farm and winery that were part of the vast estate. The New Year's Eve ball had been used as an occasion to thank those donors and volunteers who made it possible to keep the place open and running year round. It also was an event designed to remind them that operating a museum of this size and complexity required a qualified staff and lots of money.

This year's event was especially important. It was not only to be the celebration of the millennium; it was also a celebration of the 150th birthday of the completion of the estate. Following this year's ball, the house would be closed for six months of much-needed renovation and redecoration. Emily had been working on the plans for an entire year.

"Perhaps your father and I should postpone our trip at least until the new curator arrives and we see if she's truly up to the job," she said as she compared her lists to a duplicate in the notebook in front of her.

"We'll do no such thing," announced Justin Sutter as he entered the room. "You've looked forward to this trip for years. I've cleared my calendar, and we are going." He put his arms around her and kissed her forehead. "Look, honey, I know it's not the greatest thing to have to leave today instead of after the ball, but Sam will handle everything, won't you, son?"

"You have my word. Besides, in just a few hours you'll be on a plane somewhere over the Atlantic, and by the time you find out how things went, you won't care anymore."

"I just wish this snowstorm would hold off," Emily fussed, gazing out the window at the gray wintry sky. "Weatherpeople are wrong on a consistent basis. Why on earth do they have to be right today of all days?"

"Well, that's life. The storm is coming, and all indications are that we should leave today or we won't get out at all," Justin replied. "Besides, you'll be far too busy paying attention to me to worry about how things are going here." He kissed her neck and ran his hands over her arms.

Sam grinned. After forty years of marriage and five children, his parents were still like a couple of lovestruck teenagers. For years Emily had teased Justin Sutter about how she was going to have a gay old time traveling around the world on his money once he was dead and gone, since he never seemed to be able to get away from business long enough to take a real vacation. The day his father presented her with the tickets for the trip, Sam had thought she might actually faint from the shock of it.

"You are incorrigible," Emily replied, breaking away from her husband and touching her neck where he had kissed her, but she was blushing and laughing and only pretending to be annoyed.

Sam wondered if there had ever been two people more devoted to each other than Emily and Justin Sutter. More often than not it was the legend of their enduring marriage that was of interest to journalists and the tourists who regularly tramped through the estate. There were no individual portraits of them in the mansion. They were always portrayed together. From the day they married, Justin Sutter had declared that he would never have another photograph taken or portrait painted unless she was pictured at his side. Their love story was the stuff of romance novels and three-handkerchief chick flicks, Sam thought. It was also the reason that Sam himself had little interest in marrying. Logic told him that the kind of love his parents shared was rare indeed. He was a man set in his ways, and it would take a special woman to adapt to those ways. From what he had seen of modern-day women, they were not exactly into adapting to the ways of a man.

"Leave me your lists, Mom. I promise to check off each item." He stood at attention and raised his hand in a solemn pledge.

"I know you can make checkmarks," she said. "The question is, will you see to the work?"

"I'll have the new curator," he reminded her. "She can handle the work while I make the checkmarks."

A horn sounded.

"There's our cab for the airport, Emily," Justin said.

Emily went into immediate action, moving quickly out of the library to the grand hallway where the luggage stood stacked next to the door. "Oh, dear, so soon. I'm not sure I have everything I need."

"Then we can buy whatever you need," Justin replied.

"Give the lists to Sam and let's go. It's starting to snow," he added as he opened the front door and began moving luggage to the cab.

Emily glanced nervously at the sky and hesitated.

"Go," Sam prodded and took her arm. "You've waited forty years for Dad to leave the business long enough for a trip like this. Are you going to miss it now?"

Sam helped his mother with her coat while his father orchestrated the loading of the luggage into the cab. Emily gave one longing look back at the huge house as she walked out the door. "It's going to be a lovely party," she said as she stood on tiptoe to kiss Sam's cheek. "Try to enjoy yourself. Perhaps you'll meet someone," she added as if the thought had just occurred to her.

It was her standard farewell. Her one wish was to see her only unmarried child find the love of his life and settle into a marriage. In Emily's view, only a good marriage would bring him the true happiness he deserved. Of course, it would also bring her the additional grandchildren she wanted, but that was another matter.

"You've invited four hundred people, Mom," Sam teased. "I expect to meet more people than I've seen in the last year." He held the door while his parents climbed into the backseat of the cab. It occurred to him that anyone else of their wealth and station would most likely be headed for the airport in a limousine with a private chauffeur, but that had never been his father's way. The only obvious trapping of his vast wealth was the estate, and technically that belonged to Sam. His parents had established a comfortable apartment in the east wing of the house for those times when they needed to be in residence, but their main home was a sprawling contemporary located in the woods near the dairy farm.

"You know what I mean," his mother replied. "Focusing on a young woman instead of those plants of yours would be a nice change. Someone you might actually see more than twice." She placed her hand on his. "At least promise me you'll dance one dance—at midnight to see in the New Year, the new millennium."

Sam closed the door of the cab. "I promise. Now go, have a wonderful trip, and by the time you come home, it will be spring, the flowers will be in bloom, and Malmaison will be in the throes of renovation."

He watched until the cab was out of sight, following the long drive that curved for nearly a mile through the forests that surrounded the vast estate. Satisfied that his parents were indeed safely on their way, he headed back to the entrance to the grand old house.

Malmaison had been in his family for a hundred years. Sam's great-great-grandfather had acquired the place in a business deal, and it was the only home Sam or his father had ever known. Although the estate belonged to Sam, left to him by his grandfather, it was his parents who had seen to its preservation over the years. He didn't necessarily agree that it was a good idea to foster people's romantic views of the past by opening the estate up to the public. On the other hand, he could not deny that by doing so his parents had been able to preserve not only the history of the estate, but also the precious plant life that was the inheritance he prized above anything else.

Like his great-great-grandfather, Sam was focused on the future, not the past. He supposed it was of interest to people to see how the rich had lived at the turn of the last century, but he was far more interested in what he might discover that would help people live healthier and longer lives in the new millennium. His mother had been right when she reminded him that his great-great-grandfather had left him a priceless legacy by having the forethought to install native and exotic plants throughout the grounds.

The preeminent feature of the estate—at least in Sam's view—was the huge glass-enclosed conservatory set some distance from the house at the back edge of the formal gardens. From the outside, the structure, which could hardly be described as simply a greenhouse, looked like a smaller glass-walled version of the main house. Inside it was a series of large rooms, each climate-controlled for the propagation of various plant species. These days it was Sam's laboratory, his haven for focusing all of his attention on his work. When he wasn't conducting lectures at the nearby university or drafting an article for some scientific journal, he could be found in the conservatory. There he directed the work of his small staff of assistants or more likely did the work himself of pampering each seedling, recording the data, and generally worrying over the progress of each experiment. He had elected to live in the gardener's cottage because of its proximity to the conservatory, one that permitted him to get up in the middle of the night to make some adjustment that had come to him as he slept.

Sam smiled as he walked under the stone portico of the main house where guests in the previous century would have arrived by carriage and entered the house. Tomorrow the carriages of choice would more likely be luxury sedans, sports cars, or sport utility vehicles, and unless this new curator showed up soon, he was going to have to play host. It was not a role he enjoyed. Also, if the curator didn't show, he was going to have to spend hours helping Freddie Fincastle—his mother's events coordinator—and the others, to make certain all was in readiness for the big event. It meant he would have to take time away from his experiments, and they were all at a critical stage. The new curator was an essential player in this little drama. The least she could do was call.

In the library, he picked up his mother's notes. She had made lists for every contingency—the food, the entertainment, the progression of events for the evening, and even the selection of flowers for each centerpiece and arrangement. There were phone numbers with contact names for each of the vendors. There were detailed instructions about what the new curator would need to be told once she arrived and what her immediate duties would be. As far as Sam was concerned, her most immediate duty would be to relieve him of the sheaf of lists and let him get back to his research.

Sam laid the notes aside and turned his attention back to the book he had taken from the shelf earlier. He opened it to the marked page and sat down to study the full-color print of the vibrant red carnation from which the estate took its name. Malmaison. Sam studied the notes his great-great-grandfather had scribbled in the margin of the book, hardly noticing the unusual vibrancy of the color or the colossal size of the blossom. His interest lay in the potential of the plant to provide a key ingredient for a formula he was researching.

Hastily he added notes, then went in search of additional volumes that might provide more in-depth information. Absentmindedly, he buried the pages of notes left by his mother under papers of his own, and within an hour he had forgotten all about checking to be sure things were progressing for the grand ball.

It was already late afternoon when Freddie Fincastle knocked softly at the library door. "Mr. Sutter, I'm sorry to disturb you but I'm going to go ahead and send the staff home unless you have something else you need for them to complete today. We're right on schedule, and the roads are getting worse with the snow and all. Of course, with events of this magnitude, there are always a lot of things that must be left to the last possible minute."

Sam blinked and removed his glasses. Where had the time gone? He'd been vaguely aware of people scurrying around in the grand old house, but his concentration on his work had been total. He hadn't even gotten around to eating.

"I took the liberty of preparing a tray for you," Freddie continued as he entered the room and set down a tray loaded with turkey sandwiches, fresh fruit, and a bottle of wine.

"Thanks, Freddie." Sam considered the deference with which the man treated him. His mother had told him more than once that the staff thought of him as aloof. She understood that it was more because he was caught up in his work than that he was being deliberately abrupt or distant, but it explained Freddie's formality. Sam rummaged through the piles of papers on the desk until he unearthed the lists his mother had left. "Why don't you join me in a glass of wine and take a look at these? I promised Mom I would make sure everything was checked off." He smiled apologetically.

Freddie accepted the lists and the chair near the fire-place that Sam indicated. Sam uncorked the wine and poured it, wondering how he had missed someone coming in and lighting the fire. "Has the new curator shown up yet?"

"There's no sign of her. The storm has gotten pretty fierce, so she's probably been delayed. Perhaps she's called and left a message. I believe your mother gave her your number." He handed the lists back to Sam. "We've handled everything on there that was to be done today, Mr. Sutter."

"Call me Sam, and thanks. When Mom calls later, I can reassure her with a clear conscience. As for our curator, I must have left my cell phone at the cottage, but you're probably right. I'll check it when I get back there later." He smiled and raised his glass in a toast. "To the millennium."

Freddie raised his own glass. "I wondered if it would be all right with you if I stayed the night. With this storm I don't want to take the chance that I might not be able to get back here first thing tomorrow. As I mentioned, there are a lot of last-minute details that will need my attention. The good news is that the storm is expected to end on schedule later tonight. By morning, the roads should be cleared, and we can get everything delivered on time."

"Of course. Stay." Sam frowned. "There must be a

couple of rooms made up—the one for the new curator.
Take that one. I'll give her one of the other rooms for
tonight."

"Assuming she makes it," Freddie reminded him.

Sam walked to the floor-to-ceiling windows and
looked out. It was just twilight, and he could see that it
had been snowing steadily for several hours. "Good
point. Well, if you're going to stay here, I'm going out
to the conservatory to do some work and then head
home for the night. If you need me, just call."

"I'm sure everything will come off without a hitch,"
Freddie said, as if trying hard to reassure him. "After
all, we've never had to call off one of Malmaison's galas
yet," he added.

"Freddie, my man, if you pull this one off, fine. If
not, will it matter a week from now?"

Freddie looked deeply distressed. "Oh, heavens, yes.
The guests are major contributors, and your mother is
counting on this event to get them to make substantial
donations to the renovation fund. Oh, it would be just
disastrous if we had to cancel the gala—especially this
year."

"I'm sorry. Of course, you're right. You probably understand that I don't look at these things the way my
mother does. I'm really glad that you're here to look
after her interests."

Freddie smiled and stood. "Well, I'll leave you to get
back to your work. There are a few more things I want
to check on in the kitchen. I'll see you tomorrow, Sam."

"Thanks for the supper."

Freddie grinned. "Your mother asked me to check on
you. She said that you sometimes forget to eat."

"Mom worries way too much. Thanks again."

After Freddie left, Sam sat by the fire devouring the
supper and reviewing the notes he had made during the
course of the afternoon. It seemed to him that it might
be possible to recreate the unique properties of the malmaison carnation through a process of carefully grafting

more modern-day plants. It wouldn't be the real thing, but the hybrid just might work. He tossed back another glass of wine and banked the fire. Then he gathered his notes and headed for the conservatory.

Chapter 2

ALTHOUGH GINNY WAS late returning to the house, she needn't have worried. Thomas seemed barely aware that she had been gone. He did not ask to see the gown she was supposed to have gone to purchase. He kissed her cheek absently when she rushed into the library filled with stories she had made up on the trip home. She smelled the brandy on his breath and felt disappointment and a bit of irritation. Thomas was drinking too often and too early in the day for her comfort. They had argued about it, and she had decided that perhaps it would run its course, but lately she wasn't so certain. His drinking along with his moody silences had begun to frighten her.

As Ginny bustled around the library lighting the lamps, she chattered on about the preparations for the ball, hoping perhaps to stir him from the throes of the melancholy that seemed his constant companion of late. Immediately upon her return she had given the head of household, Mr. Holt, part of the cash and told him he was to make arrangements at once to see that the tradesmen were paid what they were owed and that they delivered what was needed for the gala. She was thankful to have someone like Lucas Holt in her employ, for his discretion and loyalty were absolute, and she knew that she could trust him implicitly.

"Thomas, let's take a walk out to the conservatory before dinner. The fresh air might do us both some good." Thomas loved flowers, and she thought walking among the blossoming plants in the large conservatory might cheer him. "The carnations are at their peak," she added, then felt immediately guilt-ridden.

Thomas had given her the rubies she had pawned earlier in celebration of the blooming of the beautiful malmaison carnations on their first anniversary. It had been a painful year for her, the year her parents had died, and he had wanted to do something very special to mark their anniversary. As the only heir, the estate became hers, and Thomas had tried to console her with fantasies of the lively family life they would have in the mansion, their children bounding over the grounds. They were making a new start, he had promised her, and he wanted to mark the occasion by doing something exceptional.

He had led her to the conservatory on just such a gray wintry evening as this, insisting that she wear a loose blindfold until he removed it. She could still recall the humidity and the scent of the fragrant flowers. When Thomas had removed the blindfold, she had gasped with delight, and tears had glistened on her eyelids as she slowly spun around, taking in the beauty of it all. They were standing in the midst of a hundred blooming plants lit by dozens of candles. It was as if they had left earth and landed in some fairyland.

Thomas had fastened the ruby choker around her neck, the bracelet across her wrist, and the earrings in her lobes. Each piece had been presented with passionate kisses and promises of the children they would have, the joys they would celebrate, and the happiness they would share for decades to come. "Malmaison is still your home, my darling," he had reminded her. "It will always be yours."

"Come with me," she prodded now in the oppressively dim and silent library.

"I think not," Thomas replied. "You go ahead."

"Will you be at dinner?" she asked and could not mask the weariness in her tone. She was so tired of trying to guess his mood, trying to fathom what could be behind it.

"Perhaps. I have a great deal of work to do, my dear. I will join you when I can. You go along," he urged again and smiled at her.

Ginny started toward the door and paused. She turned and saw Thomas sitting where she had left him, his brandy in one hand, his eyes focused on nothing. There was none of the usual clutter on the desk before him, only a single leather folder.

She felt such a premonition of something terrible about to happen that she could not keep still. "Thomas, I am worried about you. Will you tell me what the matter is? Are we in financial difficulty?" She had never asked the question so directly before.

She saw that her question had penetrated the fog of his drinking. His eyes widened, and he looked directly at her.

"Of course not," he replied with a false laugh. "Whatever would make you think such a thing?" He stood and moved unsteadily toward her. He was smiling, but she saw that the smile did not reach his eyes. "You know how I get when I have a number of projects in the works. It's nothing, really. I am simply distracted." He put his arm loosely around her and walked her to the door. "You go along to the conservatory and select one perfect bloom for my desk here. I promise that I will be at dinner," he assured her.

But he did not come to dinner. Ginny was forced to make excuses to the guests who had arrived early. Fortunately these guests were their dearest friends and did not question her. He remained sequestered behind the closed door of his library, and it was well after Ginny had retired for the night that she heard him moving about in his room adjoining hers.

Sometimes on nights like this, he would come to her bed, wanting to be forgiven for his behavior and to make love. She found herself hoping that he would not come tonight, and then immediately felt guilty. She lay awake, trying to decide what to do. Tomorrow she would speak to Thomas early in the day, before he had had the chance to dull his senses with alcohol. She would make him tell her the worst of it, and together they would find a solution. There was no other way.

Thomas had always insisted that they needed no one else. Friends were pleasant to have around for social occasions and festivities, but he had warned her more than once that one could not trust friends. It had always been important to Thomas that Ginny confide in no one but him and her parents. Now there was only Thomas, and how did she confide in the one person who was the source of her concern?

The bulk of their guests began arriving early the following morning for the two weeks of parties leading up to the grand ball on New Year's Eve. The large house seemed filled to bursting with the laughter and conversation of their houseguests, each of whom came accompanied with his or her own servant. To Ginny's relief, Thomas came down for breakfast and appeared to be his old self again. In fact he was so much his old self— laughing and filled with plans for entertaining their guests for the day—that she began to believe that she had perhaps made too much of his moods over the past weeks.

"I have spoken just now with the last of the tradesmen, Mrs. Thornton," Lucas Holt assured her as they went over the menu for the evening's formal dinner. "Everything will be delivered as ordered."

"Thank you, Mr. Holt. I am more certain than ever that my husband was simply distracted by his many projects. You know how he can be sometimes." She laughed gaily. "Remember that time when you had to remind him that he wasn't wearing shoes and he was about to go out in the snow?"

Holt smiled politely and nodded, but Ginny knew that he had reservations about Thomas as the manager of the household accounts—a role he had insisted on taking over when Ginny's parents died. Lucas Holt had worked for Ginny's parents. He was used to dealing exclusively with the lady of the house in these matters. It had been an awkward transition for both the servant and the master, so much so that Thomas had once suggested that perhaps it might be time to think about replacing Lucas Holt. Ginny had adamantly refused to even consider such a thought, and the matter had never been mentioned again.

"There is one thing, Mrs. Thornton," Lucas added.

"Yes?"

"The tradesmen insist that they be paid in full within two days after the New Year."

"I see." Ginny studied her hands as she tried to make sense of the jumble of emotions rushing through her. Had the debts been so noticeable that the tradesmen were only pacified and would not trust the family again? Were they spreading gossip to others? "We have never had a hint of scandal in my family, Mr. Holt," she said softly but firmly. "We will not have it now. Would it be possible to use the funds I gave you to pay for the largest orders in advance?"

"I think that would be an excellent solution, madam. I have enough left from that fund to make certain that the three most important suppliers are paid. The action should squelch any . . . further concerns."

She knew that he had stopped short of saying that the action should squelch gossip that might already be in progress. She sighed deeply. "See to it, then, Mr. Holt, and thank you."

Ginny renewed her resolve to return to New York at the first opportunity to reclaim her rubies. It would never do for them to fall into the wrong hands. She could never permit Thomas to know what she had done. She hoped that Thomas would not ask why she had elected not to wear them for the ball. To forestall that, she decided to wear her ivory lace gown that would be perfectly accessorized by the pearls. Satisfied that with the help of Lucas Holt she had avoided certain disaster, Ginny spent the day overseeing details for the gala and entertaining their guests.

It was late afternoon when she had seen the last of their guests upstairs to rest and dress for dinner and an evening of chamber music followed by charades. Ginny poured two glasses of sherry and went to the library. It had been a wonderful day, reminiscent of the earlier years of their marriage when regardless of how many people were around, they had eyes only for each other. In the early years of their marriage, she and Thomas had formed a tradition of finding a quiet moment during these holiday festivities to share alone—a moment when just the two of them could look ahead to the coming year. They would toast the coming year and pledge anew their love for each other, and even though they were days away from the actual turn of the century, Ginny had never been more certain that it was tonight that they needed this ritual, this toast.

They needed to remember what they had shared, what they had promised. The new year would bring them many new experiences, hopefully their first child. They had waited a long time for that, and Ginny felt confident that this was going to be the year they would finally conceive and start the family they both wanted.

Thomas was in the library. Ginny was relieved to see that his desk top was covered with its usual array of folders and papers. The fire crackled, and the gaslights that lit the outside garden paths revealed a light snowfall that would only add to the evening's festive mood. The scent of tobacco permeated the room, and she saw Thomas's cigar resting on the crystal ashtray she had given him for his birthday. In short, for the first time in weeks, the atmosphere in the room was normal. The entire day had felt like old times, and this was why Ginny had chosen tonight for their traditional toast.

"Darling, I have our sherry," she said, closing the door behind her. "I know that in recent years we've dropped the habit of our New Year's toast, but this is a special year ahead—beginning a new century and all." *Please God, a new beginning for us as well,* she thought, and smiled at Thomas hopefully.

Thomas turned and smiled at her. She was elated to see that he had not been drinking. His eyes were clear and calm, and his mood was cheerful, as it had been throughout the day. He held a slim volume of poetry in one hand and opened it as he approached her. "You have read my mind as usual, my darling. I had just been thinking of a perfect toast for you. Listen to this." He started to read Elizabeth Browning's masterpiece.

" 'How do I love thee,' " he began.

Ginny closed her eyes as she savored the words. She felt a lump form in her throat as he delivered the final phrase.

" 'And, if God choose, I shall but love thee better after death.' " Thomas stared at the words on the page before him.

"You'll make me cry," she said softly. "You know how I love Mrs. Browning's poetry."

"I mean every word. I wish I had written it for you," he said as he put the book aside and accepted the glass of sherry. He bent and kissed her.

"Oh, Thomas, it is going to be a good year," she promised. "Whatever problems may come our way, we can solve them together. I will be here at your side, helping you with whatever comes. You know that, and in this new year—this new century—"

He stopped her by placing his finger against her lips. "My darling, Ginny, you are always looking to the future. We have this moment, and I want to tell you I love you regardless of what has happened in the past, regardless of what may transpire in days to come to make you doubt me." He fed her a sip of his sherry to forestall any comment, then drank from the glass himself. Then he smiled. "And is this how you are to be dressed for charades?" he teased as he put down his glass, held her hands, and surveyed her day gown.

Ginny gasped. She had forgotten the time. "I must get changed," she said. "And you as well. Now don't linger here, Thomas. Everyone is so excited about tonight's entertainment."

"Yes," was his only reply, but he smiled and bent to kiss her tenderly. "You are a truly wonderful woman, Ginny," he whispered.

"Oh, Thomas, it's going to be such a lovely new year," she assured him. "You'll see." She kissed his cheek and fairly danced toward the door. As she left the room, she felt a lightheartedness that she had not known for months.

Once upstairs, she suddenly remembered some detail of the evening's menu that she had meant to tell the cook. She retraced her steps and hurried down the corridor that led to the pantry and kitchen. As she passed the library, she heard voices and thought of stopping to interrupt so that whoever was with Thomas would understand that he needed to dress for the evening. As she neared the double doors, she heard Thomas's voice raised in anger and another quieter voice, soothing, placating. She could not hear the actual words and she knew that Thomas did not like for her to interrupt him when he was discussing business.

Please don't let anything spoil this wonderful day, she prayed silently as she hesitated just outside the library.

Thomas sounded more in control, and the other person's voice was also calm. She decided to go on to the kitchen and check on Thomas on her way back. Surely by then the business with the stranger would be completed.

She had reached the passage to the kitchen when she heard the sound—a sharp crack that split the air in a single moment and then left all in silence. She froze where she stood, her hand on the brass door handle that a moment later would have taken her down the hall to the kitchen. As realization dawned, she rested her forehead against the cool, solid, carved wood of the door, her other hand clenched into a fist that slowly, steadily pounded the door as she murmured, "No, no, no."

She knew that sound. How many dozens of times had she gone out with Thomas on a bright summer's day to the woods surrounding the house where he would practice his shooting while she protested that she saw no reason for him to indulge in such a ridiculous sport? He didn't hunt, so what was the purpose? How many times had she involuntarily started at the sharp report of the gun even as she watched him pull the trigger and knew the sound would follow? How many times had she shuddered at the unique silence that seemed to follow that singular sound as it resonated in ripples through the air like a stone thrown into still water?

It took all of her strength to turn away from the solidity of that door. She was terrified at what she would discover. Had Thomas become so enraged that he had shot the other man? His temper of late had often been uncontrollable. More than once she had had to soothe things over with family, friends, and the servants. Then she began to think the unthinkable. Had Thomas been so distraught by the stranger's words that he had turned the gun on himself? Was it Thomas who lay dying? Thomas bleeding? She began to run.

By the time she reached the library, the room was filled with people. Someone tried to block her entrance. Others surrounded her, holding her, speaking unintelligible words in sorrowful funereal tones she did not want to heed. She broke free and found herself at the desk. Thomas's features were indistinguishable, no more than a horror mask of clotted blood and skin fragments. In his right hand was the gun, dangling limply, almost casually, at his side. Under his left hand was the volume of poetry, spattered now with blood.

Ginny swallowed the scream that threatened to shatter the night, and fainted.

Once revived, she retired to her room to change and then take charge of the arrangements. The police came and went. She heard the murmured "suicide," heard the pity in the policeman's voice. Friends urged her to permit them to handle everything for her. Instead she asked them to leave her and called for Lucas Holt who sat quietly taking notes as she laid out directions for attending to Thomas's body, attending to their guests, and arranging for the funeral. With quiet expertise, Lucas guided her through the process, asking for direction that he knew would lead her to think of details she would otherwise have forgotten.

Afterwards she left the library and climbed the wide stone stairway. She was aware that several of their guests were gathered in the upstairs sitting area. She was aware of the hush that fell over the small cliques of people as she made her way past them and down the hall to her room. She felt unexpected anger well within her at the thought that she had become in the last hour an object of pity.

The gown she had planned to wear for the evening was laid out across her bed. The single teardrop diamond pendant—another gift from Thomas—was on top of her dressing table. Everything was in readiness for her to dress for an evening of music and gaiety. Thomas was excellent at charades and always had their guests laughing uproariously at his antics.

She walked through the dressing room and into Thomas's bedroom where his black formal wear hung on the door just inside his dressing room and his polished black shoes stood at attention on the floor below. She caught the scent of his cologne, saw his hairbrush on the bureau. She picked it up and began gently pulling the loose hairs from between the bristles, collecting them in her hand as if she might be able to replace them on Thomas's shattered head.

She felt the first tears strike the backs of her hands as she completed her task. She put the brush aside and turned back to the bedroom. Thomas's silk dressing gown was tossed casually across the chaise where she would often sit in the mornings, talking to him about this and that before they each went about their business for the day. She sat on the chaise and fingered the silk, still clutching the soft hair in her other fist. Then she gathered the robe to her chest and buried her face in its smooth cool folds. "Oh, Thomas," she cried. "Thomas."

Lucas found her there and led her gently back to her own room where her maid, Maggie, waited. A black silk mourning gown had replaced the blue silk evening gown. Lucas crossed the room. "Mr. Thornton's solicitor is here," he said quietly. "Shall I send him away until morning?"

"No. Have him wait in the . . ." She hesitated. She had almost said that the attorney should wait in the library. "In the music room, Mr. Holt. Have the guests been offered their dinner?"

"Yes, Mrs. Thornton. They are at dinner now."

Maggie helped her dress and arrange her hair. All the while she made subtle suggestions that no one would expect her to do more tonight, that it would be perfectly fine if she decided to stay in her room until morning.

"And what would that accomplish, Maggie?" Ginny asked without malice or rancor. "I'd rather move forward with whatever we can manage tonight." *I want the nightmare to end,* she thought, knowing it would not for the foreseeable future. She could not imagine things ever being normal for her again.

It was only eight o'clock when she met with Thomas's solicitor and asked him straight out if she was destitute. He cleared his throat twice before responding.

"There are certain financial issues that I shall be happy to handle," he began.

"Will I lose Malmaison?"

The attorney seemed surprised. "I thought you knew," he said, and then added almost to himself, "Of course. That is why."

"Why what, Mr. Hudson? Do you know why my husband took his life?"

"Mrs. Thornton, wouldn't you prefer to discuss these matters after the funeral? You must be exhausted and you've had an enormous shock and—"

"Can you explain my husband's death, sir?" She said each word slowly, distinctly, as if the man were slow or hard of hearing.

Again, he busied himself shuffling papers.

"Your husband had already disposed of the estate, I'm afraid."

Ginny was certain of very little since the events of the last few hours, but one thing she knew. "Thomas would never do that. He knows . . . knew . . . what Malmaison means to me. He might have used the funds that my parents left me, but . . ."

She almost felt pity for the attorney, for his eyes were sad and filled with regret as he looked directly at her. "Your husband had already exhausted those funds when he used the estate as collateral in a very high-risk business venture, Mrs. Thornton. I tried to advise him of the risk, as did Colonel Sutter, but he insisted. The venture collapsed, and he lost his investment."

"We can repay the losses," she said as she took a mental inventory of her remaining jewels and other valuables in the house.

"I'm afraid not."

"Mr. Hudson, as you are well aware in this last year, I lost my beloved parents. Now I have lost my husband.

I cannot lose Malmaison, too," she whispered, clenching her fist to keep the tears at bay. She had never felt more alone.

The attorney reached out and covered her hand with his own larger one. "It's too late. Your husband signed the papers earlier this week. Colonel Sutter came here to dissuade him, to tell him they could work out some arrangements, but Thomas was adamant. The colonel believes that Thomas was insulted by his perception that the colonel thought Thomas would default on the deal. There was no reasoning with him. You must know that these last several weeks he has not been at all himself."

"Sutter?" Ginny repeated the name as if trying to place it in her mind. "Sutter," she said more firmly. He was the other voice. "He was here and did nothing?" She stood, and Hudson followed suit.

"Now, Mrs. Thornton, please . . ."

"You will tell Colonel Sutter that we will discuss the disposal of my home once I have buried my husband. Further, he should not assume that he will ever displace me from this property. My father built this estate. It was his pride and joy. It is and shall remain my home. This estate is all I have left, and I will not lose it. I will not."

The rest of the night and all of the following day passed in a haze of grief and anger and subliminal panic. The questions were like a persistent rhythm accompanying her actions. *Why now? Why here? Why Thomas? Why? Why? Why?*

Over the next several days, it was as if Ginny moved through wet sand. She performed the duties expected of her and more. She made the arrangements for the service. She saw to every detail herself, glad to have something to occupy her mind and keep her from thinking about what her future might hold. She accepted the condolences of dozens of people who attended the services in the family's private chapel. She watched quietly as those same people gathered in the large downstairs reception area to munch on cakes and finger sandwiches as they gossiped about what had driven poor Thomas to such disaster, and whispered about what would happen to dear Ginny now.

With each passing day, she felt the rage inside her build as she remembered all the promises Thomas had made about the life they would share, the future they would enjoy together. Thomas had always dismissed her attempts to be more involved in the business of the estate, telling her that she had all that she could handle in just managing the mansion and overseeing the gardens. As hour followed hour in the days immediately after Thomas's death, she stayed up half the night poring over the papers he had never shown her, the deals he had made without her knowledge, the money he had lost and never mentioned. In the end, there was no denying what her husband had done. Thomas had deliberately gone behind her back. He had not trusted her to understand. He had gotten them deeper and deeper in debt, and all the while he had been showering her—and himself and their friends—with extravagant gifts of jewels, art, new carriages, new clothes.

Ginny slammed shut the last of the folders and paced the room. Thomas's pride—his damnable arrogance—had always made him determined to be always the best, to *have* the best, regardless of the cost. After her parents died, she had worried about how much they were spending, recalling her father's warnings about Thomas's penchant for overspending. Thomas knew that she viewed the estate as their children's heritage and wanted nothing to endanger that. She had thought he agreed with her on that in principle, even though he laughed at her and told her that they had plenty of money. Now she recalled that of late they had argued about that very topic. The last time they had spoken of it, Thomas had ended the discussion by cruelly reminding her that since she seemed incapable of bearing a child, the point was moot. She had blamed herself and given up the argument.

It stunned Ginny to realize that with Thomas's death she was coming face-to-face with details of their marriage that she had always been able to ignore while he was alive. Before his death, there had always been the promise of tomorrow. With that promise gone, the life she had thought of as perfect seemed tarnished—even a bit tawdry. She heard the whispers of pity from her own household staff as she went about her routine. Had she been so blinded by her loyalty to him that she didn't see? It no longer mattered. What mattered now was that she could not let Thomas's death destroy everything her life had stood for, everything her parents had worked so hard to build. Where Thomas had given up, she would prevail. Where he had been weak, she would be courageous.

Malmaison was more than a grand house and acres of gardens. It was also vital to the surrounding community, providing employment and goods for the townspeople. The dairy farm, winery, and botanical gardens all had the potential to provide income until she could clear the debts Thomas had created. Day and night, Ginny continued to study her ledgers, as she met with the managers of the farm and the winery and with the head gardener. She began to lay out a plan, one that would permit her to raise the money she needed to pay off Sutter.

It was the thirtieth of December when the attorney came to call on her for the second time. She met with him in the library, sitting at the very desk where Thomas had died. She saw that her statements made Mr. Hudson uncomfortable, but she was determined to stand her ground. "I have been through everything, as I told you I would, Mr. Hudson," she began when he had seated himself across from her.

She pushed a heavy envelope across the table to him. "I have been able to raise some cash." She almost smiled as she recalled the knowing look on the pawnbroker's face when she had entered his shop earlier that day. That mocking look had disappeared, however, the moment she had opened her bag and revealed the contents. His eyes had widened, and he had been unable to disguise his disbelief at the array of items she placed in front of him. She had taken him the rest of her jewels as well as Thomas's jewels and several small silver items. The items were no more than trinkets to her now that she knew they had been purchased at the risk of their future, their very home. She had stated a price and held out her hand, indicating that there would be no bartering. He had paid the price.

Hudson opened the envelope and counted the money. "This is impressive," he said, replacing the bills in the envelope.

"It is a first payment, Mr. Hudson. Please set up a schedule for regular payments."

"You cannot possibly raise that kind of money on a consistent basis, Mrs. Thornton, even if you sell everything in the house and stables. On top of that, there are outstanding debts to contractors and other purveyors as yet unpaid for recent redecorating and repair projects. If you understood the documents you have read, you would see that."

Ginny stood up and placed both hands flat on the desk as she leaned toward him. "Mr. Hudson, do not insult me. I have not only read the documents, but also understood them completely. I am asking you to deal only with the person who cheated my husband of his property. I will attend to the other matters myself. If you cannot handle that simple request, I will retain someone who can."

Hudson raised his bushy eyebrows in surprise at her tone. "Mrs. Thornton, you are clearly overwrought. Your husband was always concerned that you would react emotionally when the issue called for pragmatic logic. That is exactly why he insisted you know nothing of these rather complex matters. I would suggest that you meet with Colonel Sutter yourself. He is not an unreasonable man and deeply regrets your loss. He—"

Ginny came around the desk to stand directly over the attorney. "That man's name is not to be mentioned in my presence," she said, her voice tight and close to breaking. "More to the point, he is never to enter this house again. Is that clear, Mr. Hudson?"

Hudson stood. "He owns this house, Mrs. Thornton. I am going to attribute this evening's dramatics to your personal loss and distress. It is understandable that you have sustained an incredible shock with Thomas's death. None of us anticipated this, but facts are facts. Colonel Sutter is the legal holder of this property."

"That is not acceptable, Mr. Hudson," she said quietly. On that note, she left the room. She stood outside the library door for a brief moment. She certainly did not want to chance seeing any of the guests who still remained in the house. She walked quickly across the winter garden and through the music room where she grabbed a paisley shawl from the back of her favorite chair as she headed out the balcony doors to the conservatory.

Oblivious to the cold and the snow soaking her shoes, she kept her eyes focused on the conservatory in the distance. Behind the building's glass walls, she could see the silhouetted outlines of her beloved plants. She brushed aside the tears as she walked and then ran along the snow-covered path beneath the grape arbor that connected the house and the conservatory. Even as a little girl, she had always found peace and serenity among her plants. In the past few days her life had changed in a way she could never have imagined possible. She must not lose Malmaison—there had to be a way.

She burst through the door of the conservatory and was assailed by the heady fragrance of the flowers and the moist warmth of the subtropical climate. Her father had designed the structure in a series of temperature-controlled sections. This room had always been her favorite, for in this place it was always summer when the

plants were at their most lush, in the full blossom of
their lives. She slowed her pace to a stroll as she savored
the most brilliant and fragrant flowers of all—her beloved red malmaison carnations. She plucked one flower
and crushed the blossom to her face, inhaling its potent
perfume. Suddenly she was reminded of Thomas lying
across that desk, the blood pooling around his head, and
she sobbed for what she had lost and for what she had
failed to see and prevent.

"You shall not win, Colonel Sutter," she vowed.
"Malmaison shall not be yours. I will find a way. I
must," she whispered. Still holding the blossom clutched
in her hand, she sank to the cold, ornately carved
wrought-iron settee and gave in to her exhaustion.

Chapter 3

SAM ALMOST TRIPPED over the sleeping woman as he entered the conservatory. He was so engrossed in his notes that he had barely noticed the long walk from the house through the arbor past the snow-covered gardens. He certainly was oblivious to the stranger asleep in his greenhouse. He was shaking clumps of snow off his shoes when he saw her reclining on the old wrought-iron settee half-hidden by the foliage. He had actually forgotten that the old piece of garden furniture was still there. Whenever he worked in the conservatory at night, he always used lanterns because he could control the amount of light and didn't like to upset the balance of light and dark for his experimental plants. He lifted the lantern higher and gave himself the luxury of studying the woman before making his presence known.

She must be the curator. There was no other explanation for a stranger in the greenhouse. She'd probably arrived earlier in the afternoon. Perhaps a member of the staff had directed her to look for him here. It would have been the logical choice, since he spent so little time in the house unless he was researching something specific in the library. He wondered why she hadn't returned to the house when she didn't find him.

She was well-dressed in what he supposed was something fashionable for these days. Sam didn't pay a lot of attention to women's clothes, but he had noticed a certain trend toward the Victorian in the garb of his female students and assistants lately. They also all seemed to be really into wearing black. He could never figure that one out. Why did perfectly lovely young women deliberately laden themselves in such a boring color? Even the Victorians had saved that somber garb for funerals and mourning. The woman on the settee was probably quite proud of her high-necked fitted dress and the embroidered shawl she had thrown over her shoulders—never mind that her choice in outerwear, not to mention her shoes, was completely inappropriate for the weather. Feminine caprice, Sam thought and smiled. The only hint of color was the flower she held clutched in one hand.

Sam set the lantern on the floor and knelt next to her, prepared to shake her gently awake. It was then that he caught a whiff of the blossom she held. It was a carnation, of that there was no doubt, but the fragrance was an uncommon blend of spicy and sweet, like cloves simmering in cider on a fall evening. Its power was unique, especially when one considered that the flower had been ripped from its source of sustenance. He stood up, looking around excitedly. Where had she plucked the blossom? What plant in his greenhouse was producing such wonders? Had she stripped the only bloom or were there more? Perhaps the hybrids . . . Sam forgot all about the woman as he searched for the source of the blossom. It was exactly the plant he had been trying to breed, exactly the potency of fragrance he had hoped to produce. The fragrance was the key, the signal that this plant contained the exact ingredient he needed for his research. It was an exciting and unexpected discovery that could possibly push his work ahead by months.

• • •

Ginny awoke with a start and immediately pushed herself upright on the uncomfortable bench. A man was there. A giant of a man standing over her, almost touching her and yet seemingly unaware of her presence.

"Do you mind, sir?" she said primly as she pulled the hem of her skirt free of his unusual shoe.

"Ah, Sleeping Beauty awakes. Welcome to Malmaison!"

He had a smile that might have been quite becoming under any other circumstances. His teeth were uncommonly even and white. Given the fact that Thomas was barely settled in his grave, however, his jovial attitude was far more than simply inappropriate. It was irritating. Ginny stood up, which did little to increase her advantage. She didn't know when she had seen such a tall man. He was at least half a foot taller than Thomas's five and a half feet, making him a full foot taller than she was. Her eyes were drawn to his bared forearm. In fact, his entire manner of dress was as unsuitable as his behavior. He was wearing no shirt, save an undergarment with sleeves and writing on the front of it. His trousers rode low on his hips and were made of some sort of tan canvas fabric. He was clean-shaven, and his thick nutmeg-colored hair was in need of a good combing, as it kept falling over his forehead. She tried to place him among the gardening staff and could not. She would have to speak to Mr. Boyle, her head gardener, about the impudence of the man.

"I apologize for not being here to meet you. You see, nobody told me you'd made it through the storm, and Freddie and I were pretty sure we wouldn't see you until tomorrow, if you made it through at all." He glanced around and inhaled deeply, closing his eyes as he savored the floral perfume. "Not a bad place to hang out and catch a nap, though," he added, opening his eyes and pushing his glasses onto the bridge of his nose. His

attention was drawn to the flower she still held clutched
in one hand. "Do you mind showing me where you
found that bloom?"

Ginny stared at the crushed red petals that were beginning to fall away from their center. "There are . . ."
She started to say that there were dozens if he would
simply look for them, but then stopped. She took in her
surroundings. She turned all around, looking at the
plants. They were different, in different locations, of different species. Nothing was as she had placed it, and
there were no brilliant red carnations.

"Ah, then, it was the only one," he said and sounded
so disappointed that she felt she should either apologize
or reassure him.

"Oh, no, not at all," she said and turned to where she
had picked the flower, only to find flats of seedlings in
its place. "It was here," she said more to herself than to
him. "Or perhaps I am mistaken. Perhaps there." Nothing made sense. How could it all have changed in the
span of only a few hours? And why, on this day of all
days, would her gardener elect to rearrange the conservatory completely?

She looked outside, saw the snow piled high around
the estate, saw lights from the house, and took some
reassurance in seeing things where and as they should
be. Still, she felt disoriented, as if she might faint. Perhaps she was dreaming. She gripped the back of the
settee and closed her eyes.

"It's no big deal," he hastened to assure her. "I just
saw the petals while you were sleeping—sounds like a
good title for a movie, doesn't it? *While You Were Sleeping?*"

He laughed at what was obviously some joke, and it
seemed only polite to smile even though she didn't have
the faintest idea what he was talking about. She gently
spread the loose petals over the palm of her hand. "You
enjoy dianthus, then?"

"Among others. Did you know that they once grew

wild? Fields and fields of them back in old Greece. I mean, it's hard not to like a flower that's been around since practically the beginning of the universe." His enthusiasm was contagious.

"My father used to add them to his recipe for mulled wine," she recalled.

"Of course," he replied, his eyes sparking with excitement, "the spicy clovelike scent." He touched the petals lightly. "I don't know that I've ever seen a variety with this coloring. The depth of it is almost like rubies," he observed.

Ginny closed her fingers around the petals protectively. Did he know about the rubies she had pawned? Was he taunting her?

"Hey, are you okay? If you don't mind my saying so, you look a little off-kilter."

Ginny turned to look at him. He spoke in such a strange manner. She understood his words, but the phrasing was different, almost insultingly casual. On top of that, for a man of his station to make any reference to her appearance at all was insubordinate. Instinctively Ginny touched her fingers to her head and found that the combs had slipped out. Her hair was as much in need of grooming as was his. She gathered it away from her shoulders and twisted it to form a chignon at the nape of her neck, but had nothing with which to secure it so gave up. She realized that to him she looked nothing like the lady of the house, and decided to forgive him his indiscretion.

She stepped away from him and almost fell as she stumbled over a loose tile in the flooring. The man immediately reached out to steady her, his fingers closing gently yet with such strength around her arm. Ginny resisted the urge to shrink from his touch.

Sam frowned. She certainly was an odd little creature—she looked and acted a little like a trapped bird, her eyes wide with unasked questions. She was quite petite, and yet there was something about her posture—

her manner—that made her seem tall and stately. He wondered if she could possibly be ill; her skin was so pale. Of course, that might just be the lighting and the contrast to her black clothing and flaming red hair. She stumbled as she moved away from him, and he instinctively reached out to rescue her. He was struck by how easily his fingers circled her arm. He made sure she was steady and then released her.

"I'm sorry for rattling on," Sam said. "You're probably starving and exhausted and anxious to get settled in." He stared at her more closely. The discussion of the flower had clearly upset her. Perhaps she thought she had made a mistake in picking the flower and was afraid of losing her job. "Don't worry about the flower. I'll check it out later. Clearly you've had a really bad day. How about some food?"

Sam saw a flicker of irritation cross her face, but she made no response. "Come on. Let's go up to the house. Did you meet Freddie? Wonderful man—organized, thoughtful. You're going to enjoy working with him."

The man was smiling again, and this time it was accompanied by the offer of his arm. His bare arm. "I'm Sam Sutter, by the way," he said as he opened the door and waited for her to precede him. "Did Mom tell you she and Dad had to take off early on their trip?"

It was unnerving the way he kept asking questions and then continued talking, never allowing the polite pause necessary for her to respond. He seemed neither to expect nor want an answer, which was actually fortunate, since Ginny had been stopped dead in her tracks at the mention of his name. *Sutter.* So this was the man who had cheated Thomas out of her beloved estate. This was the man who had driven her husband to put a gun to his head and pull the trigger. Ginny considered her options. They were alone. He appeared to be just the slightest bit demented, judging by his clothing and his manner. Clearly he could do whatever he pleased with her, and no one would ever hear her screams. It seemed the prudent thing to do was to try and go along with him until she could reach the safety of the mansion—and help. She stopped short of accepting the offer of his arm as she stepped over the threshold on her own.

He made sure he had secured the door to the conservatory, then picked up the lantern and led the way. "You must have been caught completely off guard by the snow," he said, glancing down at her ruined shoes. "I'll show you to your room, and you can change out of those wet things while I rustle us up some food in the kitchen, okay?"

He was striding along the arbor path, breaking a trail through the wet snow with his larger feet. She concentrated on following his tracks and realized that his were the only tracks on the path—two sets of them, coming and now going with no sign of her own trip from the house to the conservatory earlier. Had it snowed enough to cover her earlier tracks? How long had she slept?

"I apologize," he said as he held open the door for her and let her precede him into the house. "I'm a bit absentminded and have to admit that I've forgotten your name."

"Mrs. Thornton," she replied automatically and glanced back to see the effect the name would have on him. "Mrs. Thomas Thornton," she added for emphasis.

The man blinked and then grinned. "Thomas? Do folks call you Tommy, then? It's amazing what people name kids these days—girls with names traditionally belonging to boys and sometimes boys with names that used to be reserved for girls." He shook his head and chuckled as he walked along the hall, turning on lights as he went.

Tommy? The man was completely mad. "My given name is Virginia," Ginny said stiffly. "My late husband's name is . . . was . . . Thomas."

Sutter stopped and turned. He was immediately contrite. "I'm really sorry, Ginny—can I call you Ginny? I had no idea you were widowed. Please accept my condolences and my apologies for making light of the name thing."

The name thing? And how dare he behave in such a callous manner regarding Thomas's death?

Torn between revealing her hand and wanting to make him admit that he knew very well who Thomas Thornton was, Ginny did not acknowledge his apology. "I'd like to go to my room," she said and started down the hall ahead of him.

The man hurried to catch up with her. "You'll have to excuse the mess," he said. "I'm sure Mom told you about this annual shindig she throws every year on New Year's Eve. This year is bigger than ever, as you can well imagine."

Ginny paused. It seemed as if every word out of his mouth brought yet another surprise. "I thought the ball had been canceled for this year," she said. She was clearly dealing with a madman. Mom? He thought his mother was holding the annual ball? Had he completely blocked out Thomas's horrible death right in front of him? Perhaps the shock of watching a man put a gun to his head or the guilt of realizing that he'd stood by and done nothing had driven him insane. It would explain a great deal. Ginny decided to humor him.

"Canceled?" He laughed heartily as if she had made a most humorous joke. "Heaven forbid! The word 'canceled' is not a part of Mom's vocabulary. Nope, the event will go on as planned even if you, me, and the staff end up eating all that food."

They were passing the library and billiard room, and Ginny was relieved to see that, unlike the conservatory, everything in both rooms seemed to be as she had left it, except for one minor detail. "What are those small red lights?" she asked, realizing that she had seen them and the unusual boxlike contraption to which they appeared to be connected throughout the house.

"Security system," he replied. "We run a pretty constant tape here in the public rooms. It tends to cut down on visitors thinking we won't miss a simple little silver picture frame or gold candlestick." He pointed to the ceiling above their heads. "Sprinkler system is there along with smoke detectors. Pretty good job of concealing them without ruining the overall ambience of the place, wouldn't you say? Dad is a virtual genius at that sort of thing."

The man was rambling on again. Perhaps bringing him back to reality would be helpful. "What kind of work are you engaged in, Mr. Sutter?" She took one more glance at the red lights and wondered when Thomas had had them installed and what they had cost.

"I'm a research scientist. That's why I spend most of my time with the plants." He laughed. "Mom accuses me of liking them better than I do most people. This would be the winter garden—these glass-roofed interior garden rooms were awfully popular back then. Of course, you probably know more about that than I do."

She could not believe the audacity of the man, giving her a tour of her own home. Sarcasm seemed the only way to respond. "Is that a fact, Mr. Sutter? And those rooms we've just passed?"

"Bachelor's wing—library, billiard room, lounge. Over here we have the area used more by the females of the household." He walked quickly across the stone tiles of the winter garden and up the three marble steps to the music room through which could be seen the formal reception parlor. "Of course, these days Mom is the one most likely to be found in the library, and Dad spends a lot of time in here. He's quite a music buff—jazz more than anything else."

They had come to the grand staircase that circled its way up three stories in marble splendor. "I'll just show you the family kitchen up here and your room and then leave you to rest," he said as he bounded up the stairs. "Did somebody already take care of your luggage?"

Ginny had paused on the third step, her heart in her throat as she stared at the portrait of a woman she had never seen, dressed in a shapeless beaded gown that came to just above her ankles. Ginny had seen men with hair longer than that of this woman. But it was not her short hair or unusual garb that caught Ginny's attention. The woman was wearing the rubies Ginny had pawned.

"That's my great-grandmother," she heard the man say from his position several steps above her. "I think that portrait was done in twenty-nine, just before the stock market crashed."

Impossible. In 1829 the house had not even been conceived. She had not been born, and yet this woman stood posed in front of the gilded mantelpiece that Ginny herself had selected for the parlor after she and Thomas had taken over the house. "I don't understand," she said softly, moving closer to study the portrait. "In 1829 . . ."

He came down the stairs to stand next to her. "Not 1829," he corrected. "Nineteen twenty-nine."

She tried to focus on what he was saying to her.

"You said 1829," he repeated. "This was 1929—the end of the Roaring Twenties? The eve of the Great Depression?"

The events of the past hour whirled through Ginny's mind. The strange garb of the man. Everything changed in the conservatory. No sign of Mr. Holt or the rest of her staff. No mention of anyone familiar. The strange red lights he had explained as security. Now this portrait of a woman out of the future wearing Ginny's jewels. Perhaps it was not Mr. Sutter who had gone mad. Perhaps it was Ginny herself.

She turned to flee and was stopped by a gold banner that hung above the front entrance. *Welcome to the New Millennium! Happy New Year, 2000!* Ginny read the words once, then again. *Impossible.* She held her hands to her head, shaking herself, willing herself to awaken from this nightmare. But when she opened her eyes, the banner was still there, as was the portrait and the man called Sutter. Ginny gave in to the whirlpool of bewilderment and astonishment that assailed her and she collapsed.

"Freddie!" Sam bellowed as he rushed down the stairs to attend to the woman who was now passed out cold. *Damn.* He should have insisted she eat something. "Freddie!" he yelled again.

"Oh, my stars." Freddie gasped as he appeared at the top of the stairs. "Shall I call nine-one-one?"

"No, I think she just passed out from not eating anything all day. No telling when she got here. I found her sleeping out in the conservatory."

"Is she a street person?" Freddie asked, coming down the stairs for a closer look.

"She's the curator," Sam replied as he lifted her and started up the stairs. "Go get some tea or soup or something and bring it up to the lady's suite."

Freddie paused and seemed about to say something.

"What?" Sam asked.

"It's just that this can't be Millie Cooper, the curator, because she called about an hour ago to say she had taken another position and wouldn't be coming at all."

"This isn't Millie Cooper," Sam explained patiently. "She's . . . she's . . ." He searched his brain for the name. "Ginny. Ginny Thornton." He glanced down at the woman he held in his arms and asked the next logical question. "If she's not the curator Mother hired, who the hell is she?"

"Maybe she's one of the entertainers," Freddie guessed. "She's dressed in costume—not the most becoming costume, but period nonetheless."

"I'll carry her upstairs. Once she comes to, we'll figure out who she is and get this straightened out once and for all."

Freddie nodded and headed for the kitchen. Sam carried the woman up the stairs and down the hall to the bedroom once occupied by the lady of the house—most recently his grandmother. When his mother turned the house into a living museum, she'd had the room restored to the way it was at the turn of last century. It was extravagantly overdone for Sam's taste, but he didn't have to sleep there. He placed the woman carefully on the canopied bed, then stood back and frowned down at her.

She'd been out for several minutes. Maybe he ought to call for medical help, but then there were bound to be questions, and some reporter might get hold of it. The last thing he needed right now was trying to deal with a media circus on top of the ball. *Damn.* He considered various actions and settled on trying to loosen some of the woman's clothing to make her more comfortable. She certainly was all buttoned up tight. Not only that, but she appeared to have given new meaning to the style of layering clothing.

He had only managed to remove her shoes and open several of the tiny buttons that lined the front of her outfit by the time Freddie brought the tray of food.

"She's still out?" Freddie asked as he set the tray on the dressing table and came over to the bed.

"She's been moaning and stirring. Keeps calling for someone named Thomas. I think that was the name she gave me for her husband—her dead husband." Sam gave up on loosening the clothing and sat on the side of the bed. "Ginny," he called. "We've brought you something to eat. Time to wake up."

Finally her eyes fluttered open, then closed again immediately.

"Might be too bright," Freddie guessed. "I'll dim the lights a little."

"Okay. Try opening them again, Ginny," Sam said. "That's my girl. Now, how about some of this soup that Freddie brought up for you?" He motioned for Freddie to bring the tray closer to the bed. Cautiously lifting the hot soup bowl, he prepared to feed her.

"Where is Mr. Holt?" she asked, staring at Freddie.

"Mr. Holt? Freddie, did a Mr. Holt call?"

"I'm afraid not."

Sam lifted the spoon to her mouth. Her eyes were wide as she glanced quickly around the room. Sam missed her mouth when she turned her head slightly toward the dressing room. The hot soup sloshed over his hand and dribbled down her chin, but she seemed oblivious.

"Open that door fully, please," she instructed Freddie, who obeyed without question. Something in the tone of her voice left little room for debate. "What have you done with my clothes?" This was directed at Sam.

"I was trying to make you a little more comfortable after you passed out. I—"

"Not *these* clothes," she said, and her voice shook slightly. *"Those."* She pushed herself to the far side of the bed away from him and closer to the dressing room where Freddie was still standing next to the open door. "You may go now," she said quietly as she passed him on her way into the dressing room.

Freddie glanced at Sam. Sam nodded. "Why don't you go on back to your room, Freddie? I'll call if there's anything else."

Do you want me to call the police? Freddie mouthed as he edged his way toward the bedroom door.

Sam shook his head and indicated that Freddie should leave. Sam remained seated on the side of the bed, but he was ready to move if the woman did anything destructive.

"Ginny, we need to talk. Something has upset you. I'd like to help if I can."

She stood for a long moment with her back to him and then turned and came back into the room, closing the dressing room door behind her. She sat on the chair in front of the dressing table and glanced at herself in the mirror. With an expertise born of years of practice, she picked up the brush and began arranging her hair.

She pulled pins from the dish on the dresser as if she'd known they would be there for her use. She finished twisting her hair into its intricate design and then slowly refastened the front of her dress. She said nothing, so Sam did the talking.

"I know now that you are not the curator I was expecting. Apparently she called earlier to say she was accepting another position and would not be joining us after all. Now, what that means is that poor Freddie has got to get me through the next couple of days all on his own. I'd like to help you out, Ginny, but as you can see, we're going to be fairly busy here, not to mention short-handed."

Ginny concentrated on her image in the small tilted mirror on her dressing table. Through it she could see him behind her without his seeing her expression. The dressing table held an assortment of the usual items, but while some of them were hers, many were not. As he talked, she tried to focus on what she had seen and heard since waking up in the conservatory with this man standing over her.

The undeniable fact was that she was no longer in her own time. Somehow she had been thrust into this new time, this new century, where this horrid man and his family lived in her house, touching her things, and now ordering her about. Perhaps it was a dream—she fervently hoped so. For the moment, however, it seemed extraordinarily real, and given that, she must gather her wits and try to figure out a way to survive until such time as she could escape. It simply would not do to have this man think of her as even slightly out of her mind. That would give him the power to have her detained or locked up, and then what would she do? She took a deep breath to steady her nerves. She gathered her resolve and turned to face him.

Sam wished she would say something, but she just sat there expertly brushing and twisting her mass of red hair as he rambled on. Finally she turned to face him, and the difference was stunning. Before him sat a vision of refinement and grace. She folded her hands primly in her lap. "I would like to apologize for my earlier behavior, Mr. Sutter. I am very sorry if you feel I may have misrepresented myself. I assure you that was not my intention. You did, after all, make certain assumptions on your own." She paused, glanced around the room as if to reassure herself, then turned her focus back to him. "You see, I have been through a rather difficult time of my own. It now occurs to me that we might be of help to one another if you'll consider my proposal."

"I'm listening." Sam was intrigued in spite of his certainty that he was dealing with someone playing with a lot less than a full deck.

She took a deep breath and began. "I believe I can be of help to you because I know the history of this house very well."

"You're a student of preservation, then?" he asked. She looked older than normal to be a student.

"In a manner of speaking. You see, a number of years ago, I spent some time here." He noticed that she was choosing her words very carefully. She glanced up at him to see if he was listening, and then continued. "I believe that my knowledge of the house and grounds might be of use to you until such time as you can find a replacement for your curator."

"In exchange for what?"

"You have mentioned your interest in scientific research, Mr. Sutter. I have a project of my own that requires some research. May I be permitted use of the library perhaps? In my free time, of course."

"There are some very valuable manuscripts in there, Ginny. You have to admit that I don't really know anything about you, not to mention that the circumstances surrounding your arrival and stay here so far have been a bit unorthodox."

She actually smiled. "I cannot dispute that, Mr. Sutter. It seems that I have suffered a kind of accidental . . .

accident that has brought me into your world at a time that is clearly most inopportune for you. Nevertheless, it does occur to me that I might be of assistance. As for the manuscripts, could you not observe all of my actions in the library through your security system?"

"How do I know you're telling me the truth?"

"You cannot know that, sir. Perhaps a bit of information will assure you that I do indeed know this house. In the library there is a secret room, for example. One enters it from the balcony by pressing a button just under the bottom shelf of books near the window there. The room itself is quite small, but comfortably appointed. My . . . that is, the master of the house—at least in days bygone—would use the room for private meetings or merely as a place to escape the usual activity of the household."

Sam's eyes widened in surprise. The secret room was never mentioned in any of the literature concerning the house, because his mother didn't want to take a chance that some child would wander away from the group and get locked in there accidentally. She must have uncovered some of the original plans for the house. "Impressive," he said. "Go on."

She stood and walked around the bedroom. "This room was designed for the lady of the house. This was her private haven. That was her dressing room, leading into her husband's dressing room and then the master bedroom. Her bathroom is there." She pointed to a place where the wall covering disguised a door that indeed led to the bath. "I believe you can attest to the fact that I have not taken the opportunity to look out the windows." She turned for verification, and he nodded. "Our location faces out onto the gardens, specifically the Italian garden which is just below the balcony that runs the length of these windows."

"Who are you?" Sam asked.

"I told you earlier. I am Ginny Thornton, Mr. Sutter, and I am feeling much more like my old self. Again,

please accept my deepest apologies for my earlier behavior. I understand why it may have caused you concern."

Sam stood and paced the room while she remained
standing near the windows. "Well, I certainly can't expect you to leave tonight, and I'm willing to admit that
with no curator in sight, we need the help. I must say,
however, that I'm not entirely comfortable about this."

She waited, saying nothing.

Sam considered his options. "Here are my terms,"
he said finally. "You will stay here in this room for the
night. I warn you that any attempt to move through the
house will set off alarms and bring the police. Since your
luggage is apparently still not here, I'll ask Freddie to
find you some comfortable clothes. The soup is probably
cold by now, but there's a turkey sandwich and some
soda and fruit there. That should sustain you until the
morning."

"And tomorrow?" she asked.

"Tomorrow you will assist Freddie with the final arrangements for the gala. You will attend the gala where
I will present you as the interim curator. The estate is
about to undergo a massive renovation, Ms. Thornton.
It would not do for our guests and benefactors to think
that with my parents out of the country, there is no one
to oversee that important project. If you know as much
as you seem to about the estate, you should be able to
pull it off."

"Pull it off?"

"Mingle with the guests. Make conversation. Share
little tidbits about the house and its history. Intrigue
them so that they write nice checks to support the renovation. Can you manage that?"

She smiled. "Yes."

"Once we get past the gala, then we can discuss your
'research.' "

"Thank you, Mr. Sutter."

"Sam. It's Sam, okay?" She had gotten to him. He

had just done the most outlandish thing of his life. Every ounce of logic and rational thought he possessed told him that this woman was trouble. She was either the best scam artist in the world or she was nuttier than his aunt Mildred's banana bread. Either way, he should have his own head examined for agreeing to let her stay.

She seemed genuinely pleased with his terms, and for some unfathomable reason, that pleased him in return. "I'll be staying the night here in the house," he added.

"I imagined that you might," she replied and gave him another of her rare and lovely smiles. "Until tomorrow, then, Mr. . . . Goodnight, Sam."

A woman whose smile did weird things to his equilibrium and whose story made no logical sense whatsoever had dismissed him in his own house.

Ginny waited until he had left the room before permitting herself to take her first deep breath since she had sat down at her dressing table. She looked around the room, savoring every detail. *It all looks the same—the way I left it*, she thought. Then she remembered the portrait on the stairway, the tiny and eerie red lights throughout the house that he called a security system, and the banner announcing the new year not as 1900, but as 2000. *Impossible.*

She walked over to the tray of food the servant, Freddie, had left on the bedside table. There was a colorful metal container on it with some sort of key or lock on top. She shook it and heard what sounded like liquid. She studied the top and sides. "Coke" was the word on the label. She lifted the ring.

Whoosh! Suddenly a foamy liquid ran over the top and sides of the container and her hand. She shrieked and dropped it, then immediately retrieved it before the brown liquid could stain the Oriental rug. She licked the back of her hand to catch some of the droplets and keep them from falling on her gown. *It's good.* Sweet. A little like root beer or sassafras. She picked up the glass from the tray and poured some of the liquid into it. Sitting on the edge of the bed, she sipped the drink and eyed the fruit.

There were huge strawberries, and it was the middle of winter. She picked one up and tasted it, and her eyes closed with the sheer wonder of its rich, juicy flavor. The sandwich was equally as tasty. She devoured everything and barely heard the polite knock at the bedroom door.

She chewed quickly and swallowed a very unladylike wad of the sandwich. "Come in," she said, wiping her mouth on the linen napkin.

The servant, Freddie, entered the room. "Sam said you might need some clothing to see you through until your luggage arrives." He handed her a shapeless pair of pants and a sort of heavy jersey with writing on the front of it. "I thought sweats would be the most practical. Even with central heating, these old barns can get pretty chilly at night." He laid the costume on the bed.

Ginny eyed the clothing warily.

"It's clean," he assured her, and turned to leave.

"Thank you, Mr. Freddie. You've been most helpful." Then she remembered that Sutter's instructions had been that she was to assist the servant in handling the details of the gala. He had reversed her usual role, making her the servant to follow this man's instructions. "How may I be of assistance to you with tomorrow's gala?" she asked. "I mean, what exactly are the plans?"

The servant smiled at her and visibly relaxed. "You eat, and I'll fill you in," he said, taking a seat on one of the two matching Chippendale chairs near her fireplace. He curled one foot under his body, and she noticed that he was wearing no shoes, only heavy stockings. "It's going to be the most wonderful party. If only we can get the weather to cooperate," he added. "Everyone who is *anyone* will be here—the governor himself is coming."

"Oh, my," Ginny said, hoping to encourage the little man to reveal as much as possible.

"It's a costume ball. Emily has already picked out a gown for you—well, for the new curator—which, come to think of it, by process of elimination is you." He grinned. "Sam tells me you know a great deal about the estate, and he's counting on you to really dazzle the guests." He leaned closer, obviously prepared to share a confidence. "Sam *hates* these affairs, but he's positively devoted to his parents so he'll do his duty."

"I see. Then the estate belongs to his father?"

"Nope. Sam's the real owner. His grandfather left him the place. Of course, he likes it because of the grounds and gardens where he can experiment on his plants to his heart's content. He probably failed to mention that it's *Doctor* Sutter. Sam is one of the foremost research scientists in the field of biomedicine in the world. His mother is the romantic. She's the one who opened the place up to the public. The Sutters are truly wonderful people—all that money and just plain folks."

Ginny bristled slightly. She had to remind herself that there might have been some refinement through the generations, but the fact remained that one of the Sutters had stood by and done nothing while Thomas shot himself. "Does anyone ever talk about the previous owners of the estate?"

Freddie looked genuinely puzzled. "Previous owners?"

"Yes. The Sutters were not the original occupants, were they?"

Freddie frowned, then smiled. "Oh, you must mean the legend of how old Cashwell Sutter won the house in some kind of bet or poker game."

"It was a business investment," she replied tersely. "An illegitimate business arrangement that had disastrous consequences." She saw that her curt tone had put Freddie on guard, so she deliberately lightened her voice. "Or so I've read in some history or another. It's quite a fascinating place, isn't it?" She made a show of surveying her surroundings.

Freddie relaxed again and smiled. "It's a dream job, Ginny. Let me tell you what we've got planned for the gala."

Late into the night the two of them sat next to the fireplace, talking. Freddie told her every detail of the plans for the food, the entertainment, the festivities of the night to come. Ginny occasionally suggested a change of plans or a minor enhancement based on her own experience in giving balls at the house. Freddie reacted with something akin to glee every time she made a suggestion. "Ginny, we are going to make one hell of a team," he announced. "But for now we'd both better get some sleep. Tomorrow is going to be one of those thirty-six-hour days."

She had so enjoyed their conversation, so appreciated his flare for entertaining, that she barely noticed his profanity or the fact that he insisted on calling her by her given name. At the door he turned as if the greatest idea had just struck him.

"I remember now, Mrs. Sutter left notes about what everyone is to wear. The vintage clothing is all stored in the attic for now. One of her plans is to have a period costume museum as a part of the permanent displays. I'll take you up there tomorrow morning, and we'll get your costume and anything else you think you might need for the ball. With your slim figure, I'm sure there's not going to be a lot of need for alterations."

"I'll ask Mr. . . . I'll ask Sam if that would be all right," Ginny replied. "Goodnight, Mr. Freddie."

He laughed. "Goodnight, Ms. Ginny. Sleep tight and don't let the bedbugs bite," he said as he slipped out the door, closing it with a soft click behind him.

Bedbugs! Not in her house.

Chapter 4

WHEN GINNY AWOKE the following morning, it was light, and for an instant she thought perhaps everything that had happened had indeed been a dream—a horrible dream. She even smiled as she thought about how Thomas would tease her about her overactive imagination haunting her while she slept. Then she pushed herself up onto the pillows, prepared to ring for Maggie, and looked at what she was wearing.

She fingered the soft crude fabric of the costume. The overblouse was many sizes too large for her, the sleeves falling over her fingers. The trousers were equally rustic, and yet the entire costume was oddly comforting, a little like a favorite blanket or shawl wrapped around her. Noises from outside drew her attention. She threw back the covers and ran to the window to see what was happening. What she saw mystified her completely.

A small battalion of men in brightly colored uniforms advanced on the house. They wore heavy boots and a sort of knitted mask covered their faces as they yelled to each other above the horrendous racket of the machines they pushed along the walkways. The machines were outfitted with large shovellike contraptions mounted on their fronts, and clearly they were being used to move the piles of snow to make the advance easier.

We are under siege, Ginny thought with horror. *What more could possibly happen?*

There was a light knock at her door, followed by the immediate entrance of Sam Sutter.

"Good morning, Ginny. Glorious morning," he said enthusiastically as he balanced a tray of food and kicked the door closed behind him. "Did you sleep well?"

Was he deaf? "Malmaison is under attack, Mr. Sutter," she said, willing herself to remain calm. "Perhaps we should do something?"

He put down the tray and walked over to the window where she stood. "They do make a racket, don't they? You'd think with all the technology we've developed during this century, somebody would have been able to come up with a snowblower that runs quietly." He shrugged and looked down at her. "Nice outfit," he said with a grin.

Ginny gasped. She had been completely engrossed in the advance of the men with their machines. In the process she had overlooked the fact that Sam Sutter had come strolling into her boudoir as if it were the most normal thing in the world. Not only that, but he was standing not two feet from her, and she was not properly dressed at all.

"This is most unseemly, Mr. Sutter," she chastised him as she used the heavy drapery to cover herself.

He frowned. "Where did you go to school? Wellesley? Bryn Mawr?" He stared at her openly, as if he actually expected to have a traditional conversation.

"Mr. Sutter, do you mind? It is not at all . . ." *It is his house,* she thought, catching herself. *At least for the moment.* "That is, I would greatly appreciate it if you would be so kind as to leave me until such time as I can make myself presentable for this interview."

"Smith." He said the single word with assurance and a smile. "Sure. Have your breakfast. Catch a shower. I think Freddie said something about trunks of clothes in the attic, although personally I think you look kind of cute in those sweats." He headed back across the room toward the door. "I'll be in the library when you're ready. I'll have Freddie join us there so we can go over the final plans for the ball tonight." He rolled his eyes at the ceiling. "Mom has already called three times this morning," he confided. "I mean, it's not like she's concerned or anything." Then he did the oddest thing—he winked at her and left the room.

Satisfied that he was gone, Ginny released her grip on the drapery and crossed the room to examine the breakfast tray. She bit into the tough round bread and chewed. She surmised that the white spread that resembled a kind of butter was for the bread, but pushed it aside in favor of the strawberry jam. There was more fruit—small green slices that tasted a little like banana and a sweet melon.

She had just begun to relax and savor eating delicious food and being back in her own room, when there was another knock at the door. She quickly got into bed and pulled the covers up to her chin. "Who's there?"

"Ms. Ginny? It's Freddie Fincastle. I've brought you some regular clothes. May I come in?"

Ginny rolled her eyes in exasperation. What was it about the men in this new day and age that they thought nothing of strolling in and out of a lady's bedroom as if it were a common passageway? "All right," she replied.

Freddie smiled broadly as he entered the room. "You're going to love these." He spread a number of garments over the pair of matching armchairs. "They're Emily's—Sam's mother. She's called three times already this morning, so the last time she called, I just casually mentioned that your luggage had been misplaced or lost and you had nothing but the clothes you rode in on, so to speak. She insisted I go through her closet and bring you these."

He held up a black jumper-style day gown with what appeared to be a deep blue shirtwaist made of silk. Both were shapeless and looked as if they weighed very little compared to the ensembles she was used to donning every day. "I think you're close enough to the same size that these should get you through the day at least. Later, as I mentioned last night, we'll go up to the attic, and you can get everything you'll need for the ball tonight." He held up a pair of soft leather black slippers. "I'm afraid these are the best I could do for shoes. If you have to go outside for any reason, there should be an extra pair of boots around somewhere that you can wear."

"You're very kind, Freddie. Thank you."

"Of course, I brought several selections, so you can choose whatever fits the best. Emily insisted that I make sure you have everything you need. I think she's terrified that Sam will scare you off before she's had a chance to meet you," he confided.

So Sam Sutter was not always the convivial man he pretended to be. "It would take a great deal to 'scare me off,' as you put it."

Freddie smiled. "Good. Now I'll leave you to get dressed, and then Sam wants to meet with everybody in the library to go over all of the plans for tonight. Should I tell him we'll meet him there in about an hour?"

"That's fine," Ginny agreed. "Thank you again, Freddie. You've made me feel quite at home." Her voice caught, and Freddie gave her a sympathetic look as he briefly covered her hand with his own.

"Everything's going to work out, Ginny," he said. "The Sutters are good people."

After Freddie left, Ginny's curiosity drew her to the clothes, and she spent the better part of the hour she had trying on various combinations. She blushed when she saw that Freddie had also brought a small valise filled with toiletries and her own freshly laundered undergarments. The man was a wonder. When the French mantle clock Thomas had given her on her last birthday chimed, she realized that she had only a quarter of an hour to dress, arrange her hair, and present herself for the meeting in the library. In the end, she decided the safest course was to take Freddie's suggestion and wear the black tunic over the blue shirtwaist. The blessing was that with such simple clothing, she did not need the assistance of her maid. Her hair was another matter altogether. It would take too long to arrange it properly, so she elected instead simply to brush it back and hold it in place with a strand of black ribbon she found in one drawer of the dressing table. She stood before the mirror. She looked younger than her twenty-nine years, and knew instinctively that this fact would work in her favor. Taking a deep breath, she crossed the room and opened the door.

The day had started out so well, Sam thought. He leaned back in the desk chair where generations of Sutter men had sat and managed the affairs of the estate, and surveyed the scene before him. The spacious library suddenly felt cramped as it filled with the various staff members and temporary help who would make the evening's event a success. Everyone seemed to be talking at once. Outside the door, there was more chaos as a maintenance crew ran floor polishers and vacuum cleaners and called out directions to each other.

Sam stood and held up his hands in a plea for silence. How on earth had he allowed his mother to talk him into managing this calamity?

"Chill out, everybody!" Freddie shouted as he moved to shut out the noise of the rest of the house by closing the carved cherry doors.

"Folks," Sam began, "you are all the experts here. You each know your business. You know what you have to do, but we have to work together."

This set off a fresh barrage of requests and complaints. The guy in charge of the music needed to set up rehearsal times for the musicians, but couldn't because of the chaos of cleaning and setting up the house for the party. The woman in charge of the floral arrangements needed to have a place to work, but had been told the conservatory was off limits. The decorators in charge of making sure the house reflected the exact look of the place as it had been on New Year's Eve at the turn of the last century had been promised photographs or detailed descriptions of that time but had yet to receive them.

Sam, the introspective scientist, found himself surrounded by a bunch of temperamental creative types, and all he wanted was *out*. He glanced at Freddie who shrugged his shoulders and smiled. He recalled that it was Freddie who had dismissed the squabbling of the various players as nothing more than opening-night jitters.

"It's theater, Sam," Freddie had told him, "and once the curtain rises on tonight's gala, everybody will be friends again. You'll see." Sam hoped the guy knew what he was talking about. At the moment there were at least three people in the room who appeared to be very close to going postal on him.

The door to the library opened slowly, allowing the hustle and bustle of the cleaning chores to penetrate the room once again. Everyone turned toward the sound, their individual disputes put aside as they focused their attention on the slim young woman entering the room.

Sam watched her work her way through the crush of people. She was still dressed in black, but the modern garb was a nice contrast to the trussed-up costume she had arrived wearing. The blue of her blouse set off her deep red hair that she had pulled back in a ribbon and left free to tumble in thick curls down her back almost to her waist. She looked young and a bit intimidated, but he observed the subtle squaring of her shoulders and the determined set of her jaw as she made her way to the front of the room.

"I apologize for my tardiness," she said softly when she reached the desk. Sam saw her glance at the desk for a long moment, as if she were recalling something painful. Then she gathered herself and looked him straight in the eye. "You wanted to see me?"

It was as if they were alone in the room. She simply did not seem to pay any attention to the others, although they were all clearly fascinated with her. Sam felt an unfamiliar surge of protective feelings and had to resist the urge to place his arm around her shoulders as he made the introductions.

"I would like for all of you to meet Ginny Thornton. Ms. Thornton is the interim curator for the estate. She has just arrived, and clearly needs some time to get her bearings, but she assures me that she has a great deal of knowledge about the estate." He turned to the decorators. "Ms. Thornton's first responsibility will be to assist you in arranging the house to meet my mother's instructions that everything be as close as possible to the New Year's Eve of 1899."

She flinched. It was an almost imperceptible movement, but he observed it and filed it away as one more piece of the puzzle that made up Ms. Ginny Thornton.

"The rest of you," he continued, "will be under the capable direction and leadership of Freddie here. He has my full authority to make the decisions necessary to insure that this evening is a success, including finding alternative vendors, should there continue to be disagreements and problems created by wounded egos."

He saw a few of the vendors smile smugly, and added, "Please don't think any of you are the only game in town. You would be absolutely amazed what can be accomplished and how quickly if you throw enough money at it."

The room went still. There wasn't a person present who wasn't well aware of the vast wealth of the Sutter family. More to the point, there wasn't a person there who wanted to do anything to jeopardize the possibility of providing services to the estate in the future.

"Okay, people, we've got work to do," Freddie announced. He opened the door. "Let's get started."

Ginny started to follow the others from the room.

"Ms. Thornton, could you stay a moment?" Sam watched her pause, but she did not turn. In spite of her diminutive size, she looked positively regal standing there waiting for his next words. He took a certain delight in delivering them. "My mother wants to meet you." He held up the telephone and began pressing in the number. He saw how her eyes widened but was uncertain of the message. Was it surprise? Fear, perhaps?

"Hello, Mom," he said when Emily answered. "I have our Ms. Thornton here." He pressed the button to put the call on speakerphone and sat down at his desk.

"Good morning, Ginny, and welcome to Malmaison."

Emily's soft but lively voice filled the room. Sam watched as Ginny spun around toward the door, looking for the source of the sound. When she turned back to him, he pointed to the phone now lying on his desk. "Say hello," he mouthed.

"Hel . . . hello, Mrs. Sutter," she stammered.

"Oh, call me Emily, please. Everyone on the staff does. One doesn't need titles to get things done, don't you agree?"

"I . . . yes."

"Sam tells me that you arrived last night—that you were in some sort of accident?" Emily's voice conveyed full-blown concern. Clearly she had forgotten all about the fact that Ginny was not the person she had hired as curator. "The weather has been playing havoc with all

our lives recently. Freddie tells me your luggage is missing. Did he bring you clothing, dear?"

"Yes. Thank you."

There was a pause. "Are you sure you're all right,
Ginny? Do you need that son of mine to get you some
medical help? Sam? Are you taking care of her?"

"Yes, Mother. Ginny looks quite healthy this morning—glowing, in fact. A major improvement on the waif
I met last night." It pleased him to see that she blushed.

"Sam, I am speaking to Ginny. We all know that as
long as a body is walking and talking, you see no problem. Now, Ginny, are you sure you're up to handling
the remaining details for tonight's gala? With Freddie's
help, of course."

"I believe that everything will be fine, Mrs. . . . Emily.
Freddie is very capable."

Emily laughed. "Yes, he is. Now, let's talk about your
position as curator. We will work out the details when
I return, but is the salary package I outlined in my letter
acceptable?"

"Perfectly," Ginny said with barely a pause. Sam was
surprised. He had expected questions or explanations
about not actually being the new curator. "I believe you
will find that I know a great deal about the estate and
can be a great help to your son."

Another pause, one Sam recognized. His mother was
calculating that last statement, more in terms of match-
making than in terms of business. "I think you and Sam
should attend the ball together," she said as if the idea
were a sudden brainstorm. "You could come as Colonel
and Mrs. Sutter. There's that portrait—Sam, you know
the one I mean there in the upstairs sitting area. The
gown is in the attic, Ginny. Have Freddie show you. Oh,
it will be absolutely splendid."

"Mom, you're living vicariously again." Sam decided
to try to distract his mother, especially since Ginny
Thornton suddenly looked as if she might pass out again.

"How goes the trip?" He got up and poured a glass of water for Ginny.

"Don't try to change the subject, Sam. I want you to promise me that you will escort Ginny to tonight's ball."

"Mother, we have everything under control." He watched the slight shaking of Ginny's hand as she sipped the water.

"I know you. You'll find some reason to duck out early and hide away in the conservatory once you see that Freddie and Ginny have everything under control."

"I wouldn't do that, Mom. I know how important this is to you." He had the urge to place a comforting hand on Ginny's shoulder, but resisted. She took another sip of the water and held the glass with both hands, her eyes focused on the telephone.

"Emily, please be assured that all will be well," she said. "I will see to that."

"I have no doubt that you will, my dear. You understand that tonight is incredibly important for the future of Malmaison?"

Sam watched as Ginny straightened to her full height. He saw her deep green eyes flash with some underlying emotion. "I assure you that the future of Malmaison is extremely important to me, Emily," she said with a quiet passion that Sam found most intriguing.

He realized his mother had heard the same passion and that for her it was a relief. "Well, Samuel, with Ginny in charge, I can now afford to relax and enjoy my trip. I'll speak with you later this evening. Your father told me to remind you to make sure the stock made it through the storm all right."

"I did that already," Sam assured her. "The herd is fine. Tell him they gave a bumper crop at this morning's milking."

Emily laughed. "Good-bye, Ginny. It was lovely to meet you. Take care of my son."

"Give Dad my love and have a safe journey," Sam said and pressed the button to disconnect the phone. "We have a dairy farm on the grounds," he explained. "Dad likes to check up on the herd."

Ginny was still sitting in the wingbacked chair she had taken once she realized that Emily was not actually in the room. It was as if she'd never seen a telephone before—or at least not one with a speaker option. He sat down behind the desk and steepled his fingers as he studied her. *Who are you really, Ginny Thornton? And what is your business with this house?*

Ginny was distinctly uncomfortable once the conversation with Emily Sutter ended. She had found herself immediately liking Sam's mother and she saw that as dangerous for her purposes. These people—or at least their ancestors—had obtained Malmaison in an unscrupulous manner. Clearly the fates had somehow arranged for her to come forward in time so that she could discover some document or other evidence that would prove the estate was hers. She even dared to hope that she might be able to find the evidence necessary to turn back history and prevent Thomas's tragic death.

Sam Sutter was strangely silent. He studied her from behind the barrier of his glasses and his steepled fingertips. His silence was unnerving. "If there's nothing else," she said primly, "I will go and find Freddie. After all, time is passing, and there is much to accomplish."

"Why did my mother's suggestion that we attend the ball as my great-great-grandparents upset you, Ginny?"

She tried a disarming laugh that didn't quite work. "I wasn't upset. I was surprised . . . and honored, of course. Your mother doesn't even know me, and yet she would entrust a family member's memory to my care. I was quite flattered." She saw immediately that Sam was unconvinced. "Was there anything else?"

He stood up. "Yes, let me show you the portrait my mother mentioned. That way you'll have less trouble locating the gown in the attic."

"I'm sure Freddie . . ."

He took her arm and led the way to the door. She

could feel the strength and the heat of his hand through her sleeve. "I'll show you," he repeated as he opened the door and ushered her out.

She had the sensation that he was gauging her every reaction as together they climbed the broad marble stairway. The second floor living area was flooded in sunlight made brighter by the clear blue skies and the reflection of the light off the freshly fallen snow. The yellow silk damask covering the furniture in each of the three sitting areas as well as the rich warm oak and mahogany tables and writing desks fairly glowed. The room was large even by nineteenth-century standards. Her parents had wanted it to be spacious enough to permit a house full of guests always to find a place where they could read a book, hold a quiet conversation, or write letters.

The colors in the three Oriental rugs that defined each individual sitting area seemed even deeper and more vivid than she had ever seen them. She kept her eyes cast down to study the intricate designs as she hurried to keep up with Sam's long strides. She glanced up once and realized that his destination was the far end of the large room where the portrait hung over the fireplace.

She had thought she was prepared to see it, but it had not occurred to her that it had replaced a portrait of Thomas and her. Anger raged through her as she realized how this man and his family had displaced everything she had loved and held dear. She jerked her arm free of his grip and stopped ten yards from the fireplace.

"Mr. Sutter, this is ridiculous and completely unnecessary. Obviously it is you who are upset by the thought that I might be cast in the role of your relative. Please do not trouble yourself. I am certain that Freddie will assist me in finding something else to wear for tonight's ball. Now, if you will excuse me . . ."

"On the contrary, Ginny. I think Mom had a wonderful idea. We will receive our guests here as my great-great-grandparents would have and then escort them downstairs for dinner, followed by the musicale and then the dancing and toasts. I believe that gown would be quite stunning on you and I insist you wear it."

You insist? She whirled around and faced him. He was sitting on the fragile arm of one of her favorite Louis XVI chairs. He had pushed his ever-present glasses up to rest on top of his head, and they lay half buried in the thick, rich, unruly forest of his sable hair. He had crossed one ankle over his knee, and she saw that he was wearing some sort of moccasinlike slipper and no stockings. His trousers were of the same soft rustic fabric as the outfit Freddie had given her for sleeping, and on top he wore another version of the undergarment—this one with long sleeves and no writing.

She realized that he was deliberately baiting her, testing her. "Sam, I know you have every reason to be wary of my presence here, but I can assure you that my respect for this house and its property is without question. There is nothing I would do to bring harm or shame upon Malmaison."

"Then you should wear the gown and be here at my side when the guests arrive. They will get caught up in the romance of that, of the overall history of the estate, and they will loosen their death grips on their wallets." He stood and walked very close to her. "And that, my dear Ginny," he said softly as he gently pushed a lock of her hair back from her cheek, "is what tonight is *really* about."

He left her standing in the center of the room where she had entertained guests at innumerable weekend and more formal gatherings. Idly she ran her fingers over the writing desk where she had sat on many a cold winter day like this, answering invitations, writing thank-you notes, and making entries in her diary. She had always loved this room. In spite of its size, it had always been a cozy and comforting place to be. She strolled among the chairs and sofas, recalling conversations, laughter, and quiet evenings waiting for Thomas to return from some business meeting. She was pleased to see the fresh floral arrangements decorating the corners of the mantelpiece. She closed her eyes for a moment and then opened them and looked up at the portrait. So this was Cashwell Sutter. This was the man responsible for her husband's death and her obvious eviction from Malmaison.

Chapter 5

IT WAS COLD in the attic, and Ginny was glad that
Freddie had insisted she put on a colorful, lightweight,
puffy coat he brought her from Emily's wardrobe. She
could see her breath as she followed him up the narrow
stairway.

"I went through Emily's inventory ledger, and I'm
pretty sure I know exactly where the gown will be,"
Freddie said. "We can be in and out of here in no time
at all." He fumbled with a ring of keys and finally found
the right one. Once he had opened the lock, he pushed
the door open and stood aside for Ginny to enter.

The room was amazingly well-organized. It was a little like entering a library, only this was a library of
clothing. Each garment had been carefully packaged and
labeled. There were trunks and chests. "Accessories, un-
derwear, that sort of thing," Freddie explained as he hurried down the center aisle. He looked from the labels on
the walls to the notes in his hand until he found the area
he wanted. "Here," he called and disappeared into a rack
of clothing.

Ginny had been slowly walking along, reading the

carefully printed labels. Specially constructed cloth bags
carefully protected the hung clothing. The air was rich
with the scent of cedar and southernwood, both intended
to protect from moths and other destructive creatures.
Each piece was named and dated:

Mrs. Christine Sutter Conway, Wedding, 1958.
Miss Eileen Sutter, Graduation, 1923.
Master Byron Ross Sutter, Christening, 1904.
Colonel Cashwell Sutter, Riding Habit, 1900.

She heard Freddie's muffled commentary as he sorted
through a group of clothing. "Found it," he called and
appeared a moment later with the plain tan garment bag
in hand. He hung it on a hook on one of the supporting
posts and pointed to a trunk. "The accessories should be
there," he said.

Ginny's heart pounded. The trunk was hers. It even
showed her initials just above the lock. She walked over
to it as if in a dream. Slowly she lifted the lid. The inside
was covered in a fabric printed with tiny pink rosebuds.
The tray held an assortment of articles—gloves, evening
bags, beaded hair ornaments. The trunk smelled of
lavender. Behind her she could hear Freddie opening the
covering of the gown. Perhaps in the dim light he
wouldn't notice the tears that welled.

"You're crying," he said, and his voice was laced with
alarm.

"It's nothing," she assured him. "Truly."

He looked at the gown. "It is incredible, isn't it?
Thinking about Mrs. Sutter getting ready for her ball a
century ago just like we're getting you ready for tonight?" He reached past her and pulled out a pair of
elbow-length, cream-colored gloves. "These, don't you
think?"

Ginny turned and looked at the gown. It was beautiful.
A deep forest green silk with delicate pleating at the
low-cut neckline, a fitted bodice and a bell-shaped skirt

that flared to a slight train in back. The intricate pleating was repeated down one side of the skirt and around the hem where it highlighted a dainty handmade lace trim. The wide shoulder straps were fashioned from silk and beaded flowers. Ginny knew that there would have been matching silk flowers for her hair and a folding fan to carry over one wrist by means of a long satin ribbon.

"With your coloring and that perfect skin, you are going to be a real knockout in this," Freddie said. "Sam will have to get the jewels from the safe and bring them to you later. Is there anything else you want from up here?"

"No." She reached to close the lid of the trunk and saw the edge of her own leather diary hidden under a pile of lace handkerchiefs. Suddenly she realized that the journal might tell her how things had turned out. It would help her understand why she was in this place, this time. "Perhaps this shawl," she said and moved so that Freddie could not see her gather the diary into the fold of a lace shawl. She closed the trunk and turned, clutching the shawl to her chest. "I think that will suffice," she said with a smile.

"I'll have Peggy Wilson stop by your room later. She's responsible for maintaining all the household linens and an absolute wonder with a needle and thread. If that gown doesn't fit now, she'll make it look as if it was made for you."

"I'll just take everything to my room for now. Thank you, Freddie, for thinking of my needs."

"Don't mention it." But his broad smile told her that he was touched by her appreciation.

Downstairs, all was chaos. Freddie went off to make peace between the floral designer and the musicians, while Ginny was left with the decorators.

"We have all of this *stuff,*" one of them complained, "and no earthly idea what to do with it."

"Emily wants the house exactly as it would have been—that means every knickknack and doodad in its proper place," another chimed in, "which might have been fun if we knew where anything went."

"Why don't we give our attention first to the rooms that our guests will view this evening?" suggested a third, who then turned to Ginny. "Freddie said you knew the house, and Emily insisted that we had to wait for you to get here. Well, honey, the clock is ticking, and we've got one hell of a lot of stuff to distribute in about six hours."

Ginny tried to hide her shock at the woman's profanity. The decorator was a large and outspoken woman named Kate, and in spite of her salty language, Ginny liked her the best of the three. "I think that yours is an excellent idea. It is my understanding that our guests this evening will convene in the upstairs living area, so perhaps we should start there."

For the next several hours, Ginny worked with the trio of decorators. She found that Kate was a capable leader and quite funny in her earthy, direct manner. Ginny found herself enjoying "playing with her house," as Thomas used to tease her when she went on a spree of rearranging everything, including the furniture.

"Are you sure that chair was there?" Kate asked when they had finished setting up the music room—their last room.

"I am quite certain," Ginny declared. It was hard not to confide to the women that she was working from memories that for her were less than a week old rather than an entire century. She could not deny that perhaps the Sutter woman had come in and rearranged all of her furniture and mementos, but she was determined to make Malmaison as it had been when she was its mistress.

It amazed her how many of her things were still in place, especially the smaller items—picture frames, desk accessories, vases. Did the Sutters have nothing of their own to bring? she wondered. The mystery was explained when she followed Kate and the others back to the west

wing of the house. There she found that rooms, once
reserved for live-in servants, were now lined with
shelves and cabinets where an array of items were
tagged and stored in much the same way the clothing
had been in the attic. As she walked along the hallway,
she saw that the items filled several rooms. Clearly, the
Sutters had had a great deal of "stuff," as Kate referred
to it.

"What about these things?" Ginny asked.

"Oh, those," Kate replied with a dismissive wave of
her hand. "Emily told me we weren't to use anything
that would not have been in the house prior to 1900.
There are some very good pieces there, but it's all from
this century. Emily is a real stickler for authenticity.
She's promised Freddie and me that once the renovation
is done, she'll let us throw a twenties bash, complete
with flapper dresses and bathtub gin." The heavyset
woman launched into an impromptu dance step that involved kicking her leg out to the front and then to the
back as she sang, "Charleston, Charleston. Boop-boop-
be-doop."

Ginny couldn't help herself. She laughed, covering
her mouth with her hand at first so as not to offend the
woman. Then she saw that everyone else was laughing,
even Kate, so she released her mirth, and it felt so wonderful. For the first time in what seemed like weeks, she
felt free and truly alive. She laughed with the other
women until all of them were wiping away tears. Their
laughter would subside and then start up again, as if it
had a life of its own. When Freddie appeared in the
pantry, asking what was so funny, Kate replied simply,
"You had to be there," and they collapsed into fresh
gales of laughter.

"Come on, Ginny. Let me teach you to Charleston,"
Kate urged. "It's clear that you're way too young to
know this dance, but I would have thought in all your
research it would have come up somewhere."

She grabbed Ginny's hands and led her in the steps

of the dance while Freddie and the other two decorators hummed along. Ginny stumbled through the steps and then began to get the rhythm of it. She had always been a good dancer, had always loved to dance.

"Now you've got it. Try this!" Kate shouted above the singing of the others. She bent and did a ridiculous movement of passing her crossed hands back and forth over her knees. Ginny tried it, and her awkward attempt set them all to laughing again. It was then that she glanced up and saw Sam Sutter standing in the doorway.

"Ms. Thornton, when you have a minute," he said and turned and walked away.

Caught unawares, she nevertheless heard in his tone and saw in the faces of her compatriots that this was not likely to be a friendly meeting. "Of course," she replied and followed him down the hall.

Sam was confused and irritated by the constant inter-ruptions he was experiencing ever since Ginny Thornton had appeared in his conservatory. He had stopped by the security center of the estate to give the staff instructions for receiving guests for the ball. The security guard was reviewing the tapes completed earlier that day. As Sam stood talking to them, something had caught his atten-tion on one of the dozen or so screens behind them. Each screen reflected the recordings of one of the security cameras in various parts of the house. He saw Freddie with Ginny and recognized their location as the upstairs hallway. She was carrying some sort of bundle while Freddie carried a garment bag, no doubt the costume she was to wear for the evening.

"Can you pause and enlarge that image, please, Frank?" he asked. Leaning in close to the screen, he put on his glasses and studied the frozen image.

"Was there something in particular, Sam?" the secu-rity guard asked.

"No. I thought I saw something, but it's nothing to be

concerned about. Let it roll." It was a lie. He didn't want anyone to know that he had questions about Ginny—at least not until he could decide what was driving the nagging feeling that all was not as it seemed with her.

He watched as the action continued. Freddie and Ginny went into her room. Freddie came out almost immediately without the garment bag and went back down the hallway toward the backstairs. Ginny appeared a moment later. She was also empty-handed. Whatever he'd seen covered by the shawl had been left in her room. He was fairly certain that it was a book of some sort and that she had deliberately concealed it to get it out of the attic without Freddie's knowledge.

He had gone directly from the security office to her room. The shawl was on the bed. The garment bag had been removed, and the gown hung in the dressing room. The book was nowhere in sight. Using his investigative instincts, he considered her movements during that short span of time between when Freddie had left the room and she had appeared in the hallway empty-handed. She had hidden it hastily. He considered the way the shawl had been tossed onto the bed in a casual manner. He noticed how the edge of the bedspread had gotten caught up between the mattress and springs. He lifted the corner of the mattress and revealed the book.

MY JOURNAL,
VIRGINIA HOBBS THORNTON, 1899

He stood by the bed turning the pages, as it became clear to him what had brought Ginny Thornton to Malmaison and exactly why she had such a depth of knowledge about the estate. He snapped the diary shut and went in search of her.

Now as he strode down the hall ahead of her, past dozens of workers putting the final touches on preparations for the gala, he wrestled with anger and disappointment. Anger, because she might have said who she was from the beginning. Disappointment because he had no choice but to ask her to leave when the fact was she intrigued him—the strange formality of her diction, the regal set of her shoulders, the haunting look that came over her at the oddest moments.

He could hear her footsteps behind him. She practically had to jog to keep up, but he did not slow his pace. She followed him through the main rooms of the house to the library where he mounted the spiral stairs and opened the latch to the secret room. Only then did he pause to permit her to catch up. "I believe it was your family who liked to use this room for private business conversations," he commented as he ushered her inside and closed the door.

He indicated that she should take the straight-backed chair near the stained-glass window. He pulled the journal from his pocket and laid it on the small table next to her. He saw guilt written across her features as she stared at the leather-covered book. "Why didn't you just tell me that you are the great-great-granddaughter of Thomas Thornton and his wife Virginia?" he demanded.

"I—"

"Let me finish." She was flashing those enormous green eyes of hers at him. She must know their effect, but this was business, and he had no intention of getting caught up in the spell of her emerald eyes made even more dramatic by her unflawed skin, set off by that mass of copper hair. He realized he was staring at her and that she was waiting for him to continue speaking. "Let me finish," he repeated more calmly. "While my mother is the keeper of the flame when it comes to the legends and history associated with Malmaison, I am well aware that there was the issue of how my forefathers acquired the estate."

He took some pleasure in the fact that she could not disguise the stiffening of her spine at the mention of this unpleasant story. "I expect that the version passed down on your side of the family differs significantly from the

one that has come through the generations in my family.
The difference is that I can prove my family's story. Can
you say the same, Ginny?"

His cell phone rang, and he pulled it out of his pocket
to answer. "Sutter," he said, never taking his eyes off
Ginny as he listened. "I'll be right there." He snapped
the phone shut. "There's a problem with one of the experiments in the conservatory. I have to go." He ran his
fingers through his hair, trying to decide what to do,
trying to decide if he could trust her, knowing that Freddie needed her help to pull off the party properly. "We
aren't finished with this conversation," he said as he
leaned over and picked up the journal. "I'd like to think
that I could trust you not to go snooping around, picking
up things that don't belong to you and spiriting them
away to your room." He tapped the journal against his
thigh. Why the hell didn't she say something? It was
unnerving just having her sit there, calmly watching him
as if they'd been discussing the weather.

"May I speak now?" she asked when the silence had
gone on for a long moment, and he still had made no
move to leave.

He nodded.

"I am not a thief, Mr. Sutter. I saw the journal when
Freddie and I were in the attic. I wanted to read it. I had
no intention of stealing it. I thought that there would be
no objection to my using the documents for my research
within the confines of the house. I concealed the journal
because I did not want to have to explain it to Freddie.
Of course, now that you've deduced what my research
concerns, perhaps you are the one with something to
hide."

She stood up and swept past him. At the door, she
turned. "You have given me an assignment, one I intend
to fulfill. I assure you that I am exactly the person you
need to manage things in your mother's absence. I will
do nothing to disgrace this house. What you need to
understand is that I love Malmaison, and there is nothing

I would do—or permit others to do—to place it in harm's way. There is a great deal to be done before this evening's gala. Unless you intend to discharge me, I would respectfully suggest that you attend to your experiment and let me attend to tonight's ball." With that, she expertly pressed the combination of triggers necessary to reopen the door—a combination he had thought only owners of the house could know—and she left the room.

Sam stood in the center of the small room for several minutes after she left. He found that he was struggling to organize his thoughts, his emotions. What was it about this woman that made him want to comfort her one minute and strangle her the next? He realized he had begun tapping the journal against his thigh again. He opened it and turned the pages so he could reread the last entry.

> *December 22, 1899—Tomorrow the guests will begin to arrive. All is in readiness for the coming weeks of parties and balls and entertainment . . . at least outwardly so. Still, there is a pall that seems to penetrate our daily lives. Oh, Thomas, what is it that you are keeping from me—that has consumed you with worry and fear? Why won't you let me help you? Have I failed you so miserably in not giving you an heir? Perhaps this new century will bring us greater happiness. Perhaps . . .*

The entry stopped there as if she had been interrupted. He wondered if Thomas had walked in. More than likely it had been one of the servants or guests. From the sound of things, Thomas had not been very attentive for quite some time. From what Sam knew of the story, there was good reason why the man would be distracted. He closed the book and left the secret room. On his way to the conservatory, he handed the journal to a member of the staff and asked her to place it in Ms. Thornton's bedroom.

Ginny watched from the windows in the music room as Sam hurried through the arbor to the conservatory. In the few hours she had been in the house, she had become used to his long-legged and purposeful stride. He moved as if he always knew clearly where he was headed and what he intended to do once he arrived. She envied him that.

She thought about their interview in the secret room. At first she had thought that it was her secret that he had uncovered. When he placed her journal on the table, her heart had leapt with apprehension. Then he had given her the perfect reason for coming to Malmaison, the perfect explanation for the mystery surrounding her arrival. He thought she was her own great-great-granddaughter come to clear her family's name. His assumptions had given her a reprieve, and she could concentrate on discovering why she had been catapulted one hundred years into the future and how she might return safely to her own time.

"Ginny?"

Freddie Fincastle stood at the door. "Yes, Freddie?" Reluctantly she turned her attention back to the present.

"I thought we should have a short huddle with both the temporary and the regular staffs to go over the evening's agenda."

"A 'huddle'?"

"You know, like in football, where the team all gathers on the sidelines and discusses their next play?" She must have given him a blank stare. "A meeting?" he said as if speaking to a not-so-bright child.

"Well, of course," she replied. "What a good plan, Freddie. Where shall we meet?"

"I've asked everyone to gather in the dining room in fifteen minutes if that works for you."

"I'll be there."

He turned, and then paused and looked back. "You understand that this is your meeting as well? I mean, you should give them some pointers about how to act, how to stay in character, okay?"

Ginny smiled. "It does feel a bit like a performance, doesn't it?"

"Exactly my point. We've got a bunch of young folks out there who haven't the foggiest notion of what life was like in 1970, much less in 1899. You're going to have to coach them, Ginny. I've got my hands full just making sure everything comes out of the kitchen at the right time."

"I won't disappoint you, Freddie."

He gave a sigh of relief. "That's great. You know, even though you weren't Emily's first choice for the curator job, I for one am very glad the other one didn't show up. The way you handled Kate and the others today was nothing short of miraculous. See you in a few minutes, Gin."

Gin? If they kept shortening her name, before too long she would be known as simply "G." It was a peculiar habit, these twentieth-century people had, as if they hadn't the time to call out a proper name.

By the time the meeting had ended, Ginny just wanted to be alone. Her head was spinning as she tried to adjust to a never-ending stream of changes in the world as she had known it. There were so many people in the house, and the guests hadn't begun to arrive yet. When they did, they would come by means of conveyances in an assortment of sizes and colors, all propelled by some sort of internal motor. Apparently in the hundred years that had elapsed since her time, industry had found ways to mechanize almost everything.

There were security guards stationed discreetly

throughout the public rooms and around the grounds. The kitchen—that she had avoided all day—was a chaotic crowd of cooks, pastry chefs, and wine stewards. Throughout the downstairs rooms Kate and the other decorators were working alongside a small army of florists who were putting the final touches on the setting. There were musicians setting up equipment and warming up their instruments. And there were the hired actors—people Emily had retained to play the parts of various historic characters to add to the evening's atmosphere—being rehearsed to play their roles and given their costumes for the night.

Freddie moved quickly from room to room, making certain that all was in readiness. Somewhere in all of this, he had found time to don his costume for the evening. Ginny had been shocked to see how much he resembled Mr. Holt. He certainly was as capable as Lucas was.

She had not seen Sam since leaving him in the secret room so she assumed that he had decided to allow her to stay for the evening. She had had no time to study her journal, to see what she might have written following Thomas's death.

At Freddie's urging, she climbed the stairs to dress for her part in the evening's festivities. She was to transform herself and emerge as Mrs. Sutter, Sam's great-great-grandmother and the wife of the man who had stood by while Thomas put a gun to his head. When she entered her room, the first thing she saw was the journal lying on her dressing table. She ran to it and read the last entry.

Disappointed that it told her nothing, she turned and saw the gown she would wear for the ball hanging just inside the dressing room. She felt more like a traitor than ever and wondered how on earth she could possibly get through the evening playing her role in this farce.

• • •

Sam waited impatiently in the family living quarters. He stood beneath the portrait of his great-great-grandparents, adjusting the stiff collar of his shirt for the twentieth time. Where was she? The guests were starting to arrive. He could hear them being greeted in the downstairs vestibule, knew Freddie would soon lead the first group of them up the wide marble staircase to the living quarters where they would enjoy drinks and appetizers as they eased themselves into the ambience of the evening.

Waiters in white jackets stood by with trays of canapés, ready to circulate and serve the guests. The room was heavy with the scent of roses and evergreens. The lighting had been kept deliberately low to simulate the subdued lighting of a century earlier. A fire blazed in the fireplace, and the drapes were open to expose the view of the lit, snow-covered gardens below. *Where the hell was she?*

"Good evening, Colonel."

She was a vision. His great-great-grandmother had been a beauty in her day, but nothing to compare with Ginny Thornton. The first thing he noticed was the way the gown accented the whiteness of her shoulders and neck. The second was that she moved as if she had been dressing in corsets and ballgowns all of her life.

"You look lovely," he said and held out his hand to her.

She laid hers delicately on top of his. She was wearing soft kid gloves that reached almost to her shoulders. There was something very erotic about those gloves. Perhaps it was the way they exposed only an inch of skin between the top of the glove and the wide shoulder straps of her gown. Perhaps it was the thought that came to him unexpectedly of what it might be like to peel the glove slowly down the length of her arm.

"I have something to complete your costume," he said

as he escorted her to a chair by the fireplace.

She sat and waited. She said nothing, and it was that silence that was unnerving.

Sam took the jeweler's box from the mantel and opened it. Inside was the heavy emerald choker shown in the portrait. He placed it around Ginny's slender exposed throat, and his hands shook as he tried to work the clasp.

"I can do it," she said quietly, reaching back to fasten the necklace.

"There's a bracelet and earrings as well," he said, presenting the bracelet.

Ginny held out one hand, and he fastened the bracelet on her wrist over her glove. He bent his head to concentrate on the clasp and felt her breath on his cheek as she watched him. "You'd better do these," he said, handing her the earrings and closing the silk-lined box with a snap of its tiny metal hinges.

With a practiced hand she put on the earrings, then stood. "I think our guests have arrived," she said. "Shall we greet them?"

It was clear to him that she would be true to her word. She would play her part to perfection. He offered his arm, felt her hesitation before she placed her hand in the crook of his elbow, and together they walked the length of the room to greet their first guests.

The evening was an unqualified success. Ginny saw that Freddie could barely contain his joy at the way things were going. The invited guests quickly got into the spirit of things and were soon making up nineteenth-century roles for themselves, telling stories of life as a lumber baron, politician, or famous entertainer. When the chamber orchestra played, the guests sat on the gilded straight chairs in the winter garden or stood on the steps that led to the sunken room. They applauded each number politely as they sipped their wine.

Dinner was served in the baronial dining room at the table Thomas had had specially built to accommodate one hundred guests at one seating. The table was set with the estate's best china and crystal. It was Ginny who had corrected the plans for using tableware that she had never seen and assumed had belonged to the Sutters. Instead, she had persuaded Freddie to have the table set with the beautiful crystal, china, and silver that had been handed down through the generations of her own family. The multitiered candelabra and the chandeliers Thomas had insisted they bring home from a trip to Paris lit the room. Sam announced that the log in the enormous fireplace where three grown men could stand upright shoulder to shoulder was, in fact, the Yule log from the estate's Christmas tree.

A waiter was stationed behind each person's chair and on cue pulled the chairs away from the table so that the guests were seated simultaneously. In the same way, the battalion of waiters served the various courses of the meal. Freddie presented a course to Ginny in her role as the famous Mrs. Sutter. With her nod of approval, the food was then instantly served to all one hundred guests. It was a ballet of gourmet dining. The mood was festive, enhanced by the gentle clink of crystal stemware raised in a toast or the placement of silver knives and forks placed on bone china.

Sam had led Ginny to one end of the table and then had taken his place at the opposite end. She was aware of him watching her throughout the meal. If she laughed at something that the guest to her right or left said, his eyes were instantly on her. Each time she would meet his stare defiantly. *I am doing my job. You have my word.*

She could not stop thinking about his fingers touching her bare neck as he tried to fasten the necklace. In truth, she had stopped him and done it herself to escape the sweet torture of his touch. He was her enemy, or at least a man with whom it would be impossible even to consider more than the most businesslike relationship, and yet his fingers on her neck had made her think such shocking thoughts, had made her imagine such scandalous things.

She had seen the way he looked at her in that first moment when she had come upon him unawares. There had been no time for him to compose his expression. She knew the look a man gives a woman he finds desirable. She had seen that look on Sam's face. What's more, she had been flattered by its presence.

After dinner the party moved up the grand staircase to the ballroom. Ginny walked up with the mayor and his wife. Sam followed with a renowned and elderly philanthropist. She could feel Sam watching her even though he remained half a room away from her. She wondered if he would ask her to dance and then decided that she was getting far too caught up in the magic and romance of the setting. Perhaps she was remembering dances with Thomas, but oddly it was not Thomas who led her around the floor when she closed her eyes. The man she saw in her fantasy was Sam Sutter.

Freddie paused at her side. "It's going splendidly," he gushed. "Don't you think, Ginny? We couldn't have done it without you. Look at you—the belle of the ball."

Ginny blushed. "Be still. Someone will hear you. Do you think Sam is pleased?"

Freddie released a most ungentlemanly snort. "Pleased? The man can't take his frigging eyes off you. It's Emily who would be pleased. She's been pining away for Sam to find romance, and she would be—oh, my stars in heaven. Look at that." Freddie hurried off to rescue an obviously inexperienced waiter who was about to dump an entire tray of champagne-filled glasses on the head of the unsuspecting wife of the governor.

"Would you care to dance, Ms. Thornton?"

Ginny had been unaware of Sam's approach. She looked up at him, saw that he was smiling, and felt relief. He had obviously not heard Freddie's ridiculous prattle. "I'd be honored, Dr. Sutter," she replied.

He led her to the center of the ballroom floor. The orchestra struck up a waltz, and he held out his arms to her. Ginny was aware that no other guests were dancing. They had formed a circle and were waiting for her to complete the illusion. Colonel Cashwell Sutter and his beautiful wife leading the dance on New Year's Eve, 1899.

"Actually, it never happened," she said as Sam led her expertly around the polished parquet floor.

"What?"

"This night."

He gave her a quizzical smile. "As a scientist, Ginny, I believe I can prove that there had to have been a December thirty-first in 1899. Otherwise we would not be here tonight."

"Oh, I don't mean that the date—the day—did not occur. There simply was no grand ball."

"And you would know that because . . . ?"

He was teasing her. Thomas used to do that as well. Even one hundred years into the future, it seemed that men found women incapable of rational thought. "In that year, there was a terrible . . . accident in this house. It occurred just before New Year's Eve, and so the ball never transpired."

"You must be mistaken. My mother has researched this thoroughly. She found the menus, the entertainment, and the clothes. That necklace you're wearing was a gift from my great-great-grandfather given that very night at the stroke of midnight to mark the new century."

"It's a charming and romantic tale, Sam. It simply never happened."

She felt his hand tighten at her waist, saw his jaw flinch slightly. This was a man who did not like to be contradicted, especially when he was certain of his facts. He spun her around the room, saying nothing, his eyes locked on her face.

Ginny refused to permit him to intimidate her. She

knew very well what had and had not transpired that terrible holiday. No one danced, and it was sorrow and desolation, not gaiety, that marked the coming of the new century. "I will simply have to prove to you that your facts are wrong, Sam," she said evenly. "In the meantime, we have become the object of attention and speculation. I would suggest that a smile from you might relieve that."

He glanced briefly around the room as if he had forgotten anyone else was there. He smiled and motioned to others that they should join in the dance as he led Ginny from the floor. "We'll continue this debate another time," he said. "For now, we have guests."

"Indeed," Ginny replied and turned her attention to the elderly millionaire who immediately led her back to the dance floor.

Sam watched her. He'd spent more of the evening than he cared to admit watching her. From the moment he had turned and seen her standing there, looking exactly as if she had stepped out of the portrait over the fireplace, he had been incapable of taking his eyes off her. Now she was dancing with Sebastian Corwell, an octogenarian who could buy Malmaison and all its treasures and never feel the pinch. She was laughing, her head thrown back to expose the incredibly beautiful line of her long, slender neck. Sebastian might be old, but he wasn't dead, and he wasn't above sneaking a peek at the décolletage cleverly concealed by the tiny pleats of her gown.

"Is anything the matter, Sam?" Freddie was at his side, studying him.

"Nothing," Sam replied with a faked heartiness. He deliberately turned away from the dance floor, even though he could still hear the music of her laughter floating across the room. "What happens at midnight, my friend?"

Freddie consulted the small notebook that he had referred to for weeks as his millennium Bible. "According to Emily's research, at eleven-fifty-five, Colonel Sutter gathered all the guests on the balcony to watch the fireworks, which began, of course, at the stroke of midnight. But first he made sure everyone had champagne and gave a toast."

"And it would be my guess that Mom found the actual words of the toast?"

"Oddly, no. It was the one piece of information she failed to uncover. I'm afraid you're on your own on that one."

"You could have warned me," Sam protested.

"I know, but you'd have only fretted and worried, and it'll be better if it simply comes from your heart. You'll see. I'll go see to the serving of the champagne."

An enormous ice bucket was brought on a wheeled cart to the French doors that led to the balcony. Again, the waiters stood at attention along the walls. They balanced silver trays filled with crystal stemware. Freddie directed Sam to pop the cork on a magnum of champagne, and the sound garnered him the undivided attention of every guest. The waiters moved forward, and Freddie filled glasses, dispersing the waiters into the crowd as if commanding a battle campaign.

The orchestra had stopped playing, and now the room was filled with laughter and conversation as every guest pushed forward to secure a place close to Sam. Sam looked around the room. "Freddie, find Ginny. She should be here. Colonel Sutter's bride would have been at his side."

Ginny was found and brought forward. She and Sam exchanged wary glances as he held out his hand to her and presented her to the crowd. Freddie pressed a glass of champagne into her hand, tapped a finger on his watch to remind Sam of the time, and disappeared into the crowd.

Sam cleared his throat. "Ladies and gentlemen, we

stand here tonight as the guests of my ancestors did a century ago. If they could have looked ahead, what wonders they might have seen. Similarly, we stand here on the brink of not only a new century, but also a new millennium. For Malmaison, the new century marks a new beginning, a restoration of its beauty, its gardens, and its forests. As most of you know, I think not of the past, but of the future. Malmaison is not just a piece of history. It is a place where we can find answers for the future."

He raised his glass. "To Malmaison," he said and drank the sweet, bubbly wine.

"To Malmaison," the guests chanted in unison and drank from their glasses.

Someone in the back of the room began the countdown. The French doors were opened, and guests crowded onto the balcony. *Nine . . . eight . . .* Sam placed his hand at the hollow of Ginny's back and gently guided her onto the balcony. She glanced back at him when he touched her but showed no other reaction.

Five . . . four . . . three . . .

In that millisecond before the dawning of a new millennium, he decided that he would kiss her. He knew at the same instant that it had nothing to do with playing out a historical role. There was something about her, something about the odd way in which they had been brought together, that made the action seem exactly right. He pulled her close, knowing the tightening of his arm around her slim waist would cause her to turn and look up at him.

Two . . . one! Happy New Year!

He pulled her close and bent to meet her lips, slightly parted in surprise. He cupped her face in both his hands as he deepened the kiss. She did not resist. Sam was barely aware of the flash of the fireworks or the excited murmuring of the guests as they enjoyed the spectacle. He only knew that kissing this woman was not a casual act. It was as if the forces of the night had joined to bring them to this moment. He felt the steady throb of his own heart against her palm flattened on his chest. He felt a rush of desire such as none he had ever experienced before—unrestrained, turbulent, surging through him, driving his actions. It was a completely irrational act from a man who took pride in always considering the rationale of everything he did.

When he broke the kiss, she stood there, her face still upturned. He saw in the flare of a rocket that her eyes were closed. He allowed himself the luxury of trailing his thumbs gently across her cheeks before he released her. She opened her eyes, but said nothing. She just looked at him as if surprised to see him. It was then that he noticed the tear winding slowly down her cheek. Without a glance at the awe-inspiring display of fireworks, she turned and worked her way quickly through the crowd and back inside the house.

Sam tried to follow her, but his larger size made getting through the crowd more difficult. "Ginny!" he called as soon as he stepped into the ballroom. A waiter clearing away glasses looked up at him. The musicians paused in their conversation and glanced in the direction of the hallway. Sam took their cue. He caught a glimpse of her running down the staircase. "Ginny!"

"Leave me alone, I beg of you," she replied and did not pause as she reached the bottom of the stairs and hurried across the winter garden. He heard her footsteps on the tiled floor of the corridor leading to the lower balcony. From the windows in the upstairs living quarters he saw her running along the arbor path toward the conservatory. Something told him that he would only make things worse by going after her.

"The guests are coming back inside," Freddie reported from the entrance to the ballroom.

"Coming," Sam replied with a last look out the window. She had reached the conservatory and was safely inside.

By the time she reached the conservatory, Ginny's

sobs were uncontrollable. What was happening to her? Why could she not wake from this nightmare? How could she have willingly kissed the very man she had sworn to hate? What force of fate had propelled her forward into this time that confused and frightened her? How could she ever go back? How could she have sullied her wedding vows?

She could hear the muffled booms of the fireworks. They sounded like some distant battle, and then gradually they were silenced and she heard the orchestra striking up a new tune. Someone must have closed the balcony doors because the music was suddenly softer, more subtle, a background to her thoughts.

She stood inside the conservatory door, her back pressed against it to keep Sam away should he have decided to follow her. Gradually her sobs dwindled to the occasional involuntary shudder. As she regained control of her emotions, she found herself replaying the kiss. She examined the circumstances. It was a party and the dawning of a New Year. Kissing at midnight was not uncommon. Perhaps that was all it had been. She was making too much of it. Surely all Sam had intended was a celebratory kiss, something to play out the roles they had been assigned for the evening's festivities. If that were the case, then she was behaving like some silly schoolgirl.

On the other hand, there had been that incredible moment when their eyes had met, his hand had tightened on her waist, pulling her against him. In that moment when he had pressed his body to hers and covered her mouth with his own, the kiss had lost any semblance of innocence. To her shame, she had not resisted. Why? Why had she not pulled away, pushed him away? Instead, she had permitted herself to enjoy the sensation of his lips on hers—his wonderfully full and soft lips. To her shame, she had returned his kiss. It was he who had pulled back.

When she had finally opened her eyes and seen him

in the light of the fireworks, her emotions had over-
whelmed her. There had been no thought of Thomas, no
thought that this was not proper, no thought at all that
she had permitted the direct heir of the man who had
robbed her of her husband and her estate to kiss her with
a passion that no lady would have allowed. What had
happened to her? What would become of her? God help
her, she had wanted that kiss and in wanting it, she had
wanted him.

Chapter 6

"GOOD MORNING, DARLING." It took Sam a moment to realize that it was six in the morning and his mother was calling from somewhere on the Mediterranean.

"Morning," he croaked and then cleared his throat and pushed himself half upright in the bed. He leaned over and opened the blinds, revealing a view of the mansion enshrouded in an early-morning fog. "Mom, it's barely dawn here."

"I know, and you had a late night. I thought you might just spend the night in the main house. At any rate, I just had to tell you that I've already had half a dozen messages this morning to report on last night's gala. People actually left messages or sent E-mail. Isn't that splendid?"

Sam smiled. "Only if you didn't make them swear to contact you and give a report the minute they left," he countered.

There was a pause on the other end of the line, and he knew he'd guessed right. "Checking up on me, Mom?" he teased as he threw back the covers and pad-ded across the hardwood floor to flick on the coffee-maker. The best thing about the gardener's cottage in his view was that it was so compact. No wasted space. No wasted steps.

"Not at all. I was just anxious to know all the details and I knew I couldn't rely on you to call me. Anyway, there was one call that was totally unexpected."

Sam's interest was piqued and he started opening the blinds as he listened, waiting for the details. "And?" he prompted.

"The call was from Sebastian. He has made a pledge of five million from his foundation to be given over the next three years." Her voice was breathless with excitement. "Do you understand what this means, Sam?"

"Yeah, Mom, I do. Congratulations." Sam was genuinely happy for his mother. Malmaison was her pet project, and with an unexpected five million she could accomplish a great deal.

"There was one stipulation."

"Which was?"

"That Ms. Thornton take full charge of the restoration—at least until I return. I told him that had been the intention all along, but he made it clear that without her, he would have serious questions about supporting the project."

Sam frowned. They didn't even know if Ginny had the credentials to handle such a project, and besides, she clearly had her own agenda for the estate. "Why Ginny?" he asked, gathering his facts.

"Apparently she absolutely bowled him over during dinner with her knowledge of the history and background of the estate. Then he danced with her, and I honestly think he has a bit of a crush on the woman." Emily laughed. "He may be over eighty, but he still thinks of himself as quite the charmer."

"I think it is Ms. Thornton who has been the charmer here," Sam muttered more to himself than to his mother.

"Why, Sam, you sound almost jealous," Emily teased,

and then she was all business once again. "Whatever the cause, you must make certain that Ginny is comfortable and satisfied in her position. Have Freddie show her where everything is. I assume she was presented to the board and the architect and his people at last night's ball, but you'll have to make certain that you call a meeting of the staff and make it crystal clear that until my return, Ginny speaks for me."

The connection began to break up.

"Oh, dear, Sam, I'm losing you. Can you handle this? I'm relying on you, and on Ginny, of course. What a find! Don't you agree?"

Static overtook the connection, and she was gone.

Sam switched off the phone and headed for the shower. He needed some time to think this through, but he also wanted to make sure that he was in the main house when Ginny came downstairs for the first time since running away from the party.

Ginny had been up most of the night. She had sat in the conservatory, wishing she could just go back to her own time, her own life. On the one hand, she would have to leave Malmaison forever and mourn Thomas's tragic death while trying to reestablish her life. On the other, she would not have to face all of the conflicting issues that surrounded her now. She had closed her eyes and wished and prayed to return to her own time. When she had opened her eyes, nothing had changed. The conservatory was still filled with Sam's carefully labeled experiments rather than with her beautiful blossoms.

Once she had been certain that the ball had ended and the guests had all left, she slipped back into the house. It did not escape her notice that the balcony door had been left unlocked for her. She glanced up at the nearest red blinking security light and wondered if she was being watched. In case she was, she gave a little wave of acknowledgement and continued on to her room. There she found a curious fabric bag—a little on the order of a carpetbag—sitting on the divan with a note attached to the handle.

> *Ginny,*
> *Freddie told me your luggage had been lost and you had arrived with nothing but the clothes on your back. The girls and I decided to do a little last-minute shopping this afternoon and thought these might tide you over for a few days until your things can be located. It was fun working with you today, and we're looking forward to seeing you again soon.*
>
> > *Best regards,*
>
> *Kate and her "boop-boop-be-doop" friends.*

Ginny's eyes welled with tears at the kindness of these women who were really strangers to her. She slid open the zipper on the bag and removed several outfits. There were two long skirts with matching blouses, a sweater, two dresses that appeared of a style for day wear, a pair of sturdy flat shoes, a sort of flannel nightshirt, and a separate box filled with tiny scraps of lace and silk that could only be undergarments. There wasn't a petticoat or corset in the entire box. In the bottom of the bag, she found some heavy stockings that came only to the knee and that matched the colorful garments, and yet another of the costumes of trousers and overblouse that Freddie had loaned her in lieu of proper nightclothes.

As Ginny spread the clothing over the bed and divan, an idea came to her. Perhaps if she couldn't get back to her own time just yet, she could at least leave the estate. Dressed in these clothes, surely she could move about more freely without attracting attention. Perhaps Kate would have work for her. She could find a room in a respectable boardinghouse and work for Kate. At the same time, this would permit her to stay near Malmaison but away from Sam Sutter.

Suddenly a host of ideas came to her. She could maintain contact with Freddie. With information from him and through her own research she could gather the facts she needed to prove once and for all that Cashwell Sutter had claimed the estate unfairly. She could take her facts to the proper authorities and reclaim her property. This must be why she had been thrust forward into this new time, and once she had achieved the purpose she would be able to return to her own time.

In the back of her mind, she knew that with the kiss her primary purpose had become to stay away from Sam Sutter. He was a dangerous man, made more so by the fact that he appeared perfectly harmless. His manner was one of complete unaffectedness. His attitude toward the estate was one of nonchalance. Perhaps that came from receiving an entitlement to which he truly had no right, she thought. But it was not his position on the estate that concerned her. It was his obvious assumption that he would be able to charm her into acquiescence. She understood that this was because he thought she was his contemporary and generations removed from the events of 1899. On the other hand, given his casual and unassuming manner related to matters of the estate, she could not deny that something in her demeanor must have signaled her willingness to be kissed. She had to accept that Sam Sutter was not the only source of danger if she stayed in the house. Her own traitorous attraction to the man was also a problem.

Through the night, she worked out her plan of action, writing notes to herself about what evidence she might be able to uncover to prove her rightful ownership of the estate. At the first light of dawn she put her notes away and prepared to leave. She took one last look around the room—her room—and hoped that the next time she entered it, it would be in her own role as mistress of the estate in her own time.

She had packed everything in the colorful bag given to her by Kate and the others. She crept down the back-stairs and left a note for Freddie in the kitchen. From there she proceeded to the library where she left a note she had prepared for Sam on Thomas's desk. She stood next to the desk for a long moment, recalling the events of that tragic night, suppressing yet again the fury that overcame her every time she thought about how selfish it had seemed for Thomas to take such a horrible step without thinking of the consequences for her. Every time she entertained such thoughts, she silently reprimanded herself and wondered what kind of person she must be to be so uncharitable.

She wrapped herself in her shawl, retrieved the bag, and started across the marble floor of the foyer toward the front door. Her mind was on the security system, and she wondered how she might leave without sound-ing some sort of alarm.

"Going somewhere?"

Sam's quiet voice startled her more than if he had shouted at her to cease and desist. She turned and saw him sitting casually on the stairs. He looked as if he'd been waiting for her. At the moment his eyes were fo-cused on the bag she carried.

"I . . . I am . . ." She squared her shoulders and lifted her chin purposefully. "I am leaving," she replied calmly. "I should think you would be pleased."

That brought him off the steps at a bound. He began pacing, circling her as he attempted to deal with her announcement. "Why on earth should that please me? My mother is depending on you. Freddie is depending on you. *I* am depending on you."

"*You* do not trust me," she pointed out. "Why on earth would you want me to stay?"

He paused, and she thought that perhaps she had pin-pointed the obvious. She bent to pick up the valise again and had made it two steps closer to the door when he said, "Is it because of the kiss? That's it, isn't it? You're ticked off because I kissed you ... No! You're ticked off because you enjoyed it." He looked extremely pleased with himself, as if he had just made a momentous discovery.

Ginny felt the color rush to her cheeks. "I ..." The denial froze on her lips. She would not give him the satisfaction of debating the matter. She tightened her grip on her luggage. "Believe what you want," she replied evenly. "Now, please step out of the way—or do you intend to hold me here by force?"

This last statement was unfair. Whatever his heritage, Sam Sutter was a decent person. He was also quite attractive and clearly would not need to force his attentions on a lady. Ginny had seen the way some of the female guests had fawned over him at the ball. She had observed it and chose not to consider the fact that she didn't like them looking at him that way, flirting with him, angling for a dance with him.

"Are you threatening to call the police, Ginny?"

He was laughing at her. He might be a decent fellow, but he could be quite arrogant when he chose to do so.

"Only if you intend to hold me here against my will," she announced, meeting his eyes and refusing to back away.

"We would have an interesting tale to tell, wouldn't we?" he mused as he began pacing once again. "Let's see, we can begin with the fact that you gained entrance to the conservatory without anyone knowing of your presence. Then we can tell them about your attempt to pretend that you were the curator my mother hired. At some point, we'll have to reveal that you attempted to steal a very valuable journal from the museum's collection. And we can top it off by suggesting that it's very strange that you not only know of the existence of the secret room, but how to enter and leave it as well." He had paused in his pacing and the ticking off of each offense. He stood very close to her, so close that his breath fanned a tendril of her hair as he added, "What do you think the police will make of all that, Ginny?"

Her shoulders slumped slightly. He had a point. How on earth would she explain herself? On top of that, what kind of punishment might there be for such offenses in this day and age? For all she knew, the authorities were far more strict and even cruel in their punishments. She fought to contain an involuntary shudder. "What is it that you want?" she said through gritted teeth.

"You know what I want."

Her mind raced. In her day, if a man had made that statement, the inference would have been undeniable. He would be asking for her favors. In exchange for not ruining her reputation publicly, he would expect to ruin her in private. Surely Sam Sutter was not suggesting . . .

"I want you to stay," he continued. "I'm offering you the curator's position permanently, or at least until my mother returns." He studied her shocked expression. "I am offering you a job, Ginny. Actually my mother has already offered, and it's more important than you can imagine that you honor your agreement to accept it."

"Why is that?"

He sighed and thrust his fingers into the depths of his uncombed hair. "Is anything ever simple with you? Why isn't the job enough?"

"I want to know why this is so important to you and your mother."

He began ticking off the reasons on his fingertips. "Number one, it's important to me, because frankly I have my own work to do and this place needs the full-time attention of somebody else. Number two, Freddie is terrific, but he doesn't have the administrative skills to manage the estate. I have no reason to believe that you do either except for the fact that you knew how to work the crowd last night, and that speaks for something. That brings us to number three—you dazzled the socks off Sebastian Corwell last night, and the man is prepared to give a grant of five million dollars for the restoration project on the single stipulation that you be placed in charge of that."

"Five million?" It was a fortune, a king's ransom.

Sam nodded. "Yeah, over a three-year period." He smiled. "Just what the hell did you say to him last night at dinner?"

Ginny was so stunned at the news that his profanity did not faze her. "We discussed history," she said weakly. "He asked a lot of questions."

"Well, clearly, you had the answers." He reached down and took the bag from her. "Stay, Ginny. Please."

"There can be no repeat of . . . That is, I insist that relations between us be of a strictly business nature."

"If that's what you want," he replied evenly, but she could see that he was fighting a smile.

"I mean it," she insisted. "I will work with Freddie and the rest of the staff."

"That's fine, but I will need regular reports of your work. If it makes you more comfortable, you can type those up on the computer and E-mail them to me."

Again, he was speaking of things she did not comprehend, but she would not let him see that. "As you wish," she replied.

"Occasionally you're going to have questions that Freddie and the others will not be able to answer. Occasionally you're going to have to make decisions that will affect the entire project. In those cases, I expect you to find me and discuss them before going off on your own. Is that clear?"

"Perfectly."

"This is an enormous project, Ginny."

"As you have said before," she replied, determined not to let him see how frightened she was of the responsibility and at the same time excited because of the opportunities it would give her to find the answers to her own quest.

"Suppose we begin this morning with a working breakfast—on second thought, let's start each day with a working breakfast. That way I can go over the plans for the restoration, and you can fill me in on how things are going."

Working breakfast? She sincerely hoped that the strange term meant exactly what it sounded like. "That would be acceptable," she replied.

He laughed then, and the sound echoed off the marble floor and walls. "Ginny, you are something else," he announced heartily. "Come on, let's see what's left in the kitchen. I'm starving." He put his arm around her shoulders and then immediately removed it.

She instinctively understood that the gesture had been innocent and that he had realized how it might be mistaken for something more intimate. She also understood that she was the one who had enjoyed the gesture and had missed the comforting presence of his arm around her shoulders when he pulled away.

The kitchen was the one room of the house that Ginny had scrupulously avoided since her arrival in this new age. She had been there, of course, passing through as she worked with Freddie and the others to prepare for the party, but the differences in times there were far more obvious than anywhere else in the mansion. In all the other rooms, modern touches were concealed, visible only to someone looking for them. The kitchen was a different story, and she was greatly relieved, if confused, when she realized that Sam did not expect her to prepare a meal for him.

"You sit over there and take notes," he said, finding a pencil and pad of notepaper and handing them to her. "I'll cook and fill you in on the details of what you can expect to manage over the coming weeks and months, okay?"

"That would be fine," she agreed and took the seat he had indicated at the table. She held her pencil poised and watched him.

He placed a large glass container that looked a little like a pitcher with a lid onto the counter in the center of the room. Then he lifted what appeared to be a heavier base onto the counter and fitted the glass container on top of it. A cord ran from the back of the base to three small holes in the countertop.

"The idea here is to restore the house to the way it was when it was first built in the mid-nineteenth century by your ancestors, I believe." He peeled three bananas, broke them into pieces into the container, then turned to a large icebox and retrieved a container of orange juice and a bowl of the largest raspberries Ginny had ever seen. "Basically the place has remained pretty much untouched since the turn of the century when my ancestors bought it."

She flinched at his implication that his relatives had acquired the estate in a normal real estate transaction, but remained quiet. He poured juice into the container and added a handful of whole berries. He reminded her of the local pharmacist, mixing and measuring as if in a laboratory rather than a kitchen.

"That may be great in terms of maintaining the historical integrity of the place, but it also means that things are starting to deteriorate and are in desperate need of not only cosmetic, but also structural repair. The roof, for starters . . ." He turned and thrust a large cup under an opening on the front of the icebox. To her amazement, the machine burped and shuddered and spit out crushed ice, which he added to the concoction.

"It will be difficult for the men to manage the roof in this weather," she commented.

"Exactly," he replied as he touched a button on the side of the base. Suddenly the room was filled with a terrible grinding sound. Ginny gripped the edge of the table to keep herself from fleeing the room as she watched the whole fruit and ice whirl crazily inside the container. As quickly as it began, he made it stop with another flick of the button. "Therefore," he continued as if the annihilation of the fruit had been perfectly normal, "for the first few months we will begin inside the house, specifically in the public rooms on the first floor." He poured the thick pink liquid into two stemmed glasses and handed her one as he took a long swallow from the other.

"Eggs?" he asked, tossing three in rotation like a professional juggler.

"All right," she agreed and took a tentative sip of the drink he had handed her. It was delicious. She took another sip and savored the cool refreshing sensation of the fruity liquid.

"Do you like that?" Sam's smile told her that the question was strictly rhetorical.

"It's heavenly," she replied.

"Haven't you ever had a smoothie before?"

"A *smoothie*?" She giggled. It was a ridiculous name, and yet it was perfectly descriptive.

Since it was a holiday, perhaps he had given the servants the day off. He continued to work his culinary magic as he talked. First he expertly cracked the eggs into a small bowl and stirred them briskly with a fork. "There's a whisk around here somewhere," he said, "but in a pinch, nothing like doing it the old-fashioned way." Then he poured the egg batter into a heated pan. Carefully he maneuvered the pan so that the eggs spread evenly over the bottom. "What do you want in your omelet? Tomatoes? Mushrooms? Green pepper? How about cheese?"

At the announcement of each ingredient, she nodded more because she was fascinated by the selection than that she actually knew what it would taste like. The smell of the cooking food filled the kitchen. "Oh, no!" Sam yelled and slapped the side of his head with the flat of his hand. "I forgot coffee. Can we go with tea instead?"

"Tea is lovely," she replied. "I'll put the kettle on." She stood up and looked around for the traditional utensil.

"No, that'll take too long, and the omelets are just

about perfect. There are mugs in that cabinet there. We can nuke the water and have everything ready at the same time."

What on earth did "nuke the water" mean? Ginny took her time getting two beakers from the cabinet he had indicated and filling them with water. To her relief, he took the cups from her. "I'll take these. You get the flatware and napkins." He jerked his head in the general direction of a basket filled with freshly laundered cloth napkins next to a partitioned wire container holding forks, spoons, and knives.

Behind her she heard him open and close something, then tap in a series of signals, each one giving an answering little squeak as he pushed it. When he pushed the last signal, the entire machine lit and began making noise. Granted it was less noise than the thing he had used to create the drinks, but noise nonetheless. Was this the future? A host of noisy mechanical gadgets each designed to complete only one task, but apparently to do it quickly? The machine ceased its racket and beeped a signal.

"Get those, will you?" Sam instructed as he served up the omelets and brought the plates to the table.

Ginny stood in front of the machine where she could see the steaming cups of hot water behind a glass window. The problem was that she had no idea how to open the thing. There was a wealth of instructions, but nothing that said simply "Open."

Sam reached over her shoulder and pressed a button, and the door sprang open. "I have no idea why the manufacturers have decided to make every one of these microwaves open a different way. It's downright confusing, isn't it?" He took down the cups of hot water without use of any protection to keep from burning his hands and Ginny stifled a warning. "Tea bags are in that box over there," he said, indicating direction with a nod as he set the mugs on the table without mishap.

Ginny once again followed his direction and brought

the box to the table. He also indicated that she should sit, and took his place opposite her. He used a broad-bladed knife to cut through one of the curious round breads he had brought her that first night, then put each half into yet another machine sitting next to them at the table. He pushed down a lever, and the inside of the machine began to glow. Ginny watched in fascination, and suddenly there was a "pop" and the two pieces of bread reappeared.

"Cream cheese or butter?" Sam asked.

"This is fine," she managed to say as he placed one of the breads on her plate and deposited two more in the machine.

"So, as I was saying, the work to be done is monumental. Every room needs something. Fortunately Mom has already worked all of that through with the contractors and the architects. All you'll need to do is keep everything on schedule—a tall order with so many projects to be managed at once. It's really important that everything come together in time for the reopening in May." He paused in the chewing of his food and looked at her still-filled plate. "Aren't you going to eat anything?"

"Yes, of course," she replied, keeping one eye on the bread thing, waiting for it to pop up like some kind of jack-in-the-box.

Chapter 7

BY THE TIME they had finished eating, Ginny had several pages of notes. Sam was certainly correct in assessing the overall project as monumental in scope. "It would seem that the house has been neglected for some time if it is now in need of so much repair," she ventured.

He shrugged and carried their dishes to the sink. "Look, if Mom had her way, she'd probably pour all of the family money into maintaining this place, but that's not practical. If Malmaison can't pay its own way at least on a day-to-day operations level, then there's no point in having it open to the public."

"But surely—"

"Ginny, you need to understand that my parents and I have different views when it comes to Malmaison. I suspect that your personal views regarding the estate will also conflict with my own. The fact is, however, that Malmaison is my property, and in the final analysis I will decide its purpose going forward."

"And what would that be?" Ginny asked, an ominous fear building in her chest.

"At the moment, my interests lie mainly in the potential of the property to operate as a living laboratory for my research. The gardens and woodlands, thanks to my great-great-grandfather's foresight in selecting plantings, is a virtual treasure trove of possibilities for my research into the properties of certain plants and their ability to treat certain conditions and illnesses. As you have already discovered, I have turned the conservatory into the experimental lab for developing new species and hybrids."

"I can appreciate that your work is important to you; however, surely, you must understand—"

"My work is important for the future of people everywhere, Ginny. I don't mean that to sound egotistical. It's a simple fact that it is science that will make it possible for people to continue to improve the quality of life for future generations. I appreciate what people like you and my mother want to do in preserving our past, but I cannot allow that to be done at the expense of the future."

And what of the present? Ginny thought. *My present. My future.*

"There's a great deal of work to be done for this renovation project," he continued. "Expensive work. Mom has been able to raise a good deal of grant money to get it started. Now Sebastian has come through with his gift as well, but there is also the issue of finding craftsmen capable of replicating the work. Stonemasons aren't exactly growing on trees in this day and age. They're a dying breed."

Ginny thought of the talented craftsmen who had worked on the estate when her parents were building it. Even after she and Thomas made it their home, there had been no shortage of artisans to complete the work. "This is unfortunate," she said more to herself than to Sam.

"Mom found this one guy in Vermont. He's got the right credentials and comes highly recommended. The problem is that he's in his seventies, and I'm not sure how much of the outside work he'll be able to manage."

"Perhaps we might find a willing younger apprentice," Ginny suggested. "Then the two of them could work together on the interior repairs—the fireplace mantels, the ceilings and columns in the downstairs reception area, the stairway banister. By the time the weather improves enough to permit work on the carvings outside, the apprentice might be capable of handling those tasks—under the watchful eye of the tutor, of course."

"Ginny, that's a terrific idea." Sam was staring at her with an expression of surprise. "You have a good grasp for what needs to happen here. I can see that."

It's my house, Ginny thought, *and I am not particularly pleased at the way your family has permitted it to come to this state.* "Yes, well, it's an idea," she replied modestly.

"Why don't you place an advertisement in the local paper and see what we can turn up in the way of a willing apprentice? I'll also post something at the university. An architectural history student might be a perfect candidate." He scribbled a note to himself. "Are you comfortable working with Kate and her crew for the decorating piece of all this?"

"Oh, quite. We got along splendidly yesterday," Ginny assured him.

"I'm afraid you're going to have a skeleton staff here in the house—Kate and Freddie are the only permanent employees—aside from you, of course. Which reminds me—you're probably wondering about salary, benefits, that sort of thing. Mom had incorporated room and board as a piece of the package. You can live here in the house. The room you're in is scheduled to be among the last to be redecorated. Mom wanted to be sure she was back in town for that one, so you can stay there. She thought it made the most sense because it's close to the offices and archives."

Ginny nodded.

"The pay isn't great, I'm afraid. The offer to the other

curator was for twenty-five thousand a year. Of course, you'll have medical and dental on top of that, and a 401k."

Ginny had not heard the last part. "Twenty-five thousand dollars?" she said softly.

"Yeah, to start. With the place shut down, we lose the usual income of people coming through for the next six months. Once we're up and running again, the salary will go up. Of course, then you'll have to find a place to live, so it's a trade-off."

It was a fortune—one she could use to pay off the debt Thomas had amassed with Cashwell Sutter. With that much money she could surely buy back Malmaison. This must have been the purpose in the fates thrusting her one hundred years into the future. Her heart sang with pure joy.

"Can I assume by that smile that you'll take the job?" Sam asked.

She turned her attention back to him, and her smile froze. He was looking at her not as if they were discussing a matter of business, but as if he had other thoughts—far more private and personal thoughts. She felt herself blush and cast her eyes away from his penetrating gaze.

"There must be an understanding between us," she found herself announcing.

"So you've said."

"There can be no repeat of the . . . of last night's—"

"I won't kiss you again unless you want me to," he said softly.

She nodded.

"Is that it?"

"For the moment," she replied stiffly and risked a glance at him. The cad was grinning at her.

"You drive a hard bargain, Ginny." He stuck out his hand and clearly expected her to shake it. Did ladies do that, or was he teasing her as usual?

She shook it firmly and met his eyes defiantly. "If there's nothing else, I'll just take my things back upstairs and get started with organizing these notes," she said.

He stood still, as if reluctant to leave her.

"You can go about your own occupations, Sam. I have no plans to steal the silver today," she assured him.

He laughed. "It's not that I don't trust you, Ginny. Really. It's just that there's something about you that I can't quite figure out. In my business, that can drive a guy crazy. Call if you need anything. Otherwise, I'll look forward to seeing you at four."

As soon as he had left the room, Ginny felt as if she had been released from a sort of benign prison. For the first time since her strange arrival, she was free to roam through her house, to wander from room to room, getting her bearings among these new but familiar surroundings. It was like a wonderful gift, and she wasn't about to waste a moment of the opportunity.

Sam could not get Ginny off his mind. He had intended to head straight for the conservatory. His experiments needed constant attention, and he had been neglecting them over the past couple of days. There was data to be checked and recorded, potting trays to be turned, temperatures to measure, pollen to be collected. Yet with all of that, he found himself taking a detour to the security station.

Because of the holiday and the fact that the estate would be shut down for six months, Sam had given the security crew the day off. He told himself that this was the reason he had decided to stop by the office on his way to the lab. He told himself that he only intended to make certain that the system was working, that the cameras were recording, and that alarms were set for the outer perimeters of the estate. But as soon as he entered the small room, he turned his attention immediately to the screen that showed the kitchen he had just left. Ginny was still there. He sat down at the console and watched.

She was walking around the room, examining each appliance closely. She opened the door of the refrigerator, closed it, and then quickly opened it again. A memory of himself as a little boy came rushing back. It was the day he had tried to figure out if the light inside the refrigerator stayed on all the time. Something in Ginny's actions—the quick opening and closing of the door as if she were trying to catch the light going on or off—reminded him of that childhood memory.

She studied the stove next, then the microwave and the dishwasher. She pushed a button on the dishwasher and retreated a step when the machine obviously started its wash cycle. She seemed alarmed by this and began pushing all of the buttons in an obvious attempt to stop it, glancing over her shoulder as she did as if someone might catch her in an act of wrongdoing. What was her fascination with these ordinary household appliances?

When she was unsuccessful in turning off the dishwasher, she left the room. Sam used a series of controls to follow her movements down the corridor, past the butler's pantry and storage areas and out into the main quarters of the house. She smiled as she moved toward the winter garden. He watched as she walked directly to the three-tiered fountain in the center of the room and dipped her fingers in the splashing water. She sat on the edge of the fountain and looked up, closing her eyes and basking in the warmth of the winter sun filtered through the atrium skylight. Then she was up again, walking around the perimeter of the circular room, brushing her fingertips over the fronds of the tree-sized ferns as she went.

From the winter garden she stepped up into the main reception area of the house. She walked over to the huge carved front door and touched it, then turned and looked up the stairway to the landing and the portrait she had seen that first night. What was it she had said, just before she passed out?

"In 1829 . . ."

Sam frowned as he considered her words. Clearly the portrait was of a later period than 1829, even if she hadn't known her history or styles. Just as clearly, she was right in that the house had not been built until later in the nineteenth century. Her slip of the tongue made no sense.

She was humming as she moved through the upstairs sitting room. She moved among the furnishings as if she had been in the room dozens of times, pausing now and then to adjust a picture or straighten a collection of bi-belots on a side table. She moved with a freedom, a level of comfort that she had never exhibited before, and he wondered if it was because she thought she was unob-served. He entered the commands necessary to activate the cameras that would permit him to follow her pro-gress down the hallway to where the main bedroom suites were located, including the lady's suite where she was staying.

She passed the bedrooms and continued down the hallway toward the wing that had been restored as the children's rooms and nursery. The doors were open, and he saw her step falter as she passed them. Apparently she had been on her way somewhere else—perhaps back to the attic storage area where she had found the journal. He adjusted the controls so that he could zoom in on her features. What was it that had caught her attention?

The enlarged image was grainy, but there was no doubt of her expression. She was staring at the nursery with a wistful smile. Her entire posture had relaxed. She walked into the room and touched the hem of the chris-tening gown that was displayed on the arm of the rock-ing chair. She sat down in the chair and gathered the gown to her chest. With one toe she slowly rocked the cradle his great-great-grandfather had made for the birth of his first son. She stared out the window, and it appeared that her thoughts were on some distant memory. He watched her for some time as she sat there, lost in thought as she rocked, and then she did something that startled him. She placed the gown on the cradle and laughed.

On the day of Thomas's funeral, Ginny had come to this room. It had been empty then, except for the rocking chair. Thomas had bought her that chair when they thought she might be pregnant. It was only a few months after her parents had died, and they were just getting settled into the house. Thomas had carried her down the hall and made her close her eyes as he pushed open the door to the room with his toe. "May I present the nursery," he had announced.

She had reminded him that they weren't certain, but he had dismissed the idea. *He* was certain, so certain that he had that very day ordered the carpenter to begin making a cradle and a rocking horse for when young Master Thornton was old enough to ride. How they had laughed that sunny afternoon. Thomas had sat in the rocking chair with Ginny on his lap, and they had dreamed impossible dreams for their unborn child.

A few weeks later Ginny had awakened to terrible cramping followed by a gush of blood, and that had been the end of the dream. Thomas had said nothing when she told him. He had left her bedroom, and Lucas Holt told her later that Thomas had walked down the hall and shut the door to the nursery. He told Lucas it was to remain closed at all times. Things between Ginny and Thomas had changed after that. It was as if in losing that child, they had lost their innocence. Ginny could not remember a time after that that they were ever as carefree and filled with dreams as they had been that day when he presented her with the rocking chair. Once again, Ginny felt as if she had failed her husband. What might their life have been like if she had given him the children he so desperately wanted?

Ginny continued to rock the cradle with her toe as she released her hold on the christening gown and spread it over her lap, pressing away the wrinkles with her fingers. On the day of Thomas's funeral she had come to sit here, and the room had still been empty except for the chair. She had chosen to sit there alone because she knew no one would look for her there, and she needed to think. It was there that she had resolved to stay. It was there that she had decided that whatever it took, she would not relinquish Malmaison. She smiled as she placed the beautiful handmade gown over the edge of the cradle and looked around the room. It made her happy to think that the room had found its use as a nursery after all, and it occurred to her that Sam Sutter might well have worn that very gown for his christening. There was something about the image of the tall, muscular scientist being small enough to fit into that gown that was most amusing. In her mind she saw a tiny version of the adult Sam—glasses perched on his forehead—that made her laugh.

Ginny spent the rest of the day going through the house and making her own notes about what needed to be done. The standards for housekeeping were appalling. The finish on the wood furniture in many of the rooms was dull with years of neglect. The tapestries that hung in the vast dining room and in the high-ceilinged reception area were dust-laden and in need of some careful repair. The upholstery on the chairs in the sitting area and in the music room was threadbare in places and had been badly disguised with rudimentary patching. None of this even began to address the water-stained wall coverings in several of the rooms or the cracked and flaking plaster moldings or the chipped china and crystal.

It was after ten when Ginny went in search of Sam Sutter. She tried the library first, then the kitchen, and finally donned her shawl and marched out to the conservatory where she could see a glimmer of a lantern.

"Dr. Sutter, this is far worse than you led me to believe it would be," she announced as she threw open the door of the conservatory and waved the sheaf of notes she'd been making.

"Shut the door!" he shouted as he used his body as a protective screen between the open door and a table of plants. "Damn," he muttered when she turned to close the door.

"There's no reason for profanity, Dr. Sutter," she chastised him. "If anyone should be swearing, it is I. You led me to believe that the renovation mainly involved major structural repairs, but we have a much greater problem."

He was fussing over the seedlings like a giant mother hen. "I thought we had agreed to be on a first-name basis," he said. With great care he lowered a clear covering over the seedlings, then turned to face her. "Now, what is it that couldn't wait until morning?"

"Have you seen the state of your house, Sam? The cleaning staff has clearly neglected their chores for some time now. I'm surprised that your mother hasn't taken note of their negligence. There are a great many items that we need to add to this list of things to be accomplished. If the house does not have the most fundamental—"

"There is no cleaning *staff,* Ginny. We have a cleaning service that comes in to prepare the rooms on an as-needed basis. I know that in the old days there were up and downstairs maids and such, but it's a little tough finding people willing to work for the kind of wages those jobs command. People can flip burgers for more money."

Flip burghers? Ginny had a mental image of servants tossing businessmen and shopkeepers onto their backsides. What a strange occupation and why would anyone prefer such a thing to the fulfilling work of making sure a house was properly cleaned and managed?

"Just make a list of what needs doing and then get it done," Sam continued, sounding unusually out of sorts. "That's why you were hired."

He looked as weary and disgruntled as he sounded, and he kept checking the plants behind him as if he fully expected them to make some momentous and instant change. Ginny noticed that his brow was furrowed with worry, and he rubbed his eyes as he spoke to her.

"Yes, well, I just wanted to be sure that you understood the scope of the work," she said, and then took a step closer. "You look terrible."

He gave her a weak smile. "Thanks. You look fresh as a daisy. Clearly the prospect of overseeing the renovation of a one hundred and fifty-room house agrees with you."

"What's wrong?"

"Nothing that a little sleep won't cure. Unfortunately that will have to wait until my assistant can relieve me in the morning. Was there anything else, Ginny?"

She walked around him and gazed at the plants. "Has there been some sort of blight or disease that has destroyed the plants so that you must begin again with fresh seedlings?"

He gave her a strange look, and she knew that once again she must have said something wrong. "That is to say," she continued hastily, "one would think that in a conservatory of this magnitude, there would be full-grown plants as well as these starts."

"We're running some new experiments. We always start with the seed or rooting if we can. If that is no longer available, we have to improvise."

She walked along the rows of pots, studying the labels. "Are you developing new colors, then?"

He laughed. "I'm afraid I couldn't care less about the color, Ginny. My interest is in the medicinal properties of the plant—the possibility of developing a plant that will provide the ingredient we need to complete the cure for cancer or heart disease." He recorded some data on a small, handheld machine that looked like a miniature version of the thing in the museum office that Freddie had called a computer. "At the moment," he continued, "we're trying to develop a formula for the treatment of senescence—senility. You might say that I'm trying to find the Fountain of Youth, and I'm having just about as much luck as old Ponce de Leon did in his day."

Her eyes widened as she looked at him. "You're serious," she murmured and thought about how proud her father would have been to know that the conservatory he had insisted on adding to the plans for the original estate would be used for such good purpose.

"Your ancestors—the ones who built this place— probably thought of the conservatory here as a show-place for their plants. I'll give them credit, though—they thought about the scope of things. It's unusual to find a private conservatory that offers the normal hothouse and coldhouse plus tropical as well as cool environments all in one building. It was the main reason I was delighted when my grandfather left the estate to me."

"What exactly do you know of my ancestors?" she asked.

He shrugged. "There's never been much in the historical record. I know that your great-great-grandmother's parents built the estate, that she was their only child, and that when they died in an accident, she inherited the estate."

"Nothing more?"

He smiled. "History rarely takes note of people who live fairly normal lives, Ginny. The records related to your great-great-grandfather are much more fascinating."

Thomas. He was speaking of Thomas. Ginny's heart quickened. "In what way?" she asked.

"Why am I telling you stories you probably know far

better than I?" he asked with a laugh. "Unless, of course, you're trying to find out if my version matches your own."

He was teasing her and had no idea of how close to the truth he had come. She smiled back at him and tried to keep her voice light. "It's interesting, don't you think?"

"You really should talk to my mother, then. She has the history down cold and trains the docents and tour group leaders herself."

"But what do you know of Thom—my ancestor?"

Sam leaned against one of the potting tables and crossed one ankle over the other. He studied her for a long moment. "You're not going to like it," he warned.

"Perhaps, but it's still of interest."

"Thomas Thornton was by all accounts a philandering ne'er-do-well who used his wife's money to fund his expensive habits and in the end lost everything, including the estate. When he saw that the jig was up, he put a bullet through his brain."

Ginny swallowed once and then again as she tried to fight against the rage that threatened to overwhelm her that Thomas should be so unfairly remembered. "And his wife?" she asked quietly.

Sam shrugged and turned back to his work. "The story stops there. Obviously she went on with her life—remarried probably and finally had kids. . . ." He paused in mid-motion. Slowly he turned back to face her. "They never had children," he said. "Thomas and Virginia Thornton never had children. And if that's true, then how could you be a descendant?"

Ginny searched her mind for any possible explanation that might satisfy him. "They must have had a child," she protested. "You said yourself that there was little information about the family."

"No. I mean, that's correct, that the information is not extensive, but it seems to me that there's a Bible—a family Bible—and notations in it stop with the death of Thomas. There is no mention of a child."

She could see that his logical mind was connecting the pieces, just as Thomas himself liked to connect the pieces of the wooden jigsaw puzzles they kept in the upstairs sitting room to amuse their houseguests. Sam stood up straight and advanced one step toward her. "Who are you, Ginny Thornton?" he asked. "Is that your real name? What is it you want from my family? From this place?"

With each question, he had moved closer. Now he stood close enough that she could feel the warmth of his breath on her face.

"I have not lied about my name," she replied shakily. Was it the fact that he was getting closer to the truth or that he was so physically close that made her throat tighten and her voice tremble?

"Does that mean you have lied about other things?" he asked as he removed his glasses and focused the full strength of his gaze on her.

"Of course not," she replied haughtily, and turned.

He stopped her by catching her arm and turning her back to face him. "But there is something you've omitted," he said and he did not release his hold on her. "Ginny, I like you. I like having you here. There is no question you know what you're doing when it comes to the estate and managing the renovation project. The question is the same that it has been from the night that I first found you here: Who are you and why should I trust you?"

Ginny stared up at him. His face was very near but in shadow. She had the urge to stroke his cheek, to assure him that she meant him no harm. She only wanted what was rightfully hers. She only wanted to prove once and for all that Thomas had been forced into a situation that ultimately cost him his life and cost her the happiness and home that was all she had ever wanted. "I am Ginny Thornton," she repeated firmly.

"Virginia Thornton was childless," he reminded her, "at least while she was married to Thomas. What are you saying?"

He would never believe her. His scientific mind would not permit him to suspend every shred of logic and accept the reality that she had been cast one hundred years into the future. She straightened to her full height, which brought her mouth very close to his ear. "No one knows that better than I," she said in a low husky voice. "I *am* Virginia Thornton."

He took a step back as if she had shouted the words instead of whispering them. His eyes widened. "*You* are out of your frigging mind," he said calmly.

It was her turn to shrug, her turn to give in to the exhaustion of maintaining the ruse of the past two days. "May I go?" she asked in a tone that clearly indicated that she didn't need his permission.

"Don't leave the estate," he warned.

She did not dignify his demand with an answer.

Chapter 8

SAM WATCHED HER go, even as he forced back the unthinkable idea that what she had implied could possibly be true.

I am Virginia Thornton.

The statement echoed in the silence that surrounded him. Of course, she had meant that she was Ginny— Ginny of today. She was chastising him for implying that she had lied about her name. She had tossed her head and lifted her chin defiantly in that haughty proud way she had. She could not mean Ginny of a century earlier. That was absurd . . . impossible.

What Sam found equally impossible was concentrating on his work. His mind raced with a thousand questions. It reeled with images of the last forty-eight hours—Ginny in that old-fashioned garb asleep on the old park bench in the conservatory. Ginny seeing the snowblowers and announcing—quite seriously—that the estate was under attack. Ginny moving through the house as if she knew every corner of it. Ginny in the kitchen, not knowing the first thing about managing the microwave. Ginny in the library, startled by his mother's voice on the speakerphone.

Her words played over and over in his mind. On the stairs that first night when she had protested that the house had not yet been built in 1829, he had thought it only a slip of the tongue. In the secret room, he had assumed the diary was her ancestor's—a statement she had neither confirmed nor disputed. When he spotted the crushed petals of the flower she had clutched that first night, now carefully stored in one of his specimen boxes for study later, Sam's breath caught.

The flower was the century-old malmaison dianthus. It was extinct—had been for half a century or more. The only way she could have been holding that blossom was if she had brought it with her from the past. Sam sat down and held his head between his hands as he forced himself to go slowly back over the evidence again. Everything he knew about science told him that what he was thinking was impossible, and yet the evidence was overwhelming. Ginny Thornton had somehow transcended time to arrive here on his doorstep, clutching the very item he needed to complete his research.

Impossible, he told himself. But the evidence was before him—real . . . tangible . . . undeniable.

Sam left the conservatory and headed back toward the mansion. He glanced up and saw the lit window where she would be. He started to run. Inside the house he took the wide marble stairs two at a time, and by the time he reached her door, he was breathless with exertion and wonder. He didn't bother to knock.

She gasped as he entered the room unannounced. She was crying and had obviously been getting ready for bed. Her hair was undone, and her blouse was open. She was barefoot. She was sitting at the dressing table, her head in her hands, and when he came through the door, she gave a startled cry. He thought that he had never seen a more beautiful woman, a more desirable woman.

He thought he must be completely out of his mind.

"Are you telling me that you have come to Malmaison from another time?" he asked without preamble as he closed the door and strode across the room to where she sat.

She crossed her arms over her body to cover herself and shrank from him. "I am simply telling you my name," she replied.

"That you are Virginia Thornton?"

"Yes."

"Quick, what year were you born?" He saw her pause to calculate a lie. "Answer now," he demanded.

The chin shot up, and she swiped at her tears with the back of her hand. "Eighteen seventy," she replied, knowing that the die was cast.

He blinked as he recorded the information. "Come with me," he ordered, taking her by the hand and leading her back out into the hallway.

"I cannot leave," she protested. "I . . . I—"

"No one's going to let you leave, lady. God knows what tricks you'd be up to if I wasn't able to keep an eye on you."

She jerked her arm free of his grip and walked alongside him. "Then where are we going?"

"West wing," he answered.

She kept pace with him through the series of corridors until he reached his destination. In one of the former guest bedrooms, his mother had stored portraits that were not in current use throughout the house. He remembered that one of them had been of Thomas Thornton. He hoped there would be one of the man's wife as well, and he hoped that the woman would be six feet two, with black hair and pockmarked skin. He opened the door to the room and flicked on the light.

Ginny was clutching her arms protectively around her body and shifting from one bare foot to the other as they entered the unheated room. It dawned on him that she was no longer concerned about her state of undress. She was cold.

"Damn," Sam muttered to himself as he pulled his sweater over his head and handed it to her. Why was it that every time the woman was anywhere near him, he seemed to turn into a different person? "Put this on before you freeze to death. This won't take long."

She sniffled as she pulled the V-neck sweater over her head. It covered her almost to her knees, and the sleeves hung over her hands. She had never looked more vulnerable. He had never wanted more to hold and comfort her. He glanced at her bare feet. At least there was a rug on the floor.

"There," he said, moving across the room to the portrait of Thomas. He watched her reaction as he called her attention to the painting.

Her eyes widened, then softened. It was as if she was remembering good times, and then her expression changed. The wistful look was replaced by one of abject sadness. Sam took a deep breath and waited for her to say something. When she didn't, he studied the other portraits in the room. His search ended with the portrait in the shadows of the corner. He moved toward it as if in a dream. Ginny remained in the center of the room.

The woman was a proud and elegant beauty, and yet in her emerald eyes he saw that the artist had captured the underlying vulnerability. Her hair was done up in an intricate design. The silk taffeta of her gown ended in an incredibly sexy lace ruffle that caressed her chin and highlighted the slender length of her neck. She sat with her chin resting on one hand, looking off the canvas at something unseen. Was it Thomas? Was that half smile for Thomas?

He turned back to the flesh-and-blood woman standing alone in the center of the large room. She looked more like a waif than a woman capable of managing a nineteenth-century estate. She was trembling.

"I think I'm going to be ill," she whispered and ran from the room.

"Ginny," he called as he followed her. Damn. He always seemed to be in pursuit of this woman. It was as if she possessed something that kept eluding him—some knowledge that it would be important for him to have, and yet she was the one searching. She was the one who had traveled a hundred years to find answers.

When he reached the lady's chamber—*her* room in every sense of the word—he could hear her throwing up in the bathroom. He followed the sound, rinsed out a washcloth with cold water, and knelt next to her as he gently wiped her flushed face. "It's okay," he said huskily, not knowing what else to say.

When she seemed to have spent her sickness, he got her a glass of water and mixed in some mint mouthwash. "Here. Rinse and spit," he said.

She did as she was told and then sat back on her heels as if afraid to stray too far from the bowl of the toilet.

"Better?" he asked and flushed the toilet.

She nodded and pulled the sleeves of his sweater out of her way. He knelt beside her and wiped her face with a freshly cooled cloth. Gradually the motion became more than simply one of comforting a sick friend. With each stroke he studied the features—the flesh-and-blood features before him.

"You're very beautiful," he said with a smile, "for a woman who's over one hundred years old," he added.

She gave him her full attention then. "You believe me?"

"I don't really know what to believe, but right now it makes as much sense as anything," he admitted.

It was as if he had given her permission to let go. "Thank you," she whispered as she started to weep. Her tears were tears of relief as she opened her arms to him and hugged him. "Thank you," she repeated again and again.

It started when he kissed her temple as a gesture of

acknowledgement that things were going to be all right. "We'll sort this all out," he promised as he moved his lips over her hair and to her ear. He felt the tremor that wracked her small body as he whispered the words. She became very still, and he knew the mood had changed— for both of them.

"Ginny?"

"Hold me," she said softly and tightened her arms around him.

Now his kisses took on a new insistence, a heightened intensity. She did not pull away but moved her face and neck to give him greater access. When their mouths met, there was an instant of hesitation, and then they were kissing with no reservations. She willingly followed his lead, opening to his coaxing, permitting her tongue to join in the waltz with his, loosening her grip of need to permit her fingers to explore the depths of his thick hair. Every movement drove him to greater heights of desire.

"Ginny," he rasped as he sowed a row of open-mouthed kisses down her neck and across to where the oversized sweater had fallen away to expose her bare skin. He knew he should stop, but God help him, he had never wanted a woman more. With one hand on her slim hips he pressed her close, wanting her to know of the desire that she aroused in him.

She became very still, and he knew the moment had passed. She was, after all, a woman who had recently buried her husband, a woman of propriety, a woman from another time, another code of ethics. "It's all right," he said, loosening his hold enough to send the message that he would not force her. "We'll just talk," he added. "Okay?"

She nodded and moved away from him. "You must have a thousand questions. I know I did . . . do."

Sam pushed himself to his feet. "I think we can probably find more comfortable surroundings for this conversation," he said, glancing around the bathroom, which was spacious but not the cushiest of accommodations.

He held out his hand to help her up from the tiled floor. "Why don't I go make us some tea while you finish getting ready for bed? Go on, take a shower or bath. Take your time. I'll wait for you in there." He nodded toward the bedroom.

"Tea would be nice."

"Okay. I'll go make it—the old-fashioned way, so it will take a little time," he assured her and was rewarded by a slight blush and a smile.

"Thank you, Sam."

"No problem," he said as he left the bathroom, pulling the door closed behind him. *Enormous problem,* he thought when he reached the hallway outside the bedroom. *You have the hots for a woman who is a contemporary of your great-great-grandmother.* This made all kinds of sense, especially when he was in the midst of the most important scientific work of his career, plus he had promised to make sure the work on the estate stayed on schedule. Sam groaned as he headed downstairs to the kitchen.

Ginny moved as if in a daze as she ran the water for her bath and pinned her mass of hair up and out of the way. She retrieved her nightclothes from the bedroom and then closed and locked the bathroom door. As she pulled Sam's sweater over her head, she caught her reflection in the mirror. Her lips were swollen, and she touched them gently as she relived the feel of his mouth on hers, the way she had opened to him, needed him, desired him with no thought of Thomas or of anything else except the wonder of being in Sam's arms. She crushed his sweater to her face, inhaling the scent of him. When he had moved closer and she had been aware of his state of arousal, she had paused, not because she wanted to stop but because she didn't, and the reality of that fact was stunning.

She folded the sweater and laid it on a side bench,

then finished undressing. She considered her body in the mirror. She was too thin. The tensions of the past several days had taken their toll. And yet he had told her that she was beautiful. She ran her fingers over her throat down to the shoulder he had kissed. How her breasts had ached in need, desiring his touch there as well. *What has become of you, Ginny? What will become of you now that he knows?*

She turned off the water and stepped into the tub. She longed to just lean back and soak in the hot, soothing water for hours, but Sam would return once he had made the tea, and she did not want him to find her still in the bath. Hastily she soaped herself, rinsed, and pulled the plug to drain the water. She dried herself with one of the oversized thick towels that were definitely a modern addition to the household. She pulled on the soft flannel nightgown that had been among the gifts from Kate, and carefully opened the bathroom door.

The bedroom was empty, and there was no sign of tea. Quickly Ginny got her brush from the dresser and hurried into bed where she pulled the covers high around her. When he returned, she would beg off talking, telling him that she was exhausted. He was a decent man and would wait until morning for their conversation. That would give her some time to think.

She pulled the brush through the tangled strands of her hair, smoothing it out as she listened for the sound of his footsteps in the hallway. There was so much to sort out. Now that she had told him the truth, did he really believe her? She was fairly certain that he did. In that case, what had been intended with his kisses, his prelude to lovemaking? Had he been as surprised by that as she was? Had it been simply a natural outcome of his tenderness in ministering to her when she became ill? Or had it been something more for Sam, as it had been for her? Heaven protect her, she was attracted to him, had fought her attraction to him almost from their first meeting.

Her eyelids drooped and closed. She forced them open
and continued brushing her hair. She must think.

"Sorry," Sam said as he eased open the door with his
hip and managed the tray. "I had to check on something
in the conservatory. Here . . ."

She was asleep, her breathing coming in deep, even
sighs, her fingers relaxed around her hairbrush.

Sam set the tray on a side table and sat down on the
side of the bed. He picked up the hairbrush and turned
it over in his hands. Was this the same brush she had
used back then? Gently he brushed a strand of her long
hair that curled like a flame across the pure whiteness
of the pillow. He tried to sort out the events of this
incredible night. None of the data made sense, and yet
the proof was before him. He bent to kiss her temple.
She stirred only enough to burrow more deeply into the
covers. Sam smiled as he set the hairbrush back in place
on the dressing table and left the room.

"Have you seen Sam?" Ginny asked Freddie the following morning. Before the events of the previous evening,
they had agreed to begin each day with a meeting over
coffee to discuss the progress on the renovations and the
plans for the coming day. The fact that he was not present for that meeting made her nervous. Perhaps in the
hard light of day he had changed his mind about believing her incredible story.

"Probably in the conservatory," Freddie replied. "Now
that you're here, I doubt we'll see much of him at all."

Ginny's heart sank. She had dressed carefully in anticipation of seeing him. Her heart had pounded as she
left her room and made her way through the vast house
to the kitchen. She was both nervous at what his reaction
to her news might be in the light of day and excited at
the prospect of being near him again. When she had
wakened and seen the untouched tea tray and her brush

replaced on the dressing table, she had known he'd been there while she slept. What had his thoughts been as he stood over her?

"I imagine Sam is greatly relieved to get back to his own projects," Freddie said. "Emily was driving him bananas with all her lists and worries about the renovation, and as I believe I mentioned yesterday, Sam isn't fully convinced that opening the house up and keeping the romance of bygone days alive is such a terrific idea. He believes that people should focus on the present and the future, not the past. If you haven't heard him say it already, you will—'The past just gives people an excuse not to make life better.' "

Ginny gave her full attention to Freddie. "But that's not true," she said. "Not at all. The past is . . ." *Where my life is. It is of the most vital importance, and if generations of his family haven't protected the records, then what will become of me?*

Freddie patted her hand. "I can see that you're as passionate about this as Emily is. Bottom line? Sam has agreed that his mom can have her museum as long as it doesn't interfere with his work and as long as it can pay its own way."

"Well, then, perhaps we should proceed with our duties before he changes his mind," Ginny replied.

Day followed day, and still he did not appear. When Ginny went in search of him in the conservatory, she was told that he had gone to the university for several days. When she asked Freddie if Sam had left any messages for her, Freddie handed her copies of notes that had been scribbled on scraps of paper, all of them reminders about some detail of the renovation. In his absence there was nothing to do but oversee the work crews during the day and labor over the reports he expected each night.

On Friday she saw lights on in the gardener's cottage

at dawn, and her heart raced. He was back. Today she would finally see him. But by late afternoon she still had not seen any sign of Sam. Her nerves were on edge as she watched for him and wondered what his absence meant. As she prepared a light supper for herself in the cavernous kitchen with all of its modern appliances, she thought she caught a glimpse of him running through the woods that led up to the estate from the main road. Clearly the realization that he had this woman from another century residing in his house had driven him mad, for what other reason might there be for a grown man simply to run through the woods in the freezing cold with seemingly no destination or purpose in mind?

"Sam's back. He left a voice-mail message," Freddie said as he came through the kitchen on his way home for the day. "He'd like to meet you in the library tonight at eight. If that's not okay, I left his number on the desk in the office. You can call him back and set another time." Freddie pulled on a knitted hat and gloves and glanced out the window. "Oh, he's out for his run, so you'll get his voice mail."

"He does that running as a matter of routine, then?"

Freddie laughed. "Sam? The man is the most disciplined guy I know. He's been exercising on a regular basis since I've known him and probably way before that. He was quite the athlete in his college days—track and field. Now he runs every day regardless of rain, snow, sleet, or sunshine. Then he works out in the gym four or five times a week, and that doesn't count the times he goes cross-country skiing or rock climbing or some other fool thing. Of course, that's why he looks the way he does, and I look like this." Freddie patted his ample stomach and laughed again. "See you tomorrow, Gin."

So, he had not gone stark raving mad, Ginny thought as she took her plate of food to the office and studied the note Freddie had left. She stared at the note and then at the telephone. With a deep breath, she picked up the receiver and pressed in the numbers Freddie had written. So far she had managed to escape using the telephone, assigning any calls to Freddie or the part-time office worker who came in to manage the accounts for the estate. Ginny held the earpiece to her ear as she had observed others do, and heard a light buzzing sound, then Sam's voice.

"Hi. You dialed the number so you must know who this is. I'm not in, so leave a message. I'll call back, and we'll both be happy."

The voice was followed by an abrupt beep, then silence.

Ginny stood there in silence as well and waited. What now? "Sam?" she said finally. *He's not there—he's said as much.* She sighed. "Sam, this is Ginny . . . Ginny Thornton, and I . . ." The beeping sounded again, followed by a woman's voice.

"To send your message now, press pound."

"I give up," Ginny muttered and replaced the telephone on its base.

She glanced around the small, crowded office, her gaze falling on the thing Freddie had referred to as the "computer." Apparently he was not especially surprised that she didn't know how to use one, so the thing must be relatively new. It had some of the attributes of a typewriter, and she had used one of those. Her parents had insisted she be schooled in some clerical and secretarial skills just in case she ever needed to find employment. She had always suspected that what they really wanted was to demonstrate to her how very fortunate she was to come from such wealth and never have to worry about such mundane matters. If they could see her now they might be very glad they had insisted on her learning some rudimentary skills.

With Freddie's help, she had mastered the art of typing in the daily reports. What magic Freddie used to get them printed and sent to Sam at the university escaped her, but she did know that the thing did not really require

paper. It was a truly amazing machine. She sat at the
desk and began looking through the files Emily had left
for the new curator. Clearly Sam's mother was as disciplined and organized as her son. The files were meticulously detailed and included daily time schedules for
what needed to be accomplished to stay on schedule and
reopen the museum as planned in the late spring. Before
she could complete the day's report, she needed to find
one specific file in which Emily had laid out her color
schemes for the primary rooms.

The mantle clock chimed eight, and Ginny realized
that she had become so engrossed in the work and in
creating her report—one she had accidentally destroyed
or *deleted* as Freddie said, three times—that she had lost
track of time. She had hoped to position herself in the
library in advance of Sam's arrival for their meeting.
Now there was nothing to be done but gather her wits
and rush off to the meeting.

She deliberately slowed her steps as she approached
the half-open door. The lit fire cast a cheerful play of
shadows over the sitting area of the room. The lamp on
the desk was turned on, but Sam was not there. Ginny
took a deep breath and walked boldly into the room.
"Sam?" she called as if they met like this every day.

"Up here."

She glanced up and saw him standing on the balcony,
a book in one hand, his glasses perched on the end of
his nose as he observed her over the rims of them.

"Thank you for coming," he added as he snapped the
book shut and reshelved it, then came down the metal
spiral staircase. "Shall we sit near the fire?"

It seemed too intimate, and yet the room was large
and drafty, and that was the warmest space. "Of course,"
she agreed and on her way to a high-backed leather
chair, she paused to turn on two additional lamps.

"Are you afraid of being alone with me, Ginny?" he
asked, and there was a glint of humor in his eyes.

"Not at all. I understood we were here to review the

work on the estate. I assumed you wanted a report of the week's progress." She held up the notebook she had brought with her. "I need the light to read my notes."

"Ah, I see." Sam pulled a chair close to hers. "Then, by all means, let's review your notes."

Determined to keep the meeting on a perfectly businesslike level, Ginny sat on the edge of her chair, her spine ramrod straight as she went through the details of the overall project and then the week's work with him. She reported that all of the expected workers had shown up for work, that the various construction projects inside the mansion had begun, and that they were indeed on schedule. "Of course, this was only the first week," she reminded him. "There are bound to be unforeseen events, delays, as we go forward." She knew that throughout her report he had not taken his eyes off her face.

"Are you finished?" he asked softly.

She felt the urge to relax, to give in to the temptation of falling under the spell of his voice, of his nearness, of his arm only inches from her own. She willed herself to maintain control. "Yes. If the system we have established is satisfactory, I shall continue to provide you the daily reports in writing," she added.

"I prefer them in person. Perhaps over dinner in the winter garden."

"It is too dim in there for working," she reminded him sternly.

He smiled. "There are always candles, but you're right. We shall meet here each evening at this time. I prefer to have the reports in person . . . in the event I have questions."

"Very well." She stood. "If that is all."

"Ginny, how could that possibly be *all*?" He took her hand lightly, and she sat back down, but did not meet his gaze. "We have a great deal to discuss, don't you think?"

"I have told you what I know," she replied.

"Except why you have come. What is it that's brought you here?"

Her eyes met his. "I *live* here," she replied.

"Then," he said gently. "You lived here *then*, Ginny. Now . . ."

"There would be no *now*—at least as you know it—if things had not happened as they did. Something went terribly wrong. I believe I have come to set that right."

"And what if you find out something you don't want to know?"

"Such as?"

Sam stood and paced the length of the fireplace and back. "How should I know? I don't even know what it is you hope to find."

"I believe that I have been brought here to restore my husband's reputation."

Sam gave her a disbelieving look. "Are you serious? Have you seen the record?" He clenched one fist. "You shouldn't need to see the record—you lived it."

"Thomas was a good husband," she argued.

"Oh, really? Then you didn't mind the fact that he kept a mistress in town here? That he squandered away all of your parents' inheritance? That he—"

"Stop it right now." Ginny was on her feet and in front of him in two steps. "Now, you listen to me, Samuel Sutter. It may not occur to you that the history you have been taught has been provided by the very people who stole my inheritance from my husband. Thomas may not have been perfect, but—"

"Did you love him, Ginny? Did he love you?"

"Don't be ridiculous," she snapped and turned away.

He reached out and caught her easily, turning her to face him again. "That's no answer."

"I will not discuss my marriage with you," she said in a low, tense voice. "Now let me go." She saw in his eyes that he was thinking of kissing her again. She knew in her heart that she wanted him to do just that. *What was happening to her?*

He loosened his grip on her and turned away, placing both palms on the mantelpiece as he lowered his head and studied the flames. "I apologize. Let's start over." He paused as if searching for words. "I have no scientific basis for believing the incredible story you have offered, and yet I can't disprove it. In fact, everything I have tried has only added more validity to what you say . . . who you say you are."

"I am who I say, Sam, whether you want to believe it or not."

"That's the brunt of it—I find myself not wanting to believe this, and yet . . ."

Her heart went out to him. She knew exactly what he was feeling, for it was what she had felt in the beginning. "I handled it by fainting," she said with a smile. "Perhaps . . ."

He laughed, and she saw that he visibly relaxed. "I'm afraid I'm not the fainting type." He sat down on the edge of the sofa and stared at the flames. "So, then, how do we proceed?"

It seemed more of a rhetorical question than one to which he expected some answer, so Ginny remained silent. Instead she sat next to him and placed her hand on his. "I will promise you this, Sam. I have not come with any intention of bringing harm to you or your family."

"Could you have made that same statement that first night when we met in the conservatory?"

"No, not then," she admitted. "But now, well, perhaps I don't believe in the old adage about the 'sins of the father.' "

"I'd like to help you find the answers you need to give you some peace, Ginny."

"Even if they reveal some painful truths about *your* ancestors?"

He nodded. "Even then."

She sighed with relief and then she smiled. "I know that this is a completely improbable set of circumstances, Sam, but you have no idea how good it feels not to have to keep trying to figure out how to react to everyone and everything. It is such a relief to be able to speak about what has happened to me."

He grinned and sat back on the sofa, propping his feet on the low table in front of them. "And how do you like these modern times, Ginny?"

Her eyes widened with the wonder of the things she had seen. "It is all so incredible . . . and noisy. There are so many machines."

"We have made one or two advances during the last century."

"One or two?" Ginny was up and pacing as she ticked off everything she had seen. "Ovens that don't get hot but cook food at a speed unheard of. Telephones that take messages and allow callers to speak to everyone at once. Computers—I don't even know what they do but I suspect they are well beyond simply improving on the typewriter. Then there are the people—women who think nothing of challenging a man's opinion. Men who run through the woods for no apparent reason." She gave him a pointed look. "And the clothing. My stars, one may as well walk around half naked."

Sam was laughing out loud now, and she enjoyed the feeling that she was entertaining him, making him forget his problems, putting him at ease. She joined in his laughter. "I just wish I could get you back to my time. *Then* you would see."

He sobered immediately. "It's weird that you should say that because that may well be the answer, Ginny." His eyes flashed with excitement. "If we could both go back there, then together we could discover whatever is to be solved. We'll start here, of course. Find out everything there is to know at this end, and then . . ." He waved his hand as if it were as simple as a snap of the fingers.

"My stars, you're serious."

"Of course."

"How would you imagine we might accomplish that?" she asked.

He shrugged. "I don't know yet, but the fact is if you came forward in time, then logically speaking, there must be a way to reverse the process. We just have to figure out how to manage it," he replied.

His certainty that this might actually be possible gave her fresh hope. "You would go back with me? But why?"

He looked up at her, and the expression that came over his handsome features made her heart trip. "Well, I could say that as a scientist, I'm curious. I'm even jealous that you have had the chance to experience this phenomena of traveling through time. If I left it at that, I would have told only half a truth."

"What's the other half?"

He reached out and stroked her cheek with the backs of two fingers. "The other half is that I want to do this because when I kiss you, something happens that is wonderful and magical and I know that you feel it, too. Maybe it is for this brief moment, and if that's the case, then I'll have to accept that. But what if we could find a way to make it *forever*, Ginny?"

Chapter 9

FOREVER.

Ginny couldn't believe he'd just said that. It was un-
imaginable . . . unthinkable. She was from another time,
another era. She had been recently widowed. It didn't
matter that a century had passed. He was the ancestor
of her sworn enemy. He and his family were living in
her house, leading tours of people who were being told
that this was the *Sutter* estate. And yet she could also
not deny her attraction to the man. Whenever he touched
her, looked at her, she felt as if she had found something
precious, something she should cherish. She had the
oddest sensation that this was meant to be. At first she
had thought that what she felt was her claim to this
place, regardless of the time or the current occupants.
But in a very short time, she had begun to think of Malmaison in terms of being *with* Sam.

"Say something," he urged. "Or did I just put my size
twelve shoe squarely in my mouth?"

"It's very complicated," she replied, choosing her
words with great care. "I'm sure you can understand
that. You're a person who thrives on the adventure of

the unknown, of exploring exotic territory."

He smiled. "There certainly could be nothing more exotic than this."

"I, on the other hand, am a much less daring person. I have come here, not because I sought to do so, but because of circumstances beyond my control."

"And you want to return," he added as if considering that fact for the first time.

"I must return," she corrected. "If I don't, then what will have been the point? Thomas will have died in vain."

"Has it ever occurred to you that this isn't about Thomas?"

"Of course it's about Thomas. What else?"

"What if it's about you? What if what you are here to discover is something about yourself?"

Ginny blinked at him as if he had suddenly started to speak in a strange tongue. "That's ludicrous."

"No. It's as possible as anything else," he replied quietly. He waited a beat to allow the idea to register, and then continued. "We have a theory. Now what we must do is prove or disprove it."

"What precisely is this theory?" She was prepared to debate the matter.

"That you have been brought forward in time to find answers that will permit you to move forward with your life. Is that a fair statement?"

She considered the statement from all angles and could make no argument. "I suppose it is," she agreed.

"But?"

"But underlying all of that is the fact that I must find the means to clear Thomas's name and reputation," she insisted.

Sam sighed with exasperation. "Why? What purpose is there in that?"

She was feeling threatened, incapable of matching his greater intellect. "I will not argue this with you," she

stated with a firm determination that was her only recourse.

"All right. For tonight I'll accept that, but I've seen
you in action, Ginny, and I know that you are a bright,
clever woman. I won't permit you to fall back on some
stupid Victorian ideal of what a woman's role must be.
Loyalty is an honorable trait—when it is deserved. I
don't believe that Thomas deserves your loyalty any
more than he deserved your love."

She understood that he was deliberately badgering her
and that he wanted her to argue with him. She would
not rise to the bait. "As you are no doubt aware, it has
been a confusing day. I find that I am suddenly quite
exhausted. More to the point, there is a great deal of
work to be organized tomorrow with the working crews.
That is, after all, what you have hired me to do. May I
be excused, please?"

His eyes spoke volumes, but all he said was, "You
don't need my permission to enter or leave a room in
your own home, Ginny. Goodnight."

It was after midnight, and Ginny could not sleep. She
stood at the window of her room and looked out over
the gardens. She saw the light in the conservatory and
knew that Sam was working. She fantasized about going
to him, and her fantasy had nothing to do with contin-
uing the debate he had begun earlier in the library. Her
thoughts were only of him holding her, kissing her, murmuring her name. She turned away from the window
and faced the canopied bed and wondered what it might
be like to have Sam Sutter make love to her.

These thoughts were shocking and upsetting. She did
not want to question her morals. She had always had the
most impeccable reputation. What would people think if
they knew she was fantasizing about making love with
a man who was not her husband? She closed her eyes
to blot out the image and in so doing managed only to
heighten the titillation of her fantasy as she imagined

Sam carrying her to the bed, undressing her, and touching her in forbidden ways.

"My stars, woman, you are going completely mad," she said aloud as she opened her eyes to banish the notion once and for all. She felt the need to get away, to get out into the cold night air and clear her head. When she had been mistress of this estate, she had thought nothing of strolling through the gardens in the dead of night in summer or walking the paths through the evergreen forest at midnight in January. It helped her to think, to clear her head and find solutions to whatever problems might be plaguing her. At the moment, Sam Sutter was plaguing her, and she needed to think. How could she make sense of anything as long as she stayed in the places where she had been with him, such as this room where he had sat on her bed, watched her sleep, ministered to her when she was ill?

Already dressed in the outfit Freddie referred to as "sweats," she pulled on a pair of the heavy stockings and headed down the backstairs. She had no need of light as she moved through the kitchen and found the collection of coats, mufflers, and boots that were kept hanging near the servants' entrance. She pulled on boots, wrapped a muffler around her neck, and pulled on one of the puffy lightweight coats. She probably looked like a stuffed sausage, but why should she care? She opened the door and breathed the cleansing scent of the cold night air as she savored the silence.

Suddenly without warning, the silence of the night was split by the sound of a thousand blasting horns. Ginny covered her ears and ran for the woods to escape them.

Sam considered the possibility that he might have spent way too much time alone with his plants, especially if the idea of spending the rest of his life with a woman from a century ago was the most appealing notion he'd had in months. Had he actually suggested that they run away together to the nineteenth century?

"Not that the idea doesn't have its appeal," he commented to the foxglove. "For one thing, I would have access to dozens of plant species that have been bred into extinction in modern times. Think of all we could accomplish with that."

He frowned as he studied the flats of seedlings and thought about his efforts to raise specific plants in order to harvest the components he needed for his experiments. The ingredient he needed for his latest experiment could possibly be found in that flower Ginny had been clutching the night he had discovered her sleeping here in the conservatory. If he could travel back in time, could he also bring plants forward with him?

Who was he trying to kid? The clovelike dianthus she had brought with her might have been the focus of his interest that first night, but now Ginny was the attraction. There was something about her, a kind of undiscovered promise. He considered the analogy of how she fairly blossomed whenever he kissed her, and grinned.

"She is without doubt the sexiest woman I've ever known," he told the choir of nodding poppies. "We're not just talking about physical beauty and desirability here. We're talking brains—somebody I can actually have an intelligent conversation with. Underneath that prim and proper Victorian code of conduct—those silly nineteenth-century rules about what a woman did and did *not* do, this lady is smart and daring and courageous. I mean, think about it. She has traveled through time just to clear the name of that deadbeat Thomas. Not that I believe she consciously did it, but her desire to save her estate was so intense."

He carefully began to scrape pollen from the deep pocket of a lily. "What am I going to do about it? I'll tell you what I'm—"

Suddenly a horrendous racket shattered the stillness

of the dark night. At the same time, lights snapped on all around the property.

What now? Sam thought as he dropped the tiny tube he'd been filling with pollen and watched it shatter against the stone floor.

The security sirens wailed, and in between he could hear the approach of the police cars. Security lights illuminated the perimeter of the mansion, and a large searchlight swung its beam slowly over the house and grounds. He caught the movement of a figure away from the back entrance of the house and toward the woods.

"Damn," he muttered and headed for the side exit of the conservatory—the one that led directly into the woodland area where he cultivated wildflowers in spring. If he followed the woodland path, he might be able to catch the intruder before the guy could vault the fence and hit the road.

Sam ran the familiar path with an ease born of years of training. He spotted the intruder ahead, crashing aimlessly through the brush. The guy wasn't exactly the brightest burglar on the face of the earth. He was wearing a bright yellow ski jacket that caught the light and made him easy to follow. Sam heard the voices of the police and security officers as they checked the house and shouted their findings back and forth. He hoped Ginny was all right and chastised himself for not having gone first to check on her. If this yahoo had hurt her . . .

He doubled the pace of his stride as he gained on the bumbling idiot. The snow had melted on the path, pummeled into water by his daily runs. The path was covered with a thick carpet of pine needles that muffled his footsteps. He heard the burglar gasping for breath. The guy was out of shape and scared silly. This was going to be fun.

"Gotcha," he rasped as he caught the unsuspecting burglar in a tackle and brought him to the ground. He heard the satisfying sound of breath being knocked out of his victim by the force of the fall. He straddled the culprit and pinned the guy's arms above his head.

"Get off me," a muffled voice ordered.

"That's not going to happen, buddy." He was enjoying watching the guy thrash around trying to get free when he noticed a mouth and then a very familiar determined chin work its way out of the muffler.

"It's me, you ignoramus. Now get off," Ginny ordered, and at the same time she gave a mighty twist of her entire body that threw him off balance and forced him to release her hands.

"Ginny, what the hell—"

"I wanted to take a walk," she replied as she got to her feet and focused all of her attention on brushing herself off. "How could I have known that such a simple act would engage us in a major calamity?"

"You forgot about the security system."

"So it would seem," Ginny retorted. "Is there no way to shut those things off?" She covered her ears with her hands to protect herself from the piercing whine of the sirens.

"The security guards will enter the code as soon as they're sure there are no others."

"Others?"

"Intruders. They think somebody was trying to break *in,* not out."

"Honestly," Ginny muttered more to herself than to him, "a person simply wants to take a walk." Her words hung in the air as the sirens were silenced. "Finally," she added with a sigh of relief.

"Tomorrow, we'll make sure you know how to disarm the system should you have the urge for any more of these midnight wanderings, okay?"

"Dr. Sutter?"

They both turned at the sound of his name shouted from somewhere near the house.

"I'm out here, Frank! All's well. Just a little misunderstanding about how the system works." He helped

Ginny up and put one hand on her waist as he propelled her along with him into the light.

"Oh, Ms. Thornton," Frank said as soon as he saw the two of them emerge from the woods. Then he turned and shouted to the other men clustered near the entrance to the kitchen. "It's just the curator. She lives here. She's new. Sorry for the inconvenience, boys. I'll take it from here."

Ginny heard the others grumbling as they headed off to their automobiles. She squinted in the lights that still illuminated the house.

"You really ought to let me know if you plan on leaving after we've shut the place down for the night, Ms. Thornton," Frank instructed. "I mean, it's perfectly okay and all, but still . . ." He glanced at his watch and then at Sam. "A bit of a night owl like yourself, is she?"

Ginny distinctly heard a suggestive slur in the security guard's tone. He thought she and Sam had had an assignation in the woods at midnight. He thought . . . *Oh, my stars.* To make matters worse, Sam was having trouble containing his mirth. He was actually giving the watchman every reason to believe that he had uncovered some sort of illicit liaison.

"If you gentlemen will excuse me," she said with as much dignity as was possible when one was cold, wet, and dressed like a giant yellow sausage, "I shall retire for the evening." She started toward the house, then turned. "I am assuming it is all right for me to go back inside?"

"Yes, ma'am," Frank assured her. "I'll set the alarm again once you're back upstairs."

"Thank you," Ginny replied. She made it three steps closer to the house before she heard Sam's voice, low and sexy in the night air.

"Goodnight, Ginny. Sleep well."

You'd better not be laughing at me, Sam Sutter. He had just better not be amusing himself with Frank's assumption that there is some forbidden affair afoot here, Ginny thought as she trudged up to the mansion. She was a proper woman, and whatever her private thoughts might be about him, they must be suppressed. She had forgotten who she was—and who he was and that there was work to be done.

Sam watched her make the trip back to the house, heard her muttering under her breath as she went and fought hard not to chuckle. "Hell of a woman," he said to himself.

"If you say so, sir," Frank replied. "I'll be getting back to the post, then, if you think everything's okay."

Sam was embarrassed to realize that he had spoken aloud. "Fine, Frank. Thanks for your help. I'll make sure everything's locked up and the alarm gets reset." Sam actually felt himself blush as he realized what this might imply to the night watchman.

Frank smiled. "Whatever you say, sir." He turned and walked quickly away.

Sam continued to stand where he was until he saw the lamp come on in Ginny's room. He wondered if she would sleep now, or was she as agitated as he was? He headed back to the conservatory. He might as well work. He sure as hell wasn't going to get any sleep tonight.

The note was on her desk the following morning along with a single yellow rose.

This is intended as a peace offering in apology for my behavior last night. I would like to invite you to join me for dinner this evening in a public restaurant so that there can be no question of impropriety. Should you be so inclined, I would also like for you to attend a basketball game (NOTE: It's a sporting event) with me at the university following an early dinner. I will call for you at six unless

I hear from you via telephone before that hour. I will be at the university all day.

Cordially yours,

Sam

He was mocking her again, but his attempt at a more formal style of language amused her in spite of that, and she decided there could be nothing wrong in going out with him under these circumstances.

"Freddie? Do you know anything about . . ." She quickly consulted Sam's note. "About the sport of basketball?"

"Round ball? Sure. I'm a huge fan of the Knicks."

"The *nicks*?"

"Knickerbockers—professional New York basketball team? Not exactly a sports fan, are you, Gin?" he added with a grin.

Ginny gave him a look she hoped passed for coquettish rather than abject stupidity. "I'm afraid not. Sam has suggested that I might enjoy attending a—"

"Sam is asking you out? Praise the Lord and pass the mashed potatoes!" Freddie shouted as he raised his hands and face to the ceiling. "Our Sam? The good doctor of science? That Sam?"

Ginny nodded. "Is this unusual?"

"Unusual? Honey, this is divine intervention. Just wait 'til Emily hears the news."

"What does one wear for basketball preceded by dinner in a restaurant?"

"Dinner, too?" Freddie seemed quite beside himself.

Ginny consulted the note. "Yes, I'm quite certain. Yes, dinner in a public restaurant."

Freddie spotted the rose. "He sent flowers and a note? Oh, my sweet heavens above, this is a bloody miracle."

Ginny wondered why Freddie was suddenly speaking as if he came from Ireland. "Are you all right, Freddie?"

"Right as rain," he replied. "Now, let's consider this.

What to wear and how to prepare." He started to punch a combination of numbers into the telephone. "Kate, we need you here right now. Ginny has a date. Let me be more specific. Ginny has a date with Sam."

Ginny could hear Kate's shriek of surprise and delight from across the room.

"She'll be right here," Freddie reported as he hung up the phone. "Now, let's adjourn to the courtyard, and I'll show you a thing or two about basketball."

Freddie recruited several of the workers for something he called a "pickup" game. "There are two baskets in a real game," he explained as he stood near a tall metal post crowned by a circular hoop from which an open-ended net hung. "The idea is to put this ball through that hoop," he added.

Just then one of the workers reached over and caught the ball in the course of Freddie's bouncing. "That would be your basic steal!" Freddie shouted as he waved his hands in front of the worker's face. The other man threw the ball toward the hoop, and it went through.

"And *that*," the worker said with a grin, "would be your basic 'nothing but net.' " He sauntered off. "Time to get back to work, boys."

Freddie continued to explain the rudiments of the game as Ginny took notes to study later. The words were familiar and yet strange. *Guard. Dribble. Travel. Foul.* Her head whirled with all of the details Freddie provided.

"I believe it would be best if I just sat quietly," she suggested.

"Heavens, no. Nobody is quiet at a game. There's a lot of yelling, cheering for your favorite team. Sam will think something's the matter if you sit on your hands and don't get caught up in the spirit of the game." He seemed genuinely concerned.

"Well, of course, I shall applaud when appropriate."

Freddie rolled his eyes heavenward. "Honey, this isn't the opera. It's sports. You don't applaud." He mocked the act of delicate clapping. "You pump your fist or high five your neighbor—whether you know that person or not." He demonstrated the motions. They seemed impossibly dramatic.

"She'll need some key names," Kate suggested as she joined them in the courtyard. "Jordan is a no-brainer."

"Jordan who?" Ginny asked politely, pencil poised to add to her notes.

Kate let out one of her trademark whoops that passed for laughter. "You're kidding, right?" She observed Ginny's polite but blank stare. "Oh, my God, it's hopeless."

"Michael Jordan, honey," Freddie coached. "Until his retirement, he *was* the professional game." Then he grinned. "There's one guy on the team at the university that Sam really likes. I've heard him say that this kid could be the next Jordan. His name is Henry O'Henry, and he plays guard. Number twelve. You got that?"

Ginny scribbled and nodded. "O'Henry. Twelve."

"Sometime during the game when this kid drives to the basket, I want you to mutter under your breath something like, 'My stars, that kid is another Jordan,' like you just thought of it, okay?"

"He's going to be in a car, then, when he drives to the basket?"

Freddie blinked. Kate hooted.

"Honey, what planet did you come from?" Freddie muttered before demonstrating the concept of driving to the basket.

Sam was actually nervous as he paced the downstairs foyer waiting for Ginny. He glanced at his watch. They had plenty of time. He took his leather bomber jacket off, then put it back on. He checked his watch again.

"Am I late?"

She was standing at the landing. She wore jeans and a white T-shirt with a black blazer. Her hair was pulled back and braided. She was wearing thick-soled boots that added at least two inches to her height. She looked like something out of a fashion magazine.

"Well, aren't you looking very twentieth century to-night," he commented as she came the rest of the way down the stairs.

She blushed. "Kate insisted this was the proper attire. It is, isn't it?"

"Kate is absolutely right. Let me help you with your coat." He took the tan all-weather coat she carried and held it for her. He recognized it as one belonging to his mother. "Shall we go?"

"Whom are we playing?" she asked.

"The Huskies," he replied. "Ever hear of them?"

"I might have if you would use the name of the school—the *full* name of the school."

Sam laughed. "University of Connecticut."

"Are they good?"

"Extremely," Sam replied, amused by the fact that she was clearly working off a script prepared for her by avid basketball fans Freddie and Kate.

"Oh, dear. Then our team might . . . might get beaten up?"

"We also might get beat . . . lose." They were in the car now, and he noticed the way her eyes kept wandering over the instrument panel and how she clutched the door handle with all her might as he navigated the road from the house to the highway. "It might also be a white knuckler."

"I'm sure you're teasing me, Sam," she said as she glanced out the window at the trees flashing by.

"Not at all. A white knuckler means that the game is very exciting, and the fans clench their fists so hard that their knuckles turn white—a little like yours are now." He watched as she consciously released her grip on the door, and then accelerated onto the highway.

"Samuel!" she exclaimed and braced herself with both hands against the dashboard. "Not so fast."

"That's not fast," he said. "*This* is fast."

She refused to let him win and forced herself to settle back in the seat, her arms folded tightly across her body. "I suppose you find terrorizing people amusing," she muttered.

He laughed and slowed the car enough to make it noticeable and permit her to take a long steadying breath. "Are you hungry?"

"I was."

"Just wait until you get a whiff of Barney's sliders. Your appetite will return."

Who was Barney, she wondered, and what on earth was a slider?

The first question was answered as Sam parked the car around the corner from a huge colorful sign that read, Barney's—We're Number One in Sports Bars. He was taking her to a common tavern. She tried not to be disappointed that he had not seen fit to be seen at some finer establishment with her.

He opened the car door for her, held out his hand to assist her, and didn't let go. "Watch the traffic," he warned as he glanced both ways and then made a dash across the busy street, pulling her along.

Ginny could hear the music, muffled behind the closed double doors. The minute Sam opened the door she was engulfed by a combination of people laughing and talking—shouting, really—and the music played at a volume that was inconceivable.

"It's so loud!" she shouted, and all Sam did was grin as he pulled her inside.

"Yo, Barney, two sliders with fries and two brew-skis!" he yelled to a man behind the longest bar Ginny had ever seen. The man smiled and raised his hand in acknowledgement.

"Let's grab a table." Sam led the way through the mob of people to a small high table with no chairs.

"Two sliders," the waitress said. "Two brews." She placed the food on the tiny round table and hurried off.

She was wearing a sort of camisole that exposed her shoulders, arms, and a good portion of her breasts. The top was tucked into a skirt that barely covered her buttocks. Ginny did not know where to look, so she looked at Sam who was watching the waitress walk away. He was also smiling.

"I'm leaving," she announced and was pleased to see that her words had penetrated Sam's concentration. "It's too noisy, too hot, and these people are indecently clothed."

"Come on," he urged, catching her by the hand. "You've got to eat."

The food was tempting. In spite of its unusual and unappetizing name, it had the most heavenly smell. "I'll eat," she decided and returned to the table.

A slider turned out to be a type of chopped meat sandwich on a roll with some sort of sauce that made it difficult to hold the meat between the bread. It kept sliding around. Ginny smiled in spite of herself as she took a bite. Then she closed her eyes and savored the taste. It was heavenly.

She opened her eyes quickly when she felt Sam's finger stroking her chin. He held up his finger to show that he had actually been catching a bit of the sauce that had escaped down her chin. When he put that finger in his mouth to lick off the sauce, Ginny thought she might actually faint from the sudden surge of heat that roared through her body.

There wasn't much possibility of normal conversation, so they ate mostly in silence. She noticed that several people in the bar knew Sam. They would stop by the table to chat. Sam would introduce her as simply Ginny, and the person would smile and nod and move on.

"Finish your fries," Sam said after several minutes. "It's nearly game time."

He fished several bills from his wallet and left them

lying on the table. He drained the last of his beer.
"Ready?"

She nodded.

They became part of a general exodus from the tavern.
Everyone seemed to be going to the ball game. Out on
the street more people joined them. It seemed as if there
must be entire communities on the street, all bent on
fitting inside a huge stone building across from the tavern. Everyone was laughing and talking. Everyone was
excited, and it was contagious. Ginny felt her heart race.
She was enjoying herself. Her eyes widened in disbelief
and wonder as she glanced up and saw an enormous lit
sign—a moving sign. She tried to read it as she walked.
Apparently it was announcing other events to take place
in the large building sometime in the future. Words appeared and disappeared with what seemed like great
speed. Some words moved across the sign from left to
right, then magically dissolved, only to be replaced by
others.

Ginny stumbled, and Sam immediately took her hand.
"You look. I'll lead," he said as he led the way through
the crowd and into the building.

"Oh, my," Ginny murmured as an entirely new set of
smells, sounds, and visions assailed her. A band played.
People shouted. Vendors hawked all sorts of wares, from
food to souvenirs. Sam led the way down a corridor that
she could see widened out into a large space. She
thought she knew what to expect until she stepped into
the opening and looked around. "Oh, my stars," she
whispered.

Rows and rows of seats ringed a wooden floor with
painted markings on it. At either end of the floor was
the thing Freddie had referred to as a goal. People were
hurrying to their seats.

"We're down here," Sam said as he led the way down
a steep stairway to seats closer to the floor.

"How on earth does anyone sitting all the way up
there see the show . . . the game?" she asked.

"It is pretty high. The students refer to it as 'nosebleed country.' Fortunately being a professor does have some perks." He indicated two seats at the end of one row just a few rows up from the floor.

No sooner had they sat than everyone stood again. As noisy as the place had been, it became absolutely quiet as a quartet of uniformed young people marched to the center of the floor holding the American flag. A young woman walked onto the floor and began to sing in a sweet, strong voice. The band did not play. She sang the national anthem without accompaniment and when she had finished, there was thunderous applause.

Next, the players on the two teams were introduced. The people booed the first set of players and cheered wildly for the second. Sam was as vocal as everyone else. Ginny studied the ten young men lining up to begin the game. They were dressed in baggy silk jersey tops and long skirtlike pants—bloomers, really—and that made Ginny laugh. She studied their faces. They were so young, mere children. Several were black, which surprised her. Three men in black-and-white-striped shirts with whistles in their mouths seemed to be in charge. One of them tossed the basketball into the air, and the game began.

"Come on, O'Henry, get your act together!" Sam shouted at one of the players.

Ginny consulted the scrap of paper in her hand. *O'Henry was the next Jordan.* "Isn't he one of the best players?" she asked.

"Not tonight," Sam groused, but he gave her a strange look before turning his attention back to the game.

"Oh, dear," Ginny exclaimed several minutes later. "That young man is hitting our player. That can't be fair." She pointed to the place where the two players were on the verge of an all-out brawl, from what she could see.

"Hey, ref, you wanna watch Hoskins? He's all over Tony!" a man bellowed from behind her.

Suddenly the player called O'Henry grabbed the ball the way the workman had taken it from Freddie in the courtyard. "It's a steal!" Ginny shouted, thrilled finally to have recognized something on her own.

"You tell 'em, honey," the man behind her said as he patted her on the shoulder.

O'Henry sprinted the length of the wooden floor and tossed the ball cleanly through the goal. "Nothin' but net," Ginny announced, imitating the swagger of the worker's language.

Sam looked at her as if she had suddenly grown another head.

By the fourth quarter, Ginny was completely involved in the game. She had observed the players as individuals, noticed which of them played with the proper respect for good sportsmanship and which did not. "I don't like that young man," she observed as a player from the opposing team stepped up to take what Sam had explained was a free throw. "He's extremely rude."

The man behind her, as well as several other fans around them, nodded in agreement. "Mess up, kid!" the man bellowed. The ball hit the front of the iron hoop and bounced off.

Ginny cheered wildly and glanced at the scoreboard. Her team was behind by only one point. They would get the ball out of bounds at the opposite end of the court from where they needed to be. There was less than one second on the clock. Everyone in the place was standing. Ginny clenched her fist against her mouth as the referee handed the ball to the tallest boy Ginny had ever seen.

Suddenly O'Henry started to run for the other end of the court. The tall boy heaved the ball. O'Henry caught it at the centerline, turned, and threw it with all his strength toward the basket. Ginny held her breath along with everyone in the arena. It seemed to take forever, and then, miraculously, it went through just as the buzzer let out a raucous shout to signal the end of the game.

Bedlam resulted. Ginny pumped her clenched fist high in the air. "Yes!" she shouted along with sixteen thousand other people who were cheering and hugging and leaping up and down in the aisles.

"Oh, my God, we beat U. Conn," Sam kept saying to everyone around them as he grabbed Ginny and hugged her hard.

The man behind Ginny pounded her on the back. "You, little lady, are our good-luck charm. You come on back any time, okay? U. Conn—we beat U. Conn," he added with a broad smile. One would have thought a great battle had been won.

A chant rolled through the arena. "We're number one. We're number one."

The players remained on the floor, hugging one another and hoisting their coach high in the air as they marched around the arena, accepting the approval of their fans. It was a magical moment. Ginny had never known anything to compare. "I love this game!" she declared in a loud voice to no one in particular as she pumped her fist in the air once more. It was the most unladylike thing she had ever dared to do, and it felt wonderful.

Sam laughed and hugged her again. Then he kissed her. At first it was just a solid meeting of their lips, more evidence of their excitement. Sam pulled back, and his expression changed.

"Aw, hell," he muttered and pulled her back for a real kiss, a feel-this-down-to-your-toes kiss. Suddenly it was as if they were alone in the midst of the thousands of shouting, joyous people. The band played and people started making their way toward the exits, but Ginny was oblivious to it all. The only thing that mattered was that she was in Sam's arms, and it felt absolutely wonderful . . . as if she, too, had attained some unexpected and wholly incredible victory.

Chapter 10

GINNY AND SAM were quiet as they left the arena and walked back to the car. They were still surrounded by people from the game, which made the silence easier. He held the door for her and waited for her to get in. Then he closed the door and stood on the curb for a long moment, staring off into space. She was tempted to open the window to ask if he was ill, except she could not figure out how to open it. His face, illuminated by the yellowish street lamp, registered a kind of misery that was heartbreaking to see. After a moment he walked around to the driver's side and got in.

"I don't want you to go back," he said quietly.

Not go back? To the house? Her heart raced.

"I want you to stay . . . here . . . in this time . . . with me." He looked at her directly for the first time since they had left the arena. "I think I may be falling in love with you," he added.

His simple statement mirrored her own jumbled feelings. She had merely refused to give them credence by permitting herself to define them with words. With a single statement Sam had given them life. *I know,* she thought. *I think I may be falling in love with you as well.*

She turned away from the power of his gaze. "I must go back," was all she could think to say. She realized that she had uttered the statement as much for herself as for him. It was a reminder of why she had come, of what her purpose was.

He let out a sigh of sheer exasperation. "Why? What's the point? Thomas is dead. You came here to save Malmaison. I'm asking you to stay . . . to live here." There was anger born of frustration in his tone.

"Why can't you understand that Thomas is . . . was . . . my husband? I owe him—"

"What? You owe him what, Ginny? Your life? Your happiness? If you return and pine away for him, it won't bring him back."

"That's unfair," she snapped, her own temper on edge because she suspected he was too close to some truth that she wasn't ready to face. "Why can't you understand this from my perspective? Ever since I arrived in this century, people have talked of nothing but what *they* feel, what *they* want. Have you people no understanding of the needs of others? Even those who are dead? Thomas Thornton may not have been the smartest man who ever lived or even the best husband, but he was *my* husband, and for better or for worse I have a responsibility to honor his memory."

There was a long stretch of silence as they sat in the car, each staring out the window. The streets were deserted now, and the arena was dark. Sam turned the key, and the powerful engine roared to life. He shifted the car into gear but did not move it from the curb.

"Ginny, will you let me help you find the answers you need?"

She nodded.

"And once we have those answers, will you think about staying?"

She nodded again, and he reached over and covered her hand with his. "That's a start," he said softly.

They rode in silence until they got to the outer limits of the city. Then to her surprise, Sam chuckled.

"What is so amusing?" she asked.

"You at that game tonight," he replied, grinning at her. "Where did you get that stuff—'nothing but net' and all that other lingo?"

Ginny smiled. "Freddie and Kate tutored me," she admitted and pulled the crumbled page of notes from her pocket for him to see.

"You were using a cheat sheet?"

"Well, it was all quite confusing," she countered, but she was smiling and realized that he had deliberately broken the heaviness of their earlier mood. *Sam Sutter, you are a dear and kind man,* she thought, and resisted the urge to reach over and push back one unruly lock of his hair that kept falling over his forehead. "I had a wonderful time, Sam," she said.

He relaxed against the leather seat as he steered the car with one hand and stretched his other arm around her shoulders. "I'm glad. What shall we do tomorrow?"

"Tomorrow? I have work to do, Sam. The stonemason is beginning the repairs on the marble in the foyer and winter garden. Oh, and I almost forgot to tell you that I found a young man who is willing to take on the job of apprentice to the stonemason. After all, Mr. Justice is over seventy, and the work can be taxing."

"How did you find an apprentice? You never leave the estate."

"He's the son of one of the other workers. His father tells me that the young man is artistic, but has had a bit of a problem . . . 'finding himself' was the term he used, I believe." She giggled. "In my day, people were just grateful to have employment. What does it mean to find oneself?"

"Modern people also understand that work is important, but they believe they have a right to do something they enjoy—to find fulfillment in working."

"Do you find fulfillment in your work?"

"Oh, yes. I am fortunate enough to be doing exactly what I want to do." His voice registered his enthusiasm.

"As am I," Ginny realized. She laughed. "I suppose that makes me a thoroughly modern woman."

Sam stroked the back of her neck. "I'm glad to hear that you like being the curator for Malmasion, Ginny." He turned onto the long, winding road that led through the woods to the estate. He pulled the car into the court- yard between the house and the unused stables. "I have to go check on my experiments in the conservatory," he said as they walked the short distance to the house.

"Can I come with you? I'm curious to learn more about your work. The conservatory is so different than it was." She could see that he was genuinely pleased by her request.

"Let's pick up a snack from the kitchen, and then we'll go."

Ginny smiled. "You always seem to be hungry." It would be fun to prepare food for this man, she thought. He enjoyed everything. "Perhaps I will make you a rhu- barb pie in the spring."

The look they exchanged said clearly that each of them realized what she had just said. She was thinking of still being here in his time, in his house. "I'd like that," he said softly. "I'd like that very much."

Suddenly Ginny was overcome by a great sense of sadness, for she knew that if indeed her purpose was to restore the honor of Thomas's reputation and regain con- trol of the estate, it was impossible that she would still be here months from now. She had a job to do—a re- sponsibility to Thomas. "We'll see," she said and tried to smile.

They cut hunks of cheesecake left over from the gala and packed them in a plastic container. Sam filled a ther- mos with milk. "From our very own cows," he assured her. Ginny gathered forks and glasses and they headed for the conservatory. They took off their outer coats in the humid warmth of the greenhouse and sat on the old wrought-iron park bench to eat their cake while he explained his work to her.

"In the flower of the common dianthus—carnation—there exists a certain gene family that we think might be a key ingredient in a treatment for the senility often associated with old age. In simplistic terms, we've been able to isolate a key enzyme in polyamine biosynthesis and create a catalytic reaction resulting in a by-product that then becomes a donor in the biosynthesis of . . ."

Ginny was staring at him as if he'd just begun to speak a foreign language, which he supposed he had. "Sorry," he apologized. "It's easy to fall into the jargon of the business when you spend your days thinking about polyamines, spermines, and biosynthesis."

"It's quite fascinating, truly," Ginny assured him.

"Bottom line? We've been able to isolate two different clones—duplicates—from the petals of the common carnation and show that these elements may play a role in the degradation of a certain protein enzyme that may contribute to senescence in humans."

"And if that is so, then what?"

"If we can slow or even stop the process, then we might have the tools we need to treat the condition. In these modern times we've found the cures for a number of conditions that in your time would have meant death. That's the good news. The bad news is that by helping people live longer, we're not necessarily letting them live better unless we can provide the key for slowing the overall aging process—including the aging of the brain."

"It would never have occurred to me that flowers might be used to such ends," she said.

"Actually aromatherapy has been quite a big deal for the past decade or so. Mostly it's been used as an aphrodisiac or treatment for stress, but gradually we're discovering that the simple application of scent might be an effective tool in treating more serious medical conditions."

"You're talking of collecting the fragrant oils of the flowers as one would in making perfumes?"

"Exactly. The essential oils of some plants are known to have therapeutic effects. For example, lavender is well-known for its calming effect. If we take that one step further, we might be able to make use of it as a piece of the treatment regimen for conditions in which anxiety or nervousness play a key role."

"Such as?"

"PMS, depression, insomnia."

"What is PMS?"

"Premenstrual syndrome," he replied as if it were perfectly ordinary to mention such a topic in everyday conversation.

Ginny blushed a deep red. "I see." She didn't know where to look.

"Have I offended you, Ginny? If so, I apologize, but in this day and age, everything that has to do with a person's health and well-being is fair game for discussion."

"I see," she repeated, unable to consider how else she might respond to such astounding news. "Are there other examples?" She must be out of her head to encourage this discussion, but it was fascinating to think that flowers might also heal.

"Tons of them. What we're exploring here is really just a sophisticated version of old folk medicine. I'll bet your grandmother concocted some sort of salve to rub on your chest when you had a bad cough or bronchitis."

"She did. It was horrible, but it worked." Ginny wrinkled her nose in disgust as she recalled the terrible smell.

"Same principle applies here, except we hope the smell is a good one. In fact, the scent is probably part of the healing power."

She studied the flats of tiny seedlings. "What are these?"

"These are carnations. We're trying to reproduce the malmaison dianthus—the carnation you were carrying that first night."

"Why is it so important to have that specific variety?"

"Today's plants have been overbred for other purposes—floral beauty and stamina. We need the strength of the enzyme produced in those original plants. So far, though, we haven't been able to reproduce the blossom in sufficient strengths to make it work."

"The west greenhouse used to be filled with the plants," Ginny told him.

"I know. Mom showed me old photographs. That's what gave me the idea in the first place. Then I started checking the old logs and records in the library, which showed me that through the years the focus was on crossbreeding to obtain certain hybrids of a spectacular new color or some such nonsense. Bottom line is that they are extinct."

"No, they aren't," Ginny said slowly, then with growing excitement, she added, "If I exist, then they must exist. The night I came here, the greenhouse was filled with the color and scent of them. I could have cut dozens of blossoms that night and still had a display here among the palms and ferns. Don't you see, Sam?"

It was an impossible thought, and yet if he was to believe that she had traveled forward in time, then he also had to accept that somewhere that time—her time—still existed. If that was true, then the dianthus were there as well. Sam's heart hammered with excitement. "If we could go back," he said slowly, "I could bring the plants here, assuming once back there we could return."

His mind raced with the possibilities of what he was considering. "Ginny, if we could do that, think of the lives we might change."

"Perhaps we could even use your medicine to save Thomas from financial ruin. Surely such a discovery is worth a great deal of money."

Sam stared at her. *I don't want to save Thomas,* he

thought, and mentally berated himself for being so uncharitable. "Would that make you happy?" he asked.

"Of course. Thomas was a decent man. He didn't deserve to come to such a horrible end. If I could change that . . ."

Sam took a step closer to her, wanting to see her face in the dim light. "Would you return to him now that you've been here?" *Now that you've been with me? Kissed me?*

"We were married. I have a du . . . duty," she stammered. She seemed incapable of uttering the words with conviction.

Sam pressed his advantage. "But something has happened to you, Ginny. Something monumental. Surely there is a message in that." He moved closer and placed his hands on either side of her head, tangling his fingers in her hair as he coaxed her nearer. "I have kissed you," he whispered as he bent to kiss her now.

He stood ready to release her if she protested at all, but she didn't. She sighed and came to him. Her mouth opened under his, her arms circling his neck as if to pull him closer. Sam broke the kiss for a fraction of a second, long enough to add, "And you have kissed me as well." He saw an expression cross her features that told him she wanted to feel guilt but could not because the passion consumed her, as it did him. She placed her hand at the base of his neck and pulled him closer. It was all the encouragement he needed.

He lifted her so that she sat on the edge of one of the potting tables. He stood between her legs and pushed the blazer from her shoulders. He saw that her breasts were full and pressing against the tight fabric of her T-shirt.

"Ginny," he whispered as he kissed her eyelids and cheeks and temples. He traced patterns over her bare arms with the tips of his fingers and felt the shudder of desire that ran through her. He continued kissing her and brought his hands to her breasts, brushing them lightly at first. She stilled but did not pull away. "I want to touch you, Ginny."

"Yes," she murmured.

He covered her breasts with his hands and felt the sudden release of her breath against his ear. The sensation of that hot rush of air shot through him like a bolt of lightning. He pulled back, his breath coming in heaves as he studied her tousled hair, her kiss-swollen lips. "Ginny, do you have any idea what you're doing to me?"

"I only know that I want you to keep touching me, kissing me," she whispered miserably as she held out her arms to him.

With a groan he pulled her to him, fitting her legs around his hips as he pulled her T-shirt free of her jeans and ran his hands over her bare skin. She arched her back, exposing her neck to his open mouth. He cupped her breasts and felt her knees tighten on his hips. He lifted her, fitting her to him so that she could feel his erection through the layers of their clothes. "I want to make love to you, Ginny," he warned her. "Stop me now if you're going to." It was then he felt the dampness on her cheeks and knew it was not from his passionate kisses.

He released her enough to permit her to stand, but held her close. "Shhh," he coaxed. "It's all right. I'm sorry. You know I won't do anything you don't want, Ginny."

She gave a little hiccuping laugh. "I think you have once again identified the problem," she said in a voice that was raspy and sexy as hell. "I seem to want this very much—more than I would ever have imagined."

"But the timing is all off, right?"

She nodded, and he kissed the top of her head.

"We'll work it out," he promised. "Come on. It's been a long day. I'll walk you back to the house."

He saw her safely to the French doors that led into the downstairs living area and turned to go. "I'll stop by tomorrow. Maybe we can have dinner together, okay?"

"That would be nice. I had a wonderful time tonight, Sam. It has been such a long time since I laughed so much or felt so completely carefree. Thank you for that." She cupped his cheek with her hand, and he turned his head so that he could kiss her palm.

"Go," he said and gave her a light push to propel her into the house so he could close the door. Afraid that if he looked back he would stay, he shoved his hands into his pockets and trudged back across the gardens to the greenhouse.

By morning Ginny had decided that the only way she was going to make sense of her feelings for Sam was to come to terms with Thomas's suicide. Thomas was dead, and in a shockingly short period of time she found herself in love with another man. It did not matter that an entire century lay between the two events. For Ginny, barely six weeks had passed since that horrible night. Whether her determination to prove that Thomas had been an innocent victim of a bad business deal stemmed from her sense of duty or her sense of guilt was not the point. Either way, she must do whatever possible to find the answers.

She began the morning by meeting with the workers in charge of the various projects going on throughout the house. Assured that everything was proceeding on schedule, she met with Freddie and the rest of the skeletal staff to be sure everything under their management was under control. Then she told Freddie that she would be in the library if he needed her.

"How was the date?" Freddie asked as she gathered her notes and prepared to leave the museum's administrative office.

"It was lovely." She smiled.

"And?" Freddie prompted.

"And that's all I'm going to say," she replied.

"Not one to kiss and tell, huh?" he teased.

"A lady never discusses such matters," she said with a haughty look. Then she giggled. "I'll be in the library if you need anything."

"What if Sam calls?"

"He can also find me in the library."

"After all the help and advice I gave you, that's all you're going to tell me?" Freddie protested as she started down the hall.

"I'm afraid so. I'll see you later."

Ginny was humming to herself as she walked briskly down the stairway. She greeted several of the workers by name and stopped to see how the stonemason's apprentice was doing. By the time she reached the library and closed the double doors against the noise of construction projects going on in the downstairs area, she was feeling quite content, more like the woman she had been when she and Thomas had first married and come to live in the mansion.

Then she turned and saw the desk, and the events of Thomas's death came back to her in a rush that left her feeling melancholy. With a sigh she set her notebook on the desk and began scanning the shelves of the library. She was surprised to see that for the most part things were as they had been when she and Thomas were in residence. The volume of poetry by Elizabeth Barrett Browning caught her eye. She thought about it lying open on the desk that night, spattered with Thomas's blood. With a foreboding born of that memory, she took the volume from the shelf and opened it.

The opening pages were yellowed but spotless. Slowly she turned each brittle leaf, looking for the poem he had read to her that night—but it was not in the volume. Perhaps she was mistaken. Perhaps it had been another book, and yet the poem was listed in the contents at the beginning. Slowly she turned the pages once again. When she reached the point where the poem should have been, she saw that the pages had been carefully cut out. Why? And by whom?

She recalled that the day Sam had confronted her in the secret room she had noticed that the rows of shelves there held stacks of books and papers. She had once mentioned these to Freddie, and he had told her that those were old scrapbooks, household records, diaries, and newspapers that Emily had always intended to sort and archive. Now that Ginny was here, Freddie had suggested, perhaps she would want to take a stab at that and surprise Emily on her return.

Ginny climbed the narrow circular stairs to the balcony and the secret room. Her answers would be in the materials stored there. She was sure of it. She realized that she was still carrying the volume of poetry as she worked the combination to enter the room.

Even though there was no official cataloguing of the documents, everything in the room had been carefully stored according to type of document and time period. Ginny had already developed a liking for Emily Sutter based solely on how Sam's mother had managed the house and retained its character through time. Seeing these stockpiled resources made Ginny appreciate the woman even more. Clearly they shared a love of history, especially history that related to Malmaison. Ginny had no doubt that if she found the answers she was seeking, she would have Emily to thank for that.

She laid the Browning poetry on a side table and took down a stack of newspapers carefully bound and labeled "1899–1900." Each paper had one of those odd little self-sticking yellow papers on it with a note as to what articles were of relevance in the paper. Ginny carefully sifted through the stack until she came to the sheet that read, *Thomas Thornton Obituary*.

Drawing a deep breath, she spread the paper on a large, bare, wooden table and turned the pages until she found the article. It was filled with details of Thomas's memberships in various important societies and of his

good works. It listed his family history and survivors—
herself, a sister, an aunt. There was no mention of the
cause of death, only that private services were to be held
at the family estate.

Curious as to what news would have followed that
announcement, Ginny turned to retrieve the next paper
in the stack. It was dated six months after Thomas's
death and contained a very brief article about a summer
tea given by Mrs. Cashwell Sutter in support of the local
garden society. Ginny returned to the shelves and
scanned each paper, each date and note. Perhaps something had been misfiled, she thought. Surely the change
in ownership of Malmaison would have been news.

It took her most of the afternoon to go through the
papers, but she found nothing. Discouraged and more
than a little irritated, she was forced to abandon the
search when the daylight faded. Even with all the lamps
in the room lit, there was not enough light to continue
her work. After several hours, she had no answers—only
more questions.

"Ginny?" Sam was standing in the doorway. "Are you
all right?"

"Yes. I've just been going through some of these
things. Freddie said that it would be a nice surprise for
your mother if—"

"You don't have to pretend with me, Ginny. If you
think the answers you need are here, then you have
every right to look for them without having to make
excuses."

"Thank you." She didn't want him to be nice to her.
She had suspicions that his family had willfully destroyed pieces of history they found unpleasant or un-
flattering. "Was there something you wanted?"

"I thought we might take a walk before dinner. Would
you like that? I mean, Freddie tells me you've been shut
up in this room most of the day. Some fresh air might
be nice."

"I really should attend to . . ."

He crossed the room so that he was standing very near. "Ginny, what's wrong? What have you found that's changed everything between us? I need to know the answers, too, you know."

He was right, of course. It was unfair to take out her irritation with his ancestors on him. She sighed. "The point is that I've found nothing. There are great gaps in information that logically should be here, beginning with this." She picked up the book of poetry.

"The night Thomas died he read me a poem from this volume. The book was lying on his desk when he died. It was open to the poem and the pages were spattered with blood—*his blood.* Who would cut them out?"

Sam looked bewildered. "I don't know. Perhaps some kind soul who wanted to protect you? What other reason could there be?"

"Perhaps someone wanted to conceal evidence."

"What evidence?" He looked completely bewildered, and then his eyes glimmered with understanding. "Ginny, I know you think that somehow my great-great-grandfather might have prevented this, but if Thomas wanted to kill himself—"

"Why aren't there news reports about the change in ownership of the estate?" she challenged. "Why are those issues of the newspapers missing from these stacks?"

"I don't know, Ginny. Tomorrow you'll come with me to the library. They have all of the papers—every single day. You can go through them there."

"I will," she replied with defiance.

"Good. So how about that walk?"

"Fine," she agreed.

He grinned. "Okay, then, let's go."

He was impossible, she thought.

They walked until after dark. He told her about his work, the experiments he had successfully completed through the years. She told him of her memories of various parts of the estate as they followed the network of trails through the woods.

Suddenly he left the trail and started across a clearing. "Come with me," he urged. "I want to show you something and see if you can explain it."

"Sam, it's late and very dark."

"Come on. You know these woods as well as I do. They've been here for a hundred years, after all. It's not as if we're likely to get lost."

He was right. Ginny knew exactly where they were deep in the woods that fronted the property and offered it seclusion from the rest of the world. She kept pace with him as he picked up the trail that led to the wooden footbridge that crossed over the racing creek. The creek was frozen now, but in spring the water would bubble merrily over the stones and tree roots that lined its bed. This was one of Ginny's favorite refuges on the estate.

Just before they reached the bridge, Sam left the trail a second time and made a path for her to follow through the snow and the underbrush until he reached a small clearing. "Here," he said as he brushed snow away from a stone foundation. "What was this place, Ginny? Mom has never been able to find out anything about it, and yet on this cornerstone right here it says 1885."

Ginny bent and ran her fingers over the carved stone. "My father built me a small house here—a place to play and later to come to when I needed to escape. He said that everyone should have a place that was just for them—even children."

"I guess over the years it just deteriorated from neglect," Sam said.

"Oh, no," Ginny corrected him. "This was all there was—the foundation. Father said that my walls were the evergreens." She motioned to the tall cedars that framed the spot. "And the wildflowers created a carpet as colorful as any of the Orientals in the mansion." She stood in the center of the small area and swung her arms wide as she turned. "The sky was my roof, and when it rained, I took shelter here." She pulled aside branches of the cedars to show an area that was overgrown now but clearly had once been shaped to provide shelter.

As she moved from spot to spot renewing her acquaintance with her childhood haven, Sam leaned against a tall oak tree and watched her. "Ginny," he said after a long moment, "come home with me tonight."

She knew what he was asking and would not pretend that she did not. "It wouldn't be proper," she said softly.

He pressed his advantage. "But you want to do it."

She could not look at him so she looked at the ground and gave a slight nod. "Yes," she murmured. "God help me, I do."

He pulled her into his arms and held her. "Ginny, we both find ourselves in a strange and wonderful circumstance. We don't know what tomorrow will bring. We have tonight—this night."

She circled her arms around his waist. He was here and wanting her, and she wanted him. That was their reality. Tomorrow she might wake up and find herself thrown back in time to deal with the aftermath of what Thomas had done. Tonight she was safe and in the arms of a man who cared deeply for her. She lifted her head and looked up at him.

"I will go home with you tonight," she said.

"You do know what I'm asking?"

"Yes."

He kissed her tenderly as snow began to fall.

Chapter 11

IT WAS AS if having made the decision, they could take time to savor the moment. They walked arm in arm back to the gardener's cottage that Sam told her he had converted to his living quarters a decade earlier.

"I was something of a rebel in my younger days," he admitted sheepishly. "I grew up surrounded by the burden of all this family history and couldn't wait to get out of here. As far as I was concerned, it did little good to dwell on the past. The future was what was going to matter in the long run. To some real degree I still believe that."

"Then why did you return to Malmaison?"

"I finally understood that my great-great-grandfather had built me a laboratory right here." He made an expansive sweep of the surroundings with one hand. "Between the land and the conservatory I have everything I need to do my work." He opened the door to the cottage and stood aside to let her enter. "Home sweet home," he said with a grin.

It was clear to Ginny from the moment she entered the cottage that Sam had made the changes that were necessary to create a comfortable living and working space for himself without disturbing the overall ambience of the structure. She also understood that he had done this less because he wanted to preserve as much of the integrity of the cottage as possible and more because he simply wasn't interested in his surroundings unless they impacted his work.

Makeshift bookcases lined one wall and were filled to overflowing. A modern desk struggled to hold a computer, printer, fax machine, telephone, and a couple of other pieces of electronic equipment Ginny could not name. There were piles of books and papers everywhere, most with notes haphazardly marking pages. She could not imagine how he made sense of any of it.

"This is where you work?" she asked.

"Pretty scary, huh?" He was grinning. "I'll bet this blows holes in any stereotypical ideas you might have had about the methodical, organized scientist, right?"

"You don't have to be quite so proud of your tendency toward disarray," she replied.

"Disarray?" He laughed. "There's a good Victorian word if I ever heard one. Come with me."

She followed him down a narrow hallway and suddenly found herself in a large open room that was clearly living room, sleeping room, and kitchen. Its windows looked out on giant evergreens silhouetted against a moonlit sky. She had been in the cottage before, but this was different. "You've taken out the loft," she said.

"Sort of." He turned, and she saw that a part of the loft remained open to the room where they stood and held still more bookcases. "Are you hungry? I'm starving."

"Yes. I think I forgot lunch today." She walked around the room as he shrugged out of his jacket and hung it on a wooden peg near the door. He had kicked off his shoes at the door, and she had followed suit. She draped her coat over the back of a chair.

"Make yourself at home," he offered as he began removing things from the refrigerator. "Hit that switch there next to the mantel."

She did, and a fire sprang to life in the old stone fireplace. She looked at him in surprise.

"Gas," he told her. "Pretty neat, huh?" He brought her a glass of wine. "What shall we toast?"

She thought about why they had come back to the cottage and shyness overcame her. "I . . . I'm not sure," she stammered.

"How about life?" he suggested. "Yours . . . mine . . ."

Ours. The thought came unbidden but instantly. Ginny blushed. "Yes," she agreed, clinking her glass to his. "To life."

He sipped his wine and set the glass on the counter. "You know, Ginny Thornton, it occurs to me that I always seem to be preparing food for you. Don't you Victorian types cook?"

He had deliberately disarmed the strain of the moment again, and Ginny adored him for that. "Of course, we cook," she replied. "And we do it without all of these complex contraptions you twenty-first-century types seem to need. Step aside, sir. Take your wine into the parlor there and sit before your instantaneous fire."

Sam laughed and did as he was told. He stretched out in a leather chair that reclined when he pushed a lever. Ginny fought to show no expression.

"Pretty slick, huh?" he said.

"It's more evidence of your generation's attachment to comfort," she replied with mock exasperation. "Do you own a grater for the cheese?"

"First cabinet on the left."

She found it and took note that in contrast to his notes and papers, everything in the cabinet was meticulously neat and orderly. She peeled potatoes and onions, found a skillet, and coated it with a slab of butter. She added the vegetables and set them to cook on the stovetop while she grated cheese. Finally she diced apples, which she added to the mixture of potatoes and onions.

"How are things coming?" he asked.

"Are you worried?"

"Nope, just famished."

As she cooked, they talked about the cottage and what changes he had made. She had to admit that they were for the best. The cottage had always been a rather dark, gloomy place. Sam had removed interior walls to make three tiny rooms into the current larger one and installed large windows that framed the landscape outside on either side of the rough stone fireplace. It made the room appear much larger.

She melted the cheese. "Do you have any beer?"

"Wine *and* beer? I'm discovering some shocking things about you, Ginny."

"It's for the sauce." She opened the refrigerator and saw what she needed. "Never mind."

There was a round loaf of wheat bread on the counter. She sliced that and some tomatoes as well, then stood back and considered. "Plates?"

"Right side, second cabinet. Flatware is in the first drawer to your left. I'll refill the wine glasses, and we can eat in front of the fire." He pushed his chair out of the way and spread an old-fashioned quilt on the floor in front of the hearth, then returned to the kitchen area to refill the wine.

Ginny was serving the plates. She heaped a large portion of the onion, apple, and potato mixture with cheese sauce on one plate and added a generous hunk of bread and several slices of tomato. "Is this enough?" she asked, and her tone relayed her doubts.

"Well, now, that depends. Were you planning on feeding the *entire* population of Malmaison or just half of it?"

She blinked. "That's for you."

His eyes widened. "You expect me to eat all of this?"

"You said you were hungry," she replied uncertainly.

He smiled and kissed the top of her head. "I'm teasing you, Ginny. It's wonderful. Get yours, and let's eat.

We'll make it a winter picnic there in front of the fire." He waited for her to take her plate and then switched off the lights so that the fire's glow lit the room. "We can tell ghost stories if you like," he said as he stretched out on the quilt next to her and started to eat.

"I'll bet you know some good ones." She relaxed and realized she was almost as hungry as he appeared to be.

"When I was a boy I used to attend camp every summer. The counselors loved to try to scare us half to death with stories around the campfire. Some of them were pretty grisly, but we could always top them, and more often than not it was the counselors who had trouble sleeping."

He devoured the food with gusto, and Ginny could not help comparing his unrestrained pleasure in the simple act of eating to Thomas's eating habits. Thomas had always been suspicious of unfamiliar food. He'd sniffed it as if he thought someone might actually attempt to poison him. It had driven Ginny to distraction at first, and then, as in so many other instances, she had said nothing and merely accepted the behavior.

"This is wonderful, Ginny."

"Thank you." She was inordinately pleased with his praise of the simple meal.

"How about dessert?" He stood up and took his own spotless plate and hers to the kitchen. "Chocolate cake?"

"I don't think I could eat another bite. Truly," she protested.

"Ah, Ginny, there's always room for dessert in life. We'll share a piece. Freddie's wife made this. She thinks I'm too thin and, according to Freddie, she thinks I must forget to eat half the time. I guess he's told her that I'm pretty wrapped up in my work." He cut a large hunk of the cake and plopped it onto a plate.

"Here, try a bite." He knelt next to her, as she leaned against the reclining chair, and offered a forkful of the rich, moist cake.

Ginny had never in her life tasted anything so sinfully

rich. She closed her eyes and savored the taste of it as she slowly slid the bite of cake off the fork. "Oh, my," she murmured and opened her eyes.

Sam was staring at her, and his expression was completely serious. She licked her lips. His breath caught.

"My God, you are beautiful," he whispered and set the cake aside as he leaned in to kiss her.

His gentleness was her undoing. His lips met hers, but he did not press the advantage. Instead he settled himself on the floor next to her and pulled her into his arms. It was Ginny who deepened the kiss. It was Ginny whose hand ran restlessly over his back and shoulders, urging him closer. It was Ginny who was losing control.

She pulled away, embarrassed at her wanton behavior. "I . . . I'm . . ."

He pulled her back to him. "I want you, Ginny. I just need to be sure that it's what you want as well . . . that you'll have no regrets."

She first nodded, then shook her head. "I mean, yes, I want you . . . us . . . and no, I'll have no doubts, no regrets. Oh, Sam, just stop talking about it and kiss me properly."

He smiled and obliged.

Sam could not believe the feelings that roared through him with the realization that he was about to make love to this woman. He had fantasized about it and dismissed it as inconceivable. When she had closed her eyes and then closed her lips around that forkful of cake, he had thought he would go mad. He had visualized all sorts of erotic images in the simple act of her tasting that cake, and it had taken every ounce of restraint to keep from tearing her clothes off her and taking her right there, right then. His hand had been shaking so hard when he tried to set the cake plate aside that he was sure he had missed the table.

Now she was a willing partner in his arms, her mouth

open under his, her tongue matching his in an exotic and primal dance that communicated far more than words ever could have. He opened the buttons on her blouse far enough to permit him access to her throat, her shoulders. She arched, and he knew it was a signal of acquiescence. Her balled fists pulled at his sweater. He pulled back to strip the garment off and was rewarded by her sharp intake of breath.

He finished opening her blouse, pushing the edges back to expose her. He pulled it off her shoulders, following it down her arms with a string of kisses. Then he eased the straps of her bra from her shoulders. He looked up and saw that she was watching him. He hesitated, and she completed the act by opening the front clasp and allowing the bra to fall away. He sucked in a breath the same way a drowning man might have before going under.

He cupped her breasts, felt the fullness of them, saw how hard the nipples had grown in anticipation. He looked at her again and saw that she would not ask him to stop. With a groan he laid her back on the quilt and took one hardened nipple in his mouth, nurturing it to flower. Her response was soft whimpers, and her fingers tangled in his hair, urging him closer. He turned his attention to her other breast, and this time she murmured his name.

Gathering her in his arms, he rolled to his back. She tossed back her glorious hair and balanced her hands on his shoulders.

"Sam," she whispered just before she bent to kiss him. As if she wanted to show that she had learned her lessons well, she slid her mouth over his jaw and down his neck until he could feel the heat of her breath on his bare chest. He waited to see what she would do next. Tenderly she ran one finger over his nipple. When he responded with a slight twitch, she smiled and repeated the action, drawing it out, torturing him as she experimented with different pressures, different techniques.

"You're going to regret this," he warned, his voice a husky rasp.

She chuckled and lowered her mouth to cover him as he had her. Her hair fanned over his chest like a shawl. It smelled of cedar, but he had only a moment to savor that before his attention was riveted on what she was doing to him with her mouth and tongue. He lifted her hand from his chest and moved it lower. He pressed his erection against her flattened palm, and she suddenly went motionless.

"You do this to me, Ginny," he whispered. "I need you to finish undressing me."

It was a challenge, one he wasn't sure she was ready to accept. She sat slowly back on her heels and moved her hand away from his erection back to his chest. It seemed an eternity that she sat there, saying nothing, running her palm over his torso. Finally she brought it to rest on his belt buckle. With a shuddering sigh she unfastened his belt and opened the button on his jeans. With agonizing slowness she slid the zipper open.

"My turn," he said and reached for her. "Lie back." He pulled off the socks she wore under her skirt and kissed the instep of her bare feet. Then he ran his hands along her legs under her skirt around to her inner thighs. He felt her tighten in response. "Relax," he coaxed as he continued his massage, made more erotic by the covering of her skirt. Slowly he pulled her panties off. She was naked except for the long straight knit skirt that followed the flat planes of her stomach and legs. He knelt next to her and slowly pulled the last garment away, following its path with a trail of kisses that had her writhing and calling his name by the time he reached her feet.

"I can't wait any longer," she moaned. "I feel . . . I feel as if . . ."

"Tell me, Ginny," he urged as he ran his hands over her legs until he reached their apex. Gently he urged her to open to him. "Tell me what you're feeling."

"I'm going to explode," she whispered and then as he plunged his fingers inside her, she gasped. "Sam, you are driving me insane."

"I'm making love to you, Ginny. I'm right here. Trust me." He found the core of her and brought her to the very edge.

"Don't leave me," she cried when he pulled his fingers free and moved away to strip off the rest of his clothes.

"Never," he whispered as he moved over her. "Just one more minute," he assured her as he covered himself to protect her. He saw the question in her eyes. "It keeps you from becoming pregnant," he explained.

She let out a short and mirthless laugh. "That has never been a problem, Sam, but thank you for wanting to protect me." She opened her arms to him. "Make love to me," she whispered.

Sam moved over her. She placed her hands on his face and looked up at him with such trust and adoration that he was nearly lost before he could act. She was moist and ready for him. He lifted her hips and slid inside her and when he felt her muscles tighten around him he felt such a sense of peace and contentment, as if he'd finally found the place he was meant to be, the woman he was meant to love.

Ginny thrilled to the sensation of him filling her, of his body connected with hers, across time, across the events of their shared history. Was this why she had come? To find Sam? To love Sam? He began the rhythm of their mating with a slow steady penetration and withdrawal. But as she matched him thrust for thrust she knew that he was as close to the edge as she was, and this time neither of them would have the power to make the mating last as long as they wanted.

She had never experienced such sensations before except perhaps in the privacy of her own bed following an erotic dream. She had always thought there was something wrong with her that she had these feelings, felt these needs. But she understood that in Sam's eyes they only made her more desirable.

"Let it come," he said softly. "It's okay, Ginny, I'm right here with you."

With his assurance she surrendered to the feelings and felt them wash over her in wave after wave as she cried out her pleasure with each pulsating sensation. Sam urged her to total release with his kisses and his murmured endearments, and, true to his word, he stayed with her every step of the way, only permitting his own release and pleasure when he knew she had reached hers. In that moment her joy doubled as she heard him cry out and felt him strain against sensations rocketing through him that mirrored her own experience.

Suddenly the room was silent except for the sound of their rapid breathing as they came back to reality. She curled into his side, laying her head on his chest. He stroked her hair.

"Are you okay?" he asked.

His concern touched her. "I'm fine, Sam, truly." She raised her head so he could see her face in the firelight. "It was wonderful."

He grinned. "Aw, shucks, ma'am, that was nothing. Just wait 'til next time."

She hit him playfully. "You modern men are very cocky, aren't you?"

"And you Victorian women certainly hold up well for being . . . what is it, a hundred and thirty?"

"Twenty-nine," she corrected archly, and then they both collapsed in giggles at the preposterous idea.

They lay together in a comfortable silence. She dozed, and he covered her with the edge of the quilt. Sometime before dawn she stirred and found him watching her.

"Hungry?" he asked and reached for the chocolate cake.

"Famished," she replied and loaded one finger with the frosting before bringing it to his lips.

There was nothing there.

Ginny scanned every page of the papers on the funny screen the librarian had taught her to use in the university's archives. There was no mention of Malmaison save the articles she had found at the estate. This was impossible. There had to have been a scandal associated with Thomas's suicide, and what of her own family's long-standing reputation in the community? She scanned back to the screen with Thomas's obituary.

"Ms. Thornton?"

Ginny looked up from the harsh light of the microfilm screen and blinked.

"Sebastian Corwell, Ms. Thornton. We met at the New Year's gala?"

Ginny smiled and stood to greet the elderly gentleman. "Of course. It is so lovely to see you again." She extended her hand, and he accepted it with a courtly bow.

"What brings you to these tombs of research?"

"I . . . I needed to verify some items of history related to the estate."

"Really?" His pale blue eyes sparkled with interest and enthusiasm. "As I told you, I am something of a local history buff, Ms. Thornton. Is there anything I might do to assist you in your research?"

"Won't you please call me Ginny, Mr. Corwell?" she asked, wanting to divert his attention from the article behind her.

"Only if you agree to be on a similar first-name basis with me, my dear. Now, let's have a look . . ." He stepped around her and focused on the screen. "Ah, the death of Mr. Thornton—a relative of yours, I presume."

"Well, yes, but . . ."

"Emily told me of your unique association to the estate. It was one of the reasons I decided to give the donation for the restoration. It was clear to me at the gala that you had a special knowledge of the estate and a special attachment to it. When Emily told me that Thornton was your great-great-grandfather, I knew that you were the perfect person to see this project to its proper conclusion. You have a vested interest, a personal stake, haven't you, Ginny?"

He peered up at her from his position leaning over the screen. His face was wise, and his eyes seemed to see to the depths of her soul. She was so nervous that he would guess her secret that she could not find her voice—so she nodded instead.

"My grandparents were contemporaries of your great-great-grandparents," he continued, "and therefore I know something of them. Of course, you are named for the fair Virginia, are you not?"

Again Ginny nodded as the realization of the connection struck her. Katherine and Tucker Corwell. Of course. Thomas had not liked Tucker, had been jealous of his success and respect in the community.

"I'm afraid we share a bit of a soap opera in terms of our family histories, my dear." Sebastian chuckled and then sobered immediately. "A sad history, of course, but one the filmmakers would have a field day with were our families more nationally prominent."

"I don't understand."

"Why, I would have thought you knew." Sebastian was clearly surprised. "Thomas Thornton was in love with my grandmother, Katherine."

Sam picked that exact moment to enter the microfilm room. "Hello, Sebastian."

A thousand images and questions raced through Ginny's mind as Sam and Sebastian chatted. Sebastian's simple statement was stunning. If true, it was devastating.

"Ginny, are you all right?" Sam was looking at her with a worried frown.

"You are quite pale, my dear," Sebastian added. "Perhaps a glass of water?"

"No, thank you both. I'm just a bit tired."

"Samuel, you are working this young woman far too hard," Sebastian chided. "She needs her rest."

Sam actually blushed, and Ginny smiled. "I'm quite well, Sebastian. Thank you for your concern."

"Let me take the two of you to lunch at my club," Sebastian suggested.

"I'm afraid I have a class to teach, but, Ginny, if you'd like to go, I can meet you there."

Ginny hesitated. On the one hand, she wanted desperately to go, to hear more of what Sebastian knew. On the other hand, she was afraid. If Thomas had indeed been in love with Katherine, Ginny was not sure she could mask her own pain in hearing the details.

"I promise to be on my very best behavior, Ginny," Sebastian said.

Ginny smiled. He was a charming man, and she had nothing to fear. "I would be honored to have lunch with you. Just let me return these materials to the librarian and get my things."

Sebastian's club was the same imposing, darkly furnished bastion of male pursuits that Ginny's father and Thomas had frequented. Ginny recalled going there with her father when she was a small child. Once she reached thirteen, her father had stopped taking her, telling her that young women were not allowed. The idea had always rankled. As she entered the reception area with Sebastian, a cheery woman greeted them, and Sebastian introduced her to Ginny as the manager of the club. In the dining room Ginny was pleased to see that as many women as men occupied the elegantly set tables. Everyone was beautifully dressed in business attire, and Ginny nervously smoothed the front of her own long, straight knit skirt.

"You look quite lovely," Sebastian assured her in a quiet voice as the headwaiter led them to a table near one of the tall lead-glass windows and presented them with menus.

They ordered, and when the waiter had left, Sebastian leaned back and studied her for a long moment. "I take it that you were unaware of the affair between our ancestors, Ginny. I'm sorry if I have shocked you."

She wanted to tell him that the idea was preposterous. She wanted to tell him that Thomas had loved her and no one else. She wanted to tell him that this was but one more lie concocted to cast Thomas in a bad light. Instead, she said calmly, "I have never seen anything that would support that."

"Nor have I, directly."

The waiter delivered their food.

"Then on what basis—"

Sebastian waved his hand. "Family stories passed down through the generations. Conversations that stopped suddenly whenever as I child I might have interrupted adults reliving the past. That sort of thing." He began eating his salad. "Oh, and of course, the photograph."

"You're being deliberately obtuse, Sebastian," Ginny said.

He smiled. "I am having a bit of fun with this," he admitted. "What have you been told?"

"Nothing of the things of which you speak," she answered immediately.

"Ah, now who is being obtuse?"

"The photograph?" she asked, bringing him back to the topic he had introduced and dropped.

"It was in the New York paper in the fall of 1899, a little blurred but unmistakable. Your great-great-grandfather and my grandmother exiting a train. The story, of course, was not about them at all. It was about some newfangled parlor car that Vanderbilt had introduced. They just happened to be on the train . . . together."

"I see." Ginny swallowed the lump of salad that she

had forgotten to chew. "This then is the sum of your evidence."

He reached across the table and patted her hand. "Ginny, I apologize. I have indeed upset you. It's just that I thought the little intrigue might amuse you. After all, we are generations and an entire century removed from that event. I thought in light of the current morality, this might actually seem a bit archaic to you."

He was a kind man and he had no idea that he was breaking the news of a supposed illicit affair a man had engaged in a century earlier to that man's wife.

"It's all right, Sebastian. Actually I appreciate this opportunity to hear your version of events. Anything that may have occurred during the time period we are using as a starting point for restoring the mansion is of interest. Please tell me your own memories of the estate. You must have visited there."

"Indeed," Sebastian replied with obvious relief and spent the remainder of their time together regaling her with stories of his youth and the young Sutter children who had been his best friends.

Ginny smiled and laughed on cue, a skill she had perfected through years of appearing to listen to conversations when in fact her mind raced with details that needed her attention. The detail that demanded her immediate attention at the moment was finding that photograph.

"I must return to the library," she told Sam when he met her in front of the club. "Will it still be open?"

"It's open twenty-four hours a day, but I thought you had—"

"There is something I must see for myself. Do you think they have archived the New York papers?"

"Sure. Ginny, what is it?"

"Sebastian tells me that Thomas was having an affair with Katherine Corwell, Sebastian's grandmother. Katherine is . . . was . . . one of my dearest friends. How could I not have known about it? He must be mistaken."

"I see," he said and looked down at his shoes.

Ginny stared at him. "You knew," she exclaimed. "You knew about this horrible rumor and didn't tell me?"

"I've heard the story," he admitted. "You've been so certain that Thomas—"

"Sam, I don't need your protection. I am not some hothouse flower that will wilt under conditions of cold reality. I have traveled into the future to find the truth, and frankly if you insist on keeping things from me, you aren't being much help. Now take me to the library."

Sam smiled as she strode away and got into the car herself. She was right. He had been trying to protect her. Clearly what she needed more than protection was an ally who would help her find the truth. Someone who would be there for her when she discovered that her precious Thomas was a scoundrel who, if he hadn't shot himself, was going to break her heart in some far more devastating way.

Chapter 12

SAM WOULD HAVE done anything to spare Ginny the pain he saw flash across her face when she found the photograph. It was grainy and indistinct but clear enough for her to recognize her husband and the woman she had once considered a dear friend.

"Ginny." He touched her shoulder, and she leaned into his touch.

"There has to be some explanation," she said wearily.

"Perhaps there is," he agreed.

They were silent for a moment as she continued to study the picture.

"But what if it's true," she murmured and ran her fingers over the images.

Sam didn't know what to say. Should he tell her that it would be all right because he loved her? What kind of comfort would that be to a woman who had loved the man in the picture—who might still love that man if he were alive?

"Let's get out of here, Ginny."

"I don't think I can face going back to Malmaison just yet."

"Then we'll go somewhere else. You need to give yourself time to absorb what you've seen and heard today, to sort it out in light of what you know. Remember, Ginny, you are the single person in all of this who was there, who knows the truth . . . whatever that may be."

She clasped his hand. "You give me such hope, Sam. Thank you for that."

"So, will you come with me?"

She shrugged. "Yes, why not?"

He hated that the day's events seemed to have sucked the vitality from her. He longed to put the sparkle back in her eyes, the laughter back in her voice. "Come on."

She followed him from the library and only showed interest in their destination when he headed away from the car. "Where are we going?"

"Ice skating," he replied. "You do skate, don't you?"

"Well, yes, but—"

"Good, because I don't, and you're going to teach me."

Her eyes flickered and dulled again. "Really, Sam, this is not—"

"This is a perfect time for this. The rink is open. The students are all studying for exams—and if they're not, they should be. I can make a complete fool of myself without having it spread all over campus that Dr. Sutter is spastic. Perfect timing."

He had continued to head for the outdoor ice rink while he made his speech and he was glad to see that she had decided to follow.

"It's been years," she protested.

"I understand that it's a skill like bicycling—once you acquire the basics, they are yours for life." He approached the chalet and ordered rental skates for himself. "What size, Ginny?" he asked.

"A six," the attendant guessed. "If I'm wrong I'll give you an extra pair of socks to make them fit."

Sam paid the fees and looped both pairs of skates over his shoulder. He led the way to a park bench on the edge of the nearly deserted rink. "Sit and put these on."

"You're quite the tyrant today," Ginny fumed, and he thought he heard a hint of her old spark. Regardless, she sat and began pulling on the skates.

"Here, let me lace them for you." He knelt and laced the skates following her admonition to make them tight. "Now my turn." He sat next to her and pulled on his skates.

"Lace them tight," she instructed, "so your ankles won't buckle."

"I beg your pardon, madam," he said archly, "I do *not* have *buckly* ankles. As a matter of fact, I've been told they are quite nice." He was rewarded with the beginning of a smile. "Now then, standing up should be an interesting challenge."

He tried it, and his legs instantly took off in opposite directions as he clung to the park bench. He heard a giggle and looked down to see her watching him with one gloved fist crammed against her mouth. "Are you laughing at me, Ms. Thornton?"

She nodded and permitted the giggles to escape.

"Well, if you think it's so easy, let's see you do it," he challenged.

She stood effortlessly and took off across the ice, executing a flawless pirouette in the center of the rink. The few other skaters stopped and applauded as she skated back to Sam and slid to a stop.

"Show-off," he muttered.

She was beaming. "These new skates are wonderful," she said with delight. "They make skating so effortless. Here, give me your hands."

He looked at her with skepticism.

"Come on," she coaxed. "That's it. Now bring your feet together and stand up straight. Good. Now just one step at a time. Left . . . right . . . left . . . That's it. You've got it."

"No, I don't!" Sam yelled as he went down in a heap. "You let go," he accused.

"Now, Samuel, one cannot learn to skate without falling down occasionally."

"Well, *one* would like to have some warning that he's about to land on his . . . backside."

"This was your idea," she reminded him as she helped him to his feet.

He clung to her hands, determined not to let her release him again. "Don't let go," he growled as he concentrated on maintaining his balance.

"I'm right here beside you. There, that's much better. Now straighten up a little and lengthen your stride a bit. That's better. See how easy it is."

The sparkle was back, and she could barely conceal her mirth at his clumsiness. He had achieved his purpose. Why did he feel like such a damn fool? "This is work," he grumbled.

"It's fun," she corrected. "Now, I'm going to let go. I'll be right here."

"Not yet," he protested, and as she attempted to release his hands and he tightened his grip, they both tumbled to the ice. "That didn't work out the way you planned, did it?" he asked sheepishly as she lay sprawled on top of him.

"Not exactly."

"What do we do now?" He glanced around, looking for anything they might use to pull themselves back to a standing position.

"I'll get up first. You stay put." After a couple of attempts she managed to get to her feet. "There," she reported breathlessly. "Now you."

He held out his hand to her.

"Not this time," she called and skated away.

"You are a cruel woman, Ginny Thornton."

Her laughter echoed over the ice like sleigh bells on a winter's night. The other skaters had left. The attendant was clearly ready to call it a day. Sam rolled to his knees. Damn. The ice was cold. Whose lame idea had this been?

"I believe the gentleman would like to close up for the evening, Sam," Ginny called from her position on the far side of the ice. She was sitting on the park bench removing her skates.

Having determined that there was never a tree or telephone pole or park bench to help a man to his feet when he needed one, Sam tried standing. He made it two-thirds of the way and went flat again. "Don't you dare laugh," he called.

"Don't think about it so much, Sam. Just stand up. Just do it."

What he did *not* need at this particular moment was a Nike commercial. He glowered at her, which sent her into fresh peals of laughter. "You have a real mean streak in you, lady," he said as he struggled to his feet and remained standing. He gave her a triumphant salute by raising one fist high in the air and then clawed air as he went down for a third time.

She clicked her tongue against her teeth and shook her head. "You are hopeless."

"I am a scientist and I will solve even this problem," he announced as he proceeded to slide himself across the ice by pushing himself with his gloved hands and sliding his very cold backside along the frozen rink.

She was laughing so hard by the time he reached her that she was holding her side and could not get enough breath to speak. The attendant also seemed to be enjoying his performance. Sam pulled himself onto the bench. "You will pay for this, Ms. Thornton," he said low enough for only her to hear.

"Oh, Sam, you're soaked," she said as he stood up to hand the attendant his skates. "You'll catch your death."

"All of a sudden she's concerned," he observed, and the attendant nodded sympathetically.

"Seriously, Sam," Ginny continued as they walked back toward the car. "You need to get home and get out of those wet clothes and into bed."

Sam grinned as he caught her in a hug. "*Now* you're

talking," he said just before he kissed her.

"Sam, people will see us," she protested, but he noticed that she made no effort to move away.

"Naw, they're all studying, remember?" He kissed her again, kissed her until they were both breathless. "We have way too many clothes on," he observed as he reached for her again.

"We're outside in the middle of January," she replied as she encouraged his exploration of her neck and ear.

"We could be inside in a nice hot shower . . . the two of us." He felt her shudder with excitement. "Think about it, Ginny. I would soap your naked body, wash your hair, make love to you under the spray of the water." He whispered each suggestion in her ear, punctuating each with a kiss.

"Sam . . ." He knew that she wanted to sound a warning, but she failed miserably.

"Say yes, Ginny," he whispered and outlined her ear with his tongue.

"Sam . . ."

"Yes," he repeated.

"Yes." She sighed and melted into his kiss.

They ran the rest of the way to the car. The trip back to the estate was a blur. Ginny was only vaguely aware that he had headed straight for the gardener's cottage. They were barely inside before they were in each other's arms again, tearing at clothing, murmuring endearments. She had never done anything remotely like this. It was outrageous and thrilling. Pieces of their clothing littered the hallway from the door to the bathroom.

Sam snapped on a dim nightlight on their way to the shower. "It's the closest I'm going to come to candlelight," he said as he kissed her again and reached behind her to turn on the water.

He finished undressing her, then stripped off his own

clothes. He turned her so that her back was to him, and she could feel the full power of his erection pressing against her buttocks. His hands roamed over her breasts and down to her stomach and back again. He urged her forward into the shower.

The water was warm like a waterfall cascading over them. Sam took soap from a bottle and massaged it over the length of her body. It smelled of evergreens and fresh air. As his hands worked the intimate crevices of her body, Ginny wasn't sure she could possibly remain standing, her need for him was so great.

"Sam," she protested when he found her center and began stroking her there. "I want. . . ." She cried out as she felt the first break of climax.

"Let it come," he urged.

She abandoned any inhibition and gave in to the sensations that wracked her body. She clung to his shoulders as the tidal wave raged on. At what was surely the very pinnacle, she felt him lift her and slide inside her. He filled her both physically and emotionally, and she realized that whatever might come she would never again know a moment like this. Unexpectedly she felt the rush of a fresh crest. She felt wanton and reckless . . . and in that moment, she felt free. Free of the past. Free of its secrets and its mysteries. Free of Thomas.

Afterward they washed each other's hair and bodies and wrapped up in large fleecy towels. He combed out her hair, and she braided it while he turned back the bed covers. They did not speak, neither wanting to break the magic of what they had just experienced.

Ginny was asleep almost as soon as she curled into his body, and he wrapped her in the warmth of the covers and his arms. It was dawn when she awoke. Sam was already awake and watching her.

"I have to go back," she said.

"I know. I'm coming with you."

• • •

The trick, of course, was to figure out *how* to travel backward through time. Sam considered the problem, turned it over, and looked at it from every side as he would any experiment, any thesis. If Ginny could be propelled forward by a single traumatic event, then perhaps it was possible to go back to that exact moment when she had left the house—*her* house—and found refuge in the conservatory.

He considered his own procedures for conducting a research investigation. Conditions had to be exactly right, carefully formulated to mirror the optimum conditions that would exist if he were successful. He studied his attempts to recreate the properties of the extinct malmaison dianthus. He had done extensive research to learn everything he could about their propagation in the days before they had been bred into oblivion. The temperature. The humidity. The soil. The light. Everything must be as precise as he could make it.

He removed his glasses and pinched the bridge of his nose. "Think," he ordered himself. He walked over to the wall of glass and stared out at the mansion. It had started to snow and it was just twilight. These were the conditions the night Ginny came to him. He felt his heart pump with excitement. "What else?" he demanded of no one but himself. "Think."

He began furiously jotting notes. Clothing. Weather. Time of day. Preceding events. Sights. Sounds. Scents. *Scents.* He ran to the adjoining greenhouse and retrieved the jar in which he had stored the petals of the blossom she carried that night. He opened the lid a fraction and sniffed. There was still some potency to the dry petals. Quickly he shut the jar and headed up the arbor path to the house.

"Ginny!" he called as he shook snow from his hair and jacket just inside the kitchen. "Ginny!" he bellowed loud enough to be heard throughout the massive house.

"What is it?" She was wide-eyed with anxiety, breathless as she ran into the kitchen. "What's happened?"

"We have to recreate every nuance of that night. Even then I'm not sure it will be enough, because we would have to wait an entire year to have it be *that* night, but we must try." He pulled a chair away from the table. "Come here and tell me everything you recall. Don't leave out a single detail."

"I have told you," she protested.

"Only the surface things. We need details, Ginny, and once we have them we need to recreate them and bring that moment to life again."

She stared at him and then slowly sat. "Do you really believe we can do this?"

"Yes. You've already done it once. That proves the possibility of it. Now all we have to do is figure out how to do it in reverse. Start talking." He sat across from her, pen at the ready, and waited.

She tried desperately to give him what he wanted, but so much had happened since that time. "I feel as if it is indeed a hundred years in the past," she said when she had failed to recall yet another detail he required. "I'm sorry, Sam."

"No. It's all right. We'll get there, Ginny. It will take time, but we will." He handed her the pad and pen. "I want you to keep this with you at all times. Whenever some little memory comes back—no matter how seemingly insignificant—I want you to write it down, okay?"

She nodded and tucked the small notebook and pen in the pocket of her jumper. She understood that he was being deliberately kind to her. He had explained the importance of getting every possible detail in place—even the weather. It was evident that they would have fewer and fewer opportunities to replicate the weather as the days moved on toward spring. Time was of the essence. She *must* remember.

"Tell me how the renovation is going," he said. "Better yet, take me on a tour." He pulled her to her feet and into his arms. He kissed her tenderly. "What have you done to my house, Ms. Thornton?"

"I have treated it as my own," she teased as she stood on tiptoe to kiss him back.

He pulled her close to deepen the kiss. "And what are you doing to *me*, Ms. Thornton?" His voice was husky with desire.

Falling in love with you, she wanted to say, but instead she lifted her face for his kiss.

Arm in arm they walked slowly through the rooms of the main floor as she explained the progress of each project. Along the way she regaled him with stories of her childhood memories of hiding on the grand staircase and watching her parents' kissing after they had bid the last of their guests goodnight.

"Sometimes they would dance, and I always wondered how they could do that when there was no music." She laughed. "Even when I realized that they heard the music in their heads, I wondered how it was possible that they heard the same song."

"Perhaps your father hummed a tune you couldn't hear," Sam suggested and began humming a waltz in an off-key baritone as he held out his arms, inviting her to dance with him.

"I'm quite sure he didn't," Ginny assured him. "I would have heard that even from up there."

Sam frowned. "Your father wasn't a hummer. Your mother?"

Ginny shook her head. "Sorry."

"Then there's no other answer. They simply communicated the music." He pulled her into his arms and began a silent waltz. "Yes, this is it," he said as he spun her around the large reception area.

She could not deny that they were dancing and that there was no audible music, and yet they were in perfect step. She closed her eyes and thrilled to the pure joy of being in his arms as he whirled her around the very

space where her parents had danced so many years earlier.

"Stop," she protested with a giggle. "I'm getting
dizzy."

He slowed to a more sedate pace, swaying with little
movement as he rested his chin on top of her head.
"Ginny?"

"Hmm?" Her eyes were closed as she savored the
nearness of him.

"That portrait there . . . the one you noticed that first
night. It's out of place. Those people had not yet been
born." He stopped dancing and strode across the marble
floor for a closer look at the portrait on the landing.

"Yes, I know, but—"

"And that lamp—my parents brought that back from
Paris. It's the correct period, but it wasn't in this house
then."

"Well, no, it wouldn't have been."

He came back to her and took her by the shoulders.
"Don't you see, Ginny? We have to figure out every
move you made that night and make every room as it
was then."

Ginny was skeptical. "That will take a great deal of
work."

"Not so much in the scheme of things. These portraits
have to come down for the renovation at some point.
We'll have the workers remove them and everything else
that wasn't here. Then you'll start to fill in the pieces,
Ginny."

"But—"

"It's the only way. We'll have everything in place at
the ready. I'll monitor the weather conditions, and when
the time and conditions are exactly right, we'll go." His
eyes blazed with the excitement of the adventure of it
all.

"The rest of the staff," she protested. "Freddie and the
others—what will they think?"

"They don't have to know. During the day, you'll

manage the project, and I'll work in the conservatory. In the evenings we will prepare."

"Sam, be realistic. We are planning to return to a previous century. *Somebody* is going to notice that." She saw that she had finally gotten through to him and hated the flicker of doubt she saw dull his eyes.

He scratched his head as he paced. "Then we'll simply tell them." He made the statement as if he had just announced that they would be going out for dinner.

"Have you taken leave of your senses? We cannot tell them. They would have us committed, as Kate is fond of saying."

"We'll tell them. They won't believe us." He shrugged as if this came as no surprise. "We'll be gone, and then they'll start to wonder. Then we'll come back—"

"Come back?" She hadn't even considered the logistics of returning. "Come back? Sam, we can't even fathom how it is that we are going there in the first place. I think you need to be prepared to stay."

He laughed. "Heavens, no, woman. I like my creature comforts way too much to live in those days. Can you honestly imagine me without my microwave?"

"We must be realistic, Sam. You of all people—"

He placed a finger on her lips to quiet her. "We're going to do this, Ginny. Whatever it takes, whoever must be involved, it is going to happen. I promise."

She believed him. He was so confident, so absolutely sure that it would all work. "All right, then. What is it you want me to do?"

"Transform this place and tell me what to do to transform the conservatory. Recreate that day, that night, that environment as precisely as possible."

"I'm a little afraid, Sam," she admitted.

He put his arms around her. "So am I, sweet Ginny. So am I."

He was not afraid of the journey but of losing her back there, of having to return without her. He wanted to tell her that he loved her, but knew that this was unfair. Ginny needed to find the answers to her past before he could talk to her about a future with him. He consoled himself by holding her as they swayed gently to music heard only by the two of them.

"Honey, forgive me, but aren't we putting the cart before the proverbial horse here?" Freddie asked the following day when Ginny began directing the removal of paintings, furnishings, and decorative items that had not been in the house when she was its mistress. "I mean, this is all well and good, but it will be weeks before the work crews get to the library here."

"I know," Ginny replied calmly as she indicated another painting that needed to come down.

"As for the stairway . . ." Freddie paused. "I mean, does Sam know you've had his grandparents' portrait taken down?"

"Yes. He's in complete agreement," Ginny assured Freddie.

"Well, I'm fairly certain that Emily would not be in complete agreement," Freddie muttered more to himself than to her.

Ginny knew that she was driving the man to distraction. He had arrived that morning to find her in the throes of reorganizing the main floor of the house. Crews had been reassigned from plastering, cleaning, and painting to moving furniture in rooms where the renovation had not yet begun. "I know it appears to be a bit disorganized," she conceded.

"A bit," Freddie agreed with an ironic smile.

"I assure you it will all make sense." Of course, it would, Ginny thought. No doubt everything would be crystal clear when she explained to Freddie that she and Sam planned to travel back in time one hundred years and end up right here in this house.

"If you say so. In the meantime, I can see I'm not

going to talk you out of whatever plan you've devised overnight, so how can I help?"

"You are the dearest man," Ginny said with a relieved smile.

"Yeah, yeah, yeah. I'm sure you say that to all the guys. Now where do I begin?"

She did a quick sketch of where the room's furnishings had been located at the time of Thomas's death and handed it to Freddie. "See that the room is set up this way."

"Where are you going?" he asked as she headed for the door.

"I'll be in the storage areas trying to find the missing pieces. Let's meet in the kitchen for lunch at one." She gave a cheery wave and left the room.

"She is way too full of herself this morning," he said to no one in particular. "I wonder . . ." Then he grinned and pulled his cell phone from his pocket. "Kate? I win," he declared triumphantly. "She's slept with him, or I'm no judge of women in love. Pay up and don't give me that old check's-in-the-mail routine."

Ginny edged her way around the storeroom filled with furnishings. She peered under dust covers and into corners until she found the exact pieces she wanted. They were all there, which surprised her. She would have thought Colonel Sutter's wife would have discarded everything in the house, erased anything that might have reminded people that it had once belonged to Ginny and Thomas. Surely she would have made every effort to eradicate the scandal of Thomas's suicide.

Perhaps she had but she hadn't discarded the pieces, and Ginny felt her heart soften a bit toward the mistress of the house who had been her immediate successor. She marked the pieces with bright pieces of fabric so she could have the workers bring them to the library later. Once she had the main furnishings in place she could tackle the décor. That would be a test of her memory, but Sam assured her that once the room was arranged as it had been in that time, she would recall everything they needed to know.

She stood for a minute, staring at the leather wing chair that Thomas used for reading in front of the fire. She felt a surge of guilt as she realized how her every waking thought was of Sam, of seeing him, being with him, planning the adventure with him, and lying with him each night as he made slow, passionate love to her and then held her until she fell asleep.

These past few nights her sleep had frequently been disturbed by dreams that seemed so real, so immediate, that twice she had sat bolt upright in bed and cried out. Sam had been there to comfort her and assure her that she was safe. He had asked her about the dreams, but she had pretended not to remember. The truth was, she remembered them all too vividly. Thomas toasting her and mocking her at the same time. Thomas with Katherine. The echo of a gunshot followed by her scream.

She stroked the smooth worn leather of the chair. "Oh, Thomas, what really happened that horrible night, and might it be possible to change it all?" The words came unbidden and as a complete shock. *Why not?* she thought. *What if I could change the events of that night?*

She hurried down the hallway. She had to find Sam. She looked everywhere in the house, the conservatory, and the gardener's cottage, but he wasn't there. There was no choice but to use the telephone and leave a message—a message that wouldn't wait.

"Sam, this is Ginny. We need to go back to the day before Thomas died. It's the only way. I'm certain of it."

Chapter 13

"ABSOLUTELY NOT," SAM fumed when she tried to discuss it with him later that night. "You can't change history, Ginny."

"Oh, I see. We can blithely move back and forth between centuries but we're not permitted to touch anything along the way, is that it? Then what is the point?"

She was maddening when she tried to use logic on him, of all people. "The point is for you to get the answers you need in order to go *forward* with your life. You have an opportunity to go back and look at your own history with some incredible knowledge that others never have. Isn't that enough?"

"Why do you keep saying that this is about *me?*"

"Because if it were about Thomas, he would have been the one who rocketed through ten decades and landed on my doorstep." Sam really didn't want to fight with her, but it was frustrating to have her focused on her late husband. What if she did go back and prevented him from taking his life? What then? Where did that leave them? "Look, all I'm concerned about here is that you not be hurt anymore than you already have been."

"I appreciate your concern for my well-being, Sam, but we must think of the others in all of this."

"The *others*?"

"Thomas, Katherine and Tucker Corwell, your own great-great-grandparents."

Us, he wanted to shout at her. *What about us?* "I wouldn't think you'd be one bit concerned about Katherine Corwell," he replied and knew that he was being deliberately hurtful.

"Nothing has been proven regarding any sort of improper relationship between Thomas and Katherine," she stated archly.

"The photograph is fairly incriminating."

"On the contrary—it is little more than a form of visual gossip and insinuation. I'm quite sure that there's a logical explanation."

"You're kidding yourself," Sam said wearily. "I need to go check the timers in the conservatory. Do whatever you have to do about going back. Just understand that there are no guarantees we can even get back there. Pinpointing the exact day and hour is going to be tricky." He headed for the door.

"Sam?" For the first time since he'd received her message and come to the house to discuss it, she sounded a little uncertain.

"Yeah?" He did not turn. He couldn't look at her right now without wanting to take her in his arms, to his bed, and remind her of all they had shared these last several days.

"You will still go with me, won't you?"

He paused as he considered her request. She took his silence for the doubt that it was and pressed her case. "Because I don't honestly think I can do this without you," she added softly.

"I'll go with you," he said and left the room before he could add any of the conditions that he wanted to put on that acceptance.

• • •

For the first time since the night they had first made love, she spent the night in her own room, her own bed, alone. In some ways it reminded her of the many nights she had lain awake waiting for the sound of Thomas returning from some meeting or simply finally coming up to his room after spending hours shut away in the library. This was different in that Sam had never made love to her here in the house. They had spent their nights in the cottage, and until tonight she had never had to wonder where he was or when he might come to her.

She could not fathom why her wanting to go back to the day just before Thomas's death upset him so. Sam was a good and kind man, a caring man. She had seen the way he treated people. Perhaps it was too much to ask for him to show concern for someone who had been dead for over a hundred years. On the other hand, she would have thought that the scientist in him would have jumped at the chance to make such an incredible difference in the life of another person.

Sounds of movement in the hall outside her door caught her attention. "Who's there?" she asked nervously as she pushed herself up in bed and stared at the door.

The door swung open, and she gasped, then realized that it was Sam filling the doorway. His face was in shadow, but she heard the passion in his voice as he approached the bed and began stripping off his clothing.

"I will go back with you to any day, any hour you choose, Ginny, but before we go I want to make love to you here—in this house, in this room. Every minute that you are back there, I want you to remember this night, and I want you to remember something else as well."

She swallowed the lump in her throat that had formed the minute she realized that he had come to her. "What else?"

"I want you to remember that I love you, Ginny

Thornton," he said huskily as he lifted the covers and got into bed with her.

Tears rolled down her cheeks as she held out her arms to him and welcomed him into her bed, into her body, and into her heart. She had no idea what the days to come would bring, but Sam was right. They would always have this night. He entered her almost at once, and she realized that for the first time, he had not stopped to use the protection he had always donned in the past. She wondered if it was deliberate or simply an oversight in the passion of the moment, but quickly put the thought aside as he began to move in her, filling her, then withdrawing, then filling her again until she dug her nails into his hips to urge him to stay.

He rolled to his back, bringing her with him, and positioned her so that she straddled him as he lifted her nightgown over her head and tossed it to the floor. His hands cupped and kneaded her breasts, his thumbs toying with her nipples until her breath came in short excited gasps. Instinctively she performed the movements intended to draw him more deeply inside her and felt the climax building. Never had she felt such rapture, such bliss, such need.

"I love you, Ginny," he said as he brought her to the heights only he could create. "I love you, remember that."

She cried out his name as she felt the release come. He followed her a few seconds later, and she felt the pure joy of his seed filling her.

"You look dreadful," Freddie announced when Ginny entered the office the following morning and stifled a yawn. "At the same time," he added, peering at her closely, "there's a certain . . . contentment in those dark-shadowed eyes. What gives?"

"I don't know what you mean," Ginny replied, turning back to her work to avoid meeting his scrutiny.

"Good morning, darlings," Kate sang out as she breezed into the office with a swirl of her voluminous cape. "I bring glad tidings and breakfast." She handed Freddie a paper bag from which he unloaded bagels and cream cheese plus three steaming cups of cappuccino, while Kate removed her cape and hung it on the hall tree by the door. "Well?" she demanded. "Are we not curious?" She peered at Ginny. "My stars, woman, when was the last time you slept?"

Ginny blushed to the roots of her hair. She and Sam had gotten precious little sleep the night before. "What is your news, Kate?" she asked, deciding the best tactic was to ignore the previous question. "Glad tidings?" she prompted.

"Oh, that. It's Groundhog Day, and the little devil did not see his shadow, which I believe bodes well for an early exit to winter and all that dreadful snow and cold and bluster and an early entry for blessed spring." She lifted her cup in a mock toast. "To spring."

"To spring," Freddie echoed.

Kate and Freddie stood with their cups raised and waited for Ginny. "It would be your turn now, sweetie," Kate prompted.

"To spring," Ginny said halfheartedly. All she could think of was that Sam had said they needed the proper weather conditions as well as anything else if they were going to go back. An end to snow was *not* good news.

"Oh, now there's a ringing endorsement of the event," Freddie said. "What are you, some kind of winter-lover?"

"The snow is nice," Ginny said in a weak attempt to fend off their curiosity.

"Returning to the subject at hand," Kate boomed, "other than the circles and luggage under your eyes, you look positively radiant, my dear. Could the rumors be right?"

"I wasn't aware of any rumors." Ginny could not suppress the beginning of a smile.

"Aha," Freddie declared. "I'm right. It's you and Sam, isn't it?"

"I haven't the faintest notion what you are implying," Ginny said as she busied herself with a file of papers.

"I see," Freddie replied. "Oh, hi, Sam."

Ginny spun around and could not control the smile of expectation and love that lit her entire face. Sam was nowhere to be seen.

"As I was saying," Freddie said to Kate as if Ginny had left the room.

"I see what you mean. Definitely the hots for Sam. By all indications he has an equal attraction to her, so I would say that all is well, wouldn't you?"

"Works for me," Freddie agreed.

"You two are just mean," Ginny chided.

"But we're right, aren't we?"

Ginny had to tell someone, or she would burst. "Yes," she admitted and then started to laugh. "It's absolutely, astoundingly true."

"Well, I don't know that it's so astounding," Freddie said. "I mean, any fool who saw the way he looked at you on New Year's Eve would know—"

"Oh, it's more astounding than you can ever imagine," Ginny teased as she breezed past them and left the room.

"What the hell does that mean?" Kate boomed.

"I have to get to work," Ginny called over her shoulder as she ran lightly down the stairway. "Perhaps I'll have a little time later to tell you more. Have a good day," she called.

"Have a good day," Kate muttered under her breath as she turned back to the office. "Something's going on here," she announced.

"Well, duh, I think I told you that a week ago," Freddie replied. "And by the way, where's my money?"

Ginny could hardly wait until she finished making the rounds of the various work crews and could escape to the conservatory. She wanted to tell Sam what Kate had said about an early spring.

"Sam, Kate says that—"

He swept her into his arms and kissed her as if it had been weeks since he'd last seen her instead of only a few hours.

"Sam, someone could come in," she said but could not hide her pleasure.

"Then they'll get an eyeful," he replied and kissed her again. "Okay, what's this about, Kate?"

"She says the groundhog saw his shadow . . . didn't see his shadow . . . something of the sort. At any rate, she seems to believe that this bodes well for an end to winter in just a few weeks."

Sam laughed heartily.

"I really don't think this is a laughing matter, Sam. You said yourself that—"

"It's an old Farmer's Almanac legend, Ginny. We have far better ways of predicting weather in these modern times."

"I see. Well, if one of the workers is right, your modern meteorologists are the only people he knows who get—and I quote—'paid big bucks to be dead wrong about two-thirds of the time.' " She thought about punctuating the statement with a pretend spit of tobacco juice as the worker had done, but decided she had made her point.

"What do you suggest we do?" Sam asked, clearly fighting to contain his mirth at her imitation of the burly worker.

"I suggest we move forward with all speed."

"And that would affect the weather in what way, exactly?"

"Stop teasing me. This is serious. We must be ready to take advantage of any opportunity that may present itself, Sam."

"All right, honey. We're going to do everything we can. Come sit down, and let's make a list."

Sam's answer to world chaos would be to make a list. Ginny sighed and sat next to him on the old park bench. "There's so much to do," she said with a sigh. "Can't we just start doing it?"

"The list will help us focus. Now come on. What's first on the agenda?"

An hour later Sam had filled three pages in his small, neat script and was still writing. "We'll never get all of this accomplished in a year," he said.

"I am resisting the urge to say 'I told you so,' but it is quite difficult." She let out a dejected sigh. "This isn't going to work, is it?"

"Of course, it'll work, or at least we can take it as far as we know how and see if it works. We just need a little help."

"Freddie and Kate already think I've lost my mind. The workers are equally skeptical, although they just go about their jobs, bless them. Heavens, *I* would think I had lost my mind with some of the bizarre things I've been asking them to do these past few days."

Sam paced the tiled floor of the greenhouse, tapping his pencil against his cheek as he considered the possibilities. "We'll have to tell Freddie and Kate. That's for starters. They can stay late and help us get everything in place. In a few days we'll have to let the workers go until we can make the attempt. It won't work with all of their paraphernalia around."

"You say that as if you think Freddie and Kate will simply accept what we tell them and pitch in. Sam, they are going to think we have lost our minds."

"At first," Sam agreed, "but Freddie loves a romance, and Kate . . . well, Kate will go along with just about anything as long as it seems fairly outlandish."

He was right, although Ginny thought he might have been a bit more circumspect in his evaluation of Kate's reaction. "When shall we tell them?"

"No time like the present," Sam replied. "Let's see if they'll stay for supper. We'll feed them and then tell

them a little story about a certain young woman from
the past." He kissed the tip of her nose.

"They will never believe this," Ginny said again.

"Why not?" Sam grinned. "I did."

"Yeah, right, and I'm Teddy Roosevelt," Freddie said.
"My Rough Riders will be along any minute, and there
had better be pizza left to feed them."

Kate was silent. She kept looking from Ginny to Sam
and then back to Ginny. "You're not kidding," she said
in what for her was a whisper. "Holy—"

"Hello? Could we pause for a little reality check here?
This is not within the realm of possibility, folks," Freddie announced. "Ginny, you're a sweetheart and, my
stars, what you know about this place could fill a couple
of books. But if anybody here honestly expects me to
believe that Ginny has traveled through time and landed
here, well, lock me up now, folks, because that just ain't
gonna happen."

"Where else would she *land*, as you so aptly put it?"
Sam asked as he tore off another piece of the pizza they
had ordered and chewed it thoughtfully. "Her husband
has just shot himself. In one stunning moment she learns
not only that she is widowed, but also that she is pen-
niless. She is about to lose the very home where she was
raised, where her family had lived for generations, because her husband has gambled it away on a very risky
investment. That's a lot of stress for one individual to
deal with. Who wouldn't want to escape?"

"I have no problem with the escape. I have a *major*
problem with time travel," Freddie argued.

"Freddie, do you recall the clothes I was wearing
when I arrived? You laundered them for me." Ginny saw
that he was beginning to recall the details of that night.
"They were not a costume, Freddie. They were genuine.
You've been around the archives of this place long
enough to know that."

"Vintage clothing is very popular these days," he argued stubbornly.

"Do you recall what happened in the bedroom? How I ordered you about as if you were a servant? You even commented on my manner of speaking later when we sat together talking."

"Yes, but—"

"Believe them, already," Kate urged, "and let's get on with this. What's the plan?" she asked eagerly.

"Ginny needs to return to her own time," Sam explained. "In order to accomplish that, we're going to need to recreate the estate exactly as it was back then. We've pretty much decided that if we concentrate on the public rooms and the conservatory, and then remove any exterior distractions such as automobiles, snowblowers, and so on, we might actually be able to pull this off."

"Of course, there's also the weather," Ginny reminded him.

"Yeah, we need to replicate the weather if we can. I've been able to find weather logs for the week before New Year's Eve in 1899." He glanced at Ginny, and she knew that he was letting her know that he would help her return to the day before Thomas shot himself if he could. "In case we get lucky with the weather we have to be completely ready to take advantage of the opportunity."

"How can we help?" Kate asked. Freddie remained silent, although he was staring at Ginny as if at any moment she might vaporize into thin air.

"Starting tomorrow, we're going to tell the workers that we need to stop the work for two weeks. If at any point during that time Ginny and I go, then you can call them back to work and continue the restoration."

"You're going, too?" Freddie asked.

Sam nodded and continued to explain the plan. "As soon as the workers leave, the four of us need to go into high gear and get this place ready. Ginny can tell us what to do—some of it is already in place, thank God."

Freddie glanced at Ginny. "That's why you've been changing things this last week?"

Ginny nodded. "It's important that as nearly as possible, the rooms look exactly as they did when I lived here, Freddie."

"And that's why you cried the day we went up to the attic for the clothes?"

"I didn't think you noticed," Ginny said softly.

"You're Virginia Thornton." This time it was a statement, and Ginny knew that at last Freddie believed her.

"Yes."

"Okay," Kate boomed as she stood up and began clearing away their supper dishes. "Now that we have that cleared up, let's get to work."

They worked late into the night, laughing and making bad jokes as they tackled the final rearrangement and refurbishing of the décor in the music room. Ginny regaled them with stories of afternoon soirees her mother had held in that room, and Freddie surprised them all by playing the harp that had belonged to Ginny's grandmother.

"Let's call it a night and get started again tomorrow once the workers have left," Sam said. "If you like, why don't the two of you take rooms upstairs for the duration?"

Kate grinned broadly. "This is so much fun," she announced. "It's a little like making a movie . . . not that I've ever made a movie, but if I did, this would—"

Freddie took her by the arm and led her toward the kitchen. "Say goodnight, Katie," he instructed. "We'll see you two tomorrow," he called over his shoulder.

Sam and Ginny stood next to each other and watched them go. It occurred to Ginny that they were standing in the very spot where she had often watched her parents bid their guests goodnight. It was an overwhelmingly familiar feeling. She felt as if she had finally come home to Malmaison.

Chapter 14

THE NEXT TEN days flew by. The four of them worked long hours digging through storerooms of furniture and boxes of knickknacks to discover the exact pieces they needed. Then they had to be hauled out of storage, cleaned, and put in place. Room by room, the house took on the look and feel of the house as it had been in 1899.

Several times a day, Sam would check the weather conditions with friends at the university. Every day the weather was the same—gray and damp with temperatures rising. Ginny tried not to notice the first hint of the woodland plants poking their tight little buds above ground. As the days passed, she began to change along with the rooms. She spent long hours in the attic costume archives, retrieving clothes she had once worn.

Once they had completed the heavy work, she began dressing herself in the manner of the nineteenth century and urged the others to do the same. It was fun for Freddie and Kate. Ginny didn't tell them that she thought it was also important to the process of going back. Only Sam seemed to understand why she was doing this.

At night he would take his time opening each of the tiny buttons that often lined her dress. He would make a sensual ceremony out of removing each item of her undergarments, telling her in words and gestures how sexy he found the process. They made love only in the cottage now because Ginny was afraid that if they made love in her room, it would spoil their chances for completing the return. Often after they had made love Sam would fall into a sleep due to the exhaustion of trying to manage his work at the university, his experiments, and helping them prepare for their trip. Ginny would walk the paths of the estate, wandering the gardens, going to the conservatory, and finally up to the house.

It was her house now. Everything was as she remembered it. Every item had been placed by her hand. She had overseen the hanging of every portrait and painting and hidden the rush of memories and emotions that accompanied each one. Yet somehow Sam had known. He showed it in his respectful silence, in his hand at her waist, in the tenderness of his voice. It was at night that she began to recreate her room, filling her closet, her dresser with her own clothes, storing away the clothes she had acquired from Emily and Kate.

She felt as if she were shedding a new skin to reclaim an old one. She felt little joy in the process. What would happen if they were successful? She had been so focused on restoring Thomas's honor and winning back the estate that she had not stopped to think about her own life should she accomplish either of those things. *If Thomas lives, I will be his wife*, she thought. *Even though I don't love him. Perhaps I never did.*

Sam knew that Ginny roamed the estate at night. He had alerted Frank and the rest of the security team, who had been moved out to the gatehouse at the entrance to the estate, to pay no attention to her wanderings. He told the men that she was working on a history of the mansion and did some of her best thinking on these long nightly walks. They accepted that.

Every night Sam would wake to find her gone. He would look out and see the light in her bedroom window in the mansion. He had seen the clothing added to the dressing room there, taken notice of the collection of items on her dressing table that had never been there before. She was getting ready to go. He only hoped she wasn't also preparing to stay once they got there.

He had gotten a report from his friend at the university earlier that evening. Everything pointed to a major snowstorm moving in the day after tomorrow. They would have one chance, and Sam intended to see that they did everything possible to make it work.

The following morning he took Freddie and Kate aside and gave them the plans for setting up the conservatory. "I'm taking Ginny away for the day, and I need you to do this and then vacate the premises for the rest of the week."

Freddie understood immediately. "We'll make sure the cars are gone and the gatehouse is shut down."

Kate had tears in her eyes. "What if it works too well?" she blubbered. "What if you can't come back?"

"What shall I tell your parents?" Freddie asked somberly. "In case. . . . you know."

"I've prepared letters for them," Sam assured him. "They're in the cottage to be given only in the event we don't return before they come home. Beyond that you'll have to help them comprehend what's happened. Make them understand that I love her and I will be wherever she is."

Kate wailed.

"Oh, Katie, for heaven's sake. It's not as if they're *dying*," Freddie fumed.

"You're every bit as upset as I am," Katie snapped as she blew her nose.

Sam and Freddie shook hands, and Kate enveloped Sam in a bear hug. "Thank you both for everything,"

Sam said, even as the breath was being squeezed out of him.

"You can count on us, Sam," Freddie promised. "Now go on and get out of here. I hear Ginny downstairs."

Sam gave each of them a final hug and hurried from the room. Ginny was on her way up the stairs, and he thought she had never looked lovelier. The day gown she wore was of a soft green color that matched her eyes and highlighted her flaming hair.

"Turn right around and go back downstairs," he ordered jovially. "There will be no work today. We all need a break, and I have just given Kate and Freddie the day off. Let's go play."

"But there's still the conservatory and the carriage house and the stables—"

"They will be taken care of, but today you and I are going on a little holiday. I am going to show you *this* world so you'll have something to compare things to when we get back there."

"Sam, I really . . ." She paused on the stair and turned to stare at him. "You're telling me that we're going?"

He nodded.

"When?"

"It's supposed to start snowing just after midnight." He tried to read her expression and saw a confusion of emotions: joy, relief, anxiety. He grabbed her hand and headed for the cottage where she had deposited all of her modern-day clothing. "Let's get you changed and out into the world. Time's a-wasting."

He drove to the airport where a chartered plane waited to take them to New York City. Ginny was speechless as the plane taxied down the runway and lifted off.

"Oh, this is thrilling," she shouted above the roar of the engines.

"First flight?" the pilot asked with a grin.

Ginny nodded and then sat with her nose pressed against the glass for the rest of the trip. As they neared

New York, Sam sat close to her and pointed out all of the landmarks.

"It's so enormous," she said in wonder at the layout of the city before her.

At the airport they hailed a cab, and Sam gave the driver an address in the city. Sam grinned as Ginny clung to him during the wild ride. He saw her eyes widen until he was afraid they might pop out of her head as the taxi made its way through the side streets of midtown Manhattan.

"Good heavens, these buildings are so tall," she whispered. "Are they safe?"

"Safer than the streets, lady," the cabby replied as he cut around three other cars and headed straight for an oncoming truck before darting back into his own lane at the last possible second.

"This is good," Sam said and handed the driver several bills as they exited the cab.

For the next hour they walked along Fifth Avenue, window-shopping. Sam wanted to buy her everything, but she only wanted to look. When they reached Tiffany's, he insisted on giving her something to mark the day.

"No," she replied adamantly, and he saw tears glisten.

"Why not? What is it?"

She sighed. "Thomas used to buy me jewelry, give me things. I always told him I didn't need them, didn't want them, but he insisted."

"Understood," Sam said and hooked his arm around her waist as they walked on up the avenue.

As they neared Central Park, she began to recognize more of the surroundings—the Plaza Hotel, the museums, the park itself. Sam bought them hot pretzels from a vendor, which they munched as they walked, and she told him her memories of the city.

"Show time," he announced after glancing at his watch. He hailed another cab, and they headed for

Broadway where he had gotten them tickets for the matinee performance of *Les Misérables*.

Ginny watched the show, and he watched her. She was completely immersed in the production from the opening number. Her eyes followed the action as she sat on the edge of her seat. When the lights came up for intermission, she blinked several times as if awakening from a dream. "I never imagined theater could be like this," she said. "It's magical. Thank you, Sam, for giving me the gift of this day."

He smiled. "We aren't done yet," he told her as the orchestra struck up the opening of act 2.

After the theater, he took her to the Carnegie Delicatessen for dinner. "Nothing fancy," he warned, "but the best corned beef sandwich in town."

"I'll take your word for it."

She laughed at the brusque waiters and marveled at the sensational size of the sandwich. "I can't eat this thing," she protested.

"I can," Sam replied and made her laugh again as he did just that.

After they ate, he took her to Greenwich Village, where they wandered the streets, stopped in a couple of bookstores, and listened to some jazz in a club where the owner knew Sam.

"We went to college together," Sam explained as he introduced the man to Ginny.

"He's a good man," the club owner told Ginny.

"I know," Ginny assured him. Then she looked directly at Sam. "I know," she repeated softly.

"Time to go," Sam said after they had sat through a couple of sets of the music. They headed back to the airport where the plane waited to take them home.

Ginny watched the lights of the city until they disappeared. Sam pointed out the Statue of Liberty and Ellis Island as they flew over the harbor, then pulled Ginny into his arms for the rest of the flight.

The first flakes of snow fell as they drove from the

airport to the estate. Sam parked the car at the gatehouse, and they walked the long, winding road up to the mansion. It was completely illuminated per his instructions. "Go inside and change," he said as he left her at the front door. "I'll be back shortly."

Ginny entered the house and hurried upstairs to change. Her heart was hammering with excitement as she stripped off the modern clothes she had worn into the city and stuffed them deep inside a bureau drawer. She dressed quickly in the clothes she had been wearing the night after she had returned from the pawnbroker's in New York. She checked the room for any last sign of the twenty-first century and, finding none, went to meet Sam.

He was standing at the foot of the stairway, dressed in the gardener's clothing they had decided he should wear. "I have one more surprise," he told her as he offered her his arm and led the way through the balcony doors and onto the arbor path.

She could see that the conservatory was illuminated from within, and it looked different, more like the place she remembered.

"Close your eyes," Sam told her as they neared the entrance.

She heard the leaded glass door click and open. The scent of cloves assailed her. "Dianthus," she whispered.

"Open your eyes," he said.

The palm court had been restored, and the room was lit with a dozen lanterns. Throughout the room were large pots filled with red carnations. It was enchanting. "Oh, Sam, how did you do this?"

"I've discovered that Freddie can work magic once he believes in something."

"But your experiments?"

"Safely moved to another greenhouse in the back there. I don't think they will interfere with our plan. The carnations are hybrids, of course. If you get enough of them in a humid room, they give a pretty good imitation of your malmaison blossoms."

He put his arms around her. "I love you, Ginny. Whatever happens, never forget that." He kissed her, and she returned his kiss, wanting never to let him go.

"I love you." It was the first time she had said it aloud. She saw his surprise. "Whoever I was, whoever I have become, it is you that I love." She caressed his cheek with her palm. "Only you."

"Then stay with me now. Forget the past," he urged. "It's not too late to stop this whole thing."

She shook her head sadly. "I must do this, Sam."

"For Thomas," he said with resignation.

"For us," she corrected as she reached up to kiss him.

They stayed like that for several long moments. Kissing and touching and holding each other.

"It's starting to snow harder," he said. "You'd better go now."

For the first time she was genuinely afraid. "I want you with me."

He shook his head. "It won't work that way. Your only chance is to go to the house and stay there tonight alone. Tomorrow, we will either awaken to yesterday or still be in the present. There's only one chance, Ginny. If you want it, you have to go now."

She kissed him once more with a passion that would have to last them perhaps a lifetime, and then ran from the conservatory without a backward look. When she reached the house, she went straight to her room, but as she passed the library, she thought she caught the faintest hint of cigar smoke coming from behind the closed doors. She paused on the stair and looked back at the library door, then decided she had been imagining things.

Once in her room, she followed the plan as Sam had instructed. She sat at her dressing table and closed her eyes and thought about everything that had happened that night when she had returned from the pawnbroker.

She had given Lucas Holt the money and then gone in search of Thomas.

Thomas had been sitting alone at his desk in the library. He had been drinking—probably for hours.

She had urged him to come up and dress for dinner. He had assured her he would be at dinner. He had not come, and she had been forced to make excuses for him yet again as she entertained their guests by herself.

Now as she sat at her dressing table with her eyes closed, remembering that night—details that she had failed to consider before became part of her memory now. Katherine had seemed quite nervous that evening, or was she imagining that in light of the story Sebastian Corwell had told her? One thing was certain—Tucker Corwell had been unusually gregarious.

Katherine had taken her usual place to Ginny's left. Tucker sat across from his wife. Katherine's ethereal blond beauty was as striking as ever. In her presence Ginny always felt a bit dowdy. They had been the best of friends since childhood, their families close neighbors and friends. When Katherine had married Tucker, Ginny had cried for a week, certain that she had lost her best friend forever.

After Ginny married Thomas, the two couples visited back and forth for long weekends and summer holidays. The two women stayed in touch with a constant stream of notes and detailed letters. Once Ginny and Thomas took ownership of Malmaison after the death of Ginny's parents, the two couples had been practically inseparable—until recently.

This was the first time they had seen each other since they had rented a house together at the seashore the summer before. Ginny recalled thinking that Katherine had changed, was quieter than usual. Had she not been so worried about Thomas, she probably would have taken Katherine aside and asked her if anything was wrong.

When Ginny had finally given up on having Thomas

join them at the dinner table, she had said something to the effect that these days he was so busy with various business projects, she was lucky if she saw him at all. Tucker had laughed heartily and said something like, "I know just what you mean, Ginny. Katherine here has acquired a taste for meetings and charities that keeps her away from home far more than usual."

Katherine had blushed. Ginny was sure of it. Then Tucker had gone on about how proud he was of his wife's good works and that he enjoyed teasing her about becoming one of those "modern working women."

That statement immediately moved the conversation to the topic of the changing times and the turn of the century and what the new century might bring. Ginny had been grateful to Tucker for turning the attention away from Thomas's absence and her feeble attempt to excuse it.

She took a deep breath and continued the exercise. After dinner, Thomas had made an appearance. He was full of excuses and apologies. He had invited the men to the billiards room. Ginny had joined the ladies in the music room. Everyone had gathered in the upstairs living quarters for dessert and liquors before retiring for the night. The evening had passed.

After seeing their guests off to their rooms, Ginny had begun clearing the glasses and dessert plates.

"Ring for the help," Thomas had said irritably. "Sometimes, Ginny, you act as if you are no more than a hired servant rather than one of the wealthiest women in the state."

"It's late," Ginny replied. "Mr. Holt will see that everything is cleared before anyone is about tomorrow morning. I'll just move a few things." Through the years she had learned that the best way to disarm Thomas was simply to remain calm and go about her business. His piques of anger passed as quickly as they came over him. "Are you coming to bed?" she asked.

"In a while. I think I'll read." He had kissed her cheek. "You go along, darling."

"Thomas, I really want you to be part of the day we planned for tomorrow. The guests miss you when you aren't around."

He had smiled. "I'll be the life of the party. Now go along and get your rest." She remembered that she had stood at the banister and watched him descend the stairs.

She opened her eyes and left her room. She walked over to the place where she had stood, and imagined Thomas on the stairs unaware that she was watching him. He looked tired and beaten. His shoulders slumped, and he walked with a heavy step. He entered the library and closed the door with a firm click of the latch.

Ginny turned and started back to her room. The clock on the mantel struck half past midnight. She was aware of movement at the far end of the family sitting room. "Sam?"

"No, madam."

Lucas Holt picked up a tray loaded with dessert plates and liquor glasses and turned to face her. "I'm sorry if I startled you. I thought perhaps I should clear these things tonight."

"Lucas." Ginny's voice was husky with emotion. Her heart pounded, and her eyes filled with tears. *It has happened*, she thought.

"Yes, madam?" Lucas was staring at her with a curious expression. "Is anything the matter?"

"No." She cleared her throat and spoke with more conviction. "I just wanted to say how truly lovely everything was this evening. Thank you, Lucas."

"It is my great pleasure, Mrs. Thornton." He stood holding the heavy tray, and she realized that he was waiting for her either to dismiss him or go on about her business. He would never leave a room without her permission or before she did.

"That will be all," she said softly. "Have a good evening, Mr. Holt."

He gave a slight bow and carried the tray back down the hall that led to the backstairs. Ginny ran to the top of the grand staircase and looked down. There was a light coming from underneath the library door. She hurried along the passageway that led to all the guest rooms and miraculously heard voices and stirrings behind the doors, smelled the scent of perfume as if someone had recently passed this way. She glanced up and realized that there were no security cameras, no sprinklers in case of fire. It was 1899, and those things had not yet been invented, much less installed. Ginny felt the ridiculous urge to giggle.

She wanted to find Sam, to tell him that it had worked. She hurried back along the hallway toward her room. From there she would be able to look out and see the conservatory. She and Sam had arranged a signal. She would place a single lit candle in her window. He would answer with a lantern in the conservatory. That would have to do until they could meet in the gardens the following day.

She had almost reached her room when she heard the opening and closing of a door. She glanced back and saw Katherine Corwell leaving her room and hurrying along the hallway toward the stairs. The memory came back to her with a jolt.

Of course. That night Ginny had left her room to remove the dishes from the living quarters before Thomas came to bed and saw them there. She was going to put them in her room and have Maggie take them to the kitchen the following morning. But Lucas Holt had been there before her, just as he had tonight, and she had been returning to her room when Katherine had come out of hers.

"Katherine? Is everything all right?"

Katherine gave a startled gasp and then laughed. "Oh, Ginny, I didn't see you there."

Ginny studied her friend. She was nervous. Her voice

always took on a giggly, light air whenever she was anxious about something.

"Was there something you needed?"

"I . . . that is, I . . ." She giggled and touched her hair. She was still dressed in the gown she had worn to dinner. It showed off her pale translucent skin and upswept white gold hair to perfection. "I couldn't sleep," she managed to say. "I thought perhaps something from the library . . ." She allowed her voice to drift off as if it were only a passing thought.

"I believe Thomas is still down there. Perhaps he can assist you in selecting something," Ginny replied evenly.

Katherine hesitated. She looked closely at Ginny, and something in Ginny's expression must have caused her to change her mind. "You know, I'm being very silly. I'm certain that if I simply give myself enough time, sleep will come. I certainly don't want to disturb Thomas at this time of night," she added with a laugh.

Everything they said to each other was exactly what they had said that night. Only Ginny's perception of it had changed. "I'm sure Thomas would be delighted to recommend a book," Ginny said, finishing out her piece of their little script. "You know how he is about his precious books. Go along. I'll see you in the morning."

Ginny turned the knob on her bedroom door and entered the room. She closed the door behind her and leaned against it. Could it be true, then? Katherine and Thomas had planned to carry on an affair under her very nose, in her very own house? She felt the bile of raw anger pump its way to her throat. How dare they!

She ought to march down there and throw open the library door and tell them a thing or two. Better yet, she should take Tucker with her. Sam wouldn't like it, of course. He kept reminding her that she couldn't change history. *Sam!*

She ran to the window and fumbled with the match

to light the candle, then turned out the gas lamps that lit the room. She looked out toward the dark conservatory. *Be there*, she pleaded. *I don't think I can do this without you.*

Chapter 15

"WHO THE DEVIL are you, and what are you doing out here this time of night?"

Sam must have dozed off. He'd come to the conservatory, as planned, to work on the plants and wait to see if indeed this would be the night that the plan would work.

"Well?" The gruff-voiced little man was pointing a gun at him. Obviously Freddie had failed to let the third-shift security guard know of the plan to take a couple of weeks off.

"Look, Mr. . . ." He fumbled for a name. Ginny had learned the name of every single worker who came through the house in just a few days. He should be able to keep the regulars straight.

The man waved the gun. "Don't you be concerned about who I am. Just state your business before I blow your fool head off."

Sam paid closer attention to the gun. It was not exactly standard security guard issue . . . at least not for modern times. He fought a smile as he took in his surroundings and the garb of the man in front of him. *We did it,* he thought, and fought the urge to crow with delight.

"You got one more minute," the man warned.

"My name is Sam, and Ms. . . . Mrs. Thornton invited me here. I'm to meet with the head gardener, Mr. Boyle." He had changed the story that he and Ginny had agreed upon where he would pose as a hired assistant to the head gardener. In the face of the man holding a loaded gun on him, he thought Ginny might forgive him if he exaggerated his position a bit.

The man squinted up at him. "Mrs. Thornton never mentioned nothing about this to me. It's the dead of winter. It's not likely she'd want to take on extra help this time of year."

"Exactly," Sam said. "But she said something about wanting to develop some new variety of dianthus and thought I might be of some assistance."

Boyle actually chuckled and lowered the pistol a little. "She's a caution, that one. Known her since she was knee-high to a grasshopper and she was always wanting to try something new." He glared at Sam. "What might you know about such things?"

Sam pushed the old-fashioned wire-rimmed glasses he'd had made for the trip up on his nose. "I've been somewhat successful in propagating other plants in my work with the university."

"You're a professor, then?" Respect colored the older man's voice. "Well, why didn't you say so? I've been able to learn a lot from you fellows over the years. Mrs. Thornton's daddy introduced me to a bunch of your kind years back, and we've been working together ever since. Can't say as I remember seeing you there." Suspicion was back.

"I haven't been there long. Just moved here from Michigan."

"Great tulips up that way, hey?" He laid the gun on a potting table. "You gave me a start being out here in the middle of the night like this. I woulda given you the grand tour myself if I'd knowed you was coming."

"Mrs. Thornton had provided me with directions and suggested I take a look around before she introduced me to you and the rest of the staff tomorrow. I'm afraid I got a little distracted and lost track of time. I didn't think there would be any harm in coming on out."

"Bit of a night owl, are you?" Boyle chuckled. "Me too. Can't tell you how many times I've sat bolt upright in bed at three in the morning recalling some chore I forgot to do over here. Drives the missus crazy, but I tell her plants don't work on people-time."

Great, Sam thought. He had planned on being able to use the conservatory as a logical meeting place for him and Ginny. With Boyle popping in and out, that wasn't going to be so practical.

"Where you staying?" Boyle asked, clearly prepared to settle in for a nice long chat.

"The gard . . ." Sam caught himself just in time. "I have a place near the university, but while we're working on this project, Mrs. Thornton has kindly offered me a room here at the estate." *Where, I haven't a clue, but we don't have a choice.* It was a small detail they had failed to consider.

"Great. You'll have to stop by the cottage and meet the missus. I'll warn you right now, though. She's gonna try to fatten you up."

"I'll take my chances," Sam replied with a grin and offered his hand.

Boyle pumped it enthusiastically. "Well, I'll let you get back to your nosing around. Frankly I think you tend to pick up more that way. Taught Mrs. Thornton that when she was no more than a twig." He laughed and shook his head in admiration. "She's got a mind of her own, that one. Just like her blessed mother."

He was leaving. *Thank you, God.*

"I'll see you in the morning, then," Boyle added as he headed out through the back greenhouses that were closer to the cottage.

"It's going to be an honor to work with you, sir," Sam called after him. Boyle waved and continued on his way.

Satisfied that he was finally alone, Sam practically ran to the entrance to the palm court. From here he had the best view of Ginny's room. The candle was there—a lone flickering flame in the otherwise darkened window. He found the lantern they had stashed in a corner of the conservatory and lit it.

"Please, be there, Ginny," he muttered to himself as he held the lantern high and swung it slowly back and forth. Nothing.

He waited several minutes, during which lights in various upstairs windows went dark and the candle burned on. Then he lifted and swung the lantern again. *Where are you?* If they had truly made it back, then the house was full of people—people who might look out and see a strange lantern signaling in the night, and alert others.

Suddenly the candle was extinguished, and then immediately it flared to life again. *She was there.* He strained to see her in the window and was able to make out the movement of the curtains as she lifted the candle to light her face. She was smiling.

Ginny barely slept that night. She sat in bed, listening to the sounds of the suddenly revived house. She heard Thomas come to his room. His stumbling movements told her that he had had still more to drink, and she wondered if it was because Katherine had decided against showing up for their assignation. When all was quiet, she considered slipping out of the house to find Sam. It occurred to her that the one thing they had failed to plan was where he would sleep. She hoped he would be all right at least for one night in the conservatory, for it was far too risky for her to attempt to leave the house with so many guests plus their servants and hers in residence.

She must have dozed, for the next thing she knew it

was dawn and she could hear the servants quietly going about the business of preparing the house for the day. She smiled as she heard the distinct sound of the scrape of a shovel against the stone steps leading to the garden. It was not a snowblower. They were not under attack.

Her first thought was of Sam and how he had made it through the night. She would have to make certain he found a warm place to stay for as long as they were here. *For as long as they were here.* It stunned her to realize that she was planning to return to the future even before she had discovered the answers she had come to find. Did that mean that she already knew the answers in her heart of hearts? Did that mean that even if she could save Thomas she would leave him?

She rang for Maggie, anxious for the day to move forward—to what conclusion she did not yet know, but she had traveled forward and back again across time to relive this day and she had no intention of missing a single moment of it.

Sam awoke to the heady fragrance of a greenhouse filled with malmaison dianthus. He could barely contain his excitement as he realized that these were no second-rate imitations. These were the real things. He moved from plant to plant, studying the details of the blossom at its various stages, furiously scribbling notes. If only there were some way to transport these beauties forward in time, to revive them and let them deliver their potential benefits to the world. It was thrilling just to have the opportunity to see them, touch them, smell them. He savored the moment.

"Good morning, Professor," Boyle called out as he hustled through the back door of the conservatory, making sure the door was closed and latched against the blustery wind that was blowing the fresh powdered snow all around the estate. "She's a cold one today," he added.

"Good morning, Mr. Boyle. I was wondering if you

might be willing to tell me everything you know about
this particular variety of dianthus."

"Aye. We call the others 'the pinks,' but that one is
special. She's no delicate little thing—strong, vibrant,
hardy—that's our lady there."

"Yes, but . . ." Sam pumped the man for information
for over an hour and was delighted with Boyle's knowledge and experience in growing and propagating the
plant. He was so engrossed in his discussion that he
failed to notice Ginny entering the conservatory.

"Morning, ma'am," Boyle said, instantly on his feet.

"Good morning, Mr. Boyle. I see the two of you have
met." Sam noticed how she looked to him for cues, but
Boyle was way ahead of him.

"Yes, ma'am. Me and the professor got to know each
other last night."

Sam saw how the corner of Ginny's mouth twitched
when Boyle referred to him as the "professor." Origi-
nally they had decided that it made the most sense for
him to be a simple gardener added to the staff to assist
with the heavy work, given his size.

"I see," Ginny said. "And how were your accommodations, Professor?"

"I told Mr. Boyle here how you had been kind enough
to offer me a room in the main house while we conduct
our research on the dianthus."

"I see," Ginny repeated, letting him know that she was
following his story. "I came to invite you to join us for
breakfast, Professor; that is, if you can spare the time
from your work here."

"Oh, you go on, Doc," Mr. Boyle urged. "I'll make
sure things are shipshape here." He moved past Ginny
and added under his breath, "He's quite a talker, that
one."

Sam saw Ginny stifle a giggle. "I'd be delighted to
join your guests for breakfast," he said. "Perhaps you
would permit me to escort you back to the main house

where I could freshen up and change before meeting the others?"

Ginny was clearly impressed with his formal manners and gentility. "I would be honored," Ginny replied and placed her hand on his arm.

As they walked along the arbor path, Sam grilled her on the events of the previous night. She told him everything that had happened, including the encounter with Katherine.

"How does that make you feel?" he asked.

She smiled sadly. "Sam, this is the nineteenth century. Married women are not supposed to *feel*. We are supposed to *adjust*."

Sam certainly didn't like that answer, and as soon as they had entered the deserted hallway of the main house, he pulled her into his arms and kissed her thoroughly. "Adjust to *that,* Mrs. Thornton." He released her and strode down the hall. "Which is to be my room?"

Ginny called for Lucas Holt to show Sam to one of the spare rooms away from the other guests. She used the reasoning that he was not here for the festivities, but to conduct research, and would need a quieter place than the others. She also requested clothing be brought for him since his luggage had gone astray.

She saw Sam's surprise at her use of the same excuse she had given when she found herself in his world with nothing but the clothes on her back.

"He's quite large, Mrs. Thornton," Lucas observed, looking Sam over as if he were some prize specimen.

"Yes, he is," Ginny replied with a wicked smile that only Sam could witness. To her satisfaction, he blushed. "Perhaps something from my father's trunks?"

"Perhaps," Lucas replied with thinly veiled skepticism. "If you'll follow me, sir."

Sam did as he was requested. "Right behind you, Mr. Holt."

• • •

When Thomas appeared at the breakfast table, Sam took an instant dislike to the man. He hoped it had nothing to do with his feelings for Ginny and knew that this was impossible. Of course, it had everything to do with Ginny, but there was more—an underlying slyness about the man that put Sam instantly on his guard.

Sam took notice of the way Thomas surveyed the people in the room, mentally calculating their importance and power. He showed an interest in Sam only because Sam was unknown.

"We have not met," Thomas said.

"This is Dr. Samuel Sut—"

"Sutherby," Sam interrupted her. "Thank you for permitting me to enjoy the hospitality of your home during my research."

Thomas glanced at Ginny and awaited an explanation. Clearly he did not like to be out of the loop on anything that had to do with Malmaison.

"You remember, darling, I told you about Dr. Sutherby last evening. He's going to be working with Mr. Boyle on the development of a new strain of dianthus."

Thomas smiled, and it did nothing to warm his cold gray eyes. "Welcome to my home, sir." He gave a brief courtly bow and turned his attention to the wealthiest man in the room—Tucker Corwell. "Tucker, did you rest well?"

"Quite," Corwell replied, and it was evident to Sam that Sebastian's grandfather did not like Thomas Thornton any more than Sam did.

"And you, fair Katherine, how did you pass the night?" His voice had softened to an almost blatantly seductive purr.

Sam glanced at Ginny and saw her sharp intake of breath. He knew that she was reliving a moment that she had given no meaning to the first time around. He saw that she did not miss the almost imperceptible brush of

Thomas's fingers along the back of Katherine's shoulder as he moved toward his place at the head of the table. He sat and snapped his cloth napkin across his lap and waited to be served. "Ginny, tell us what you have planned for the day." Before Ginny could reply, he continued. "My wife is brilliant at entertaining, as we all know, but I believe that this time she has truly surpassed herself, haven't you, my darling?" He leaned over and kissed her cheek, making a show of fondling her neck as he did so.

Sam thought he might actually throw up. How could she ever have loved this man? Ginny smiled and laid out the schedule of activities for the day. It was indeed an impressive agenda, running the gamut from outdoor hikes and winter sports to parlor games and musicales.

Thomas applauded the list once she had completed it. "Shall we get started, then?" he announced as he poured an excessive amount of maple syrup from the silver pitcher at his elbow onto his pancakes.

After breakfast Sam excused himself and prepared to return to the conservatory. Ginny caught up with him in the room he had been assigned where he had gone to retrieve his notebook.

"You can't desert me," she said in an urgent whisper as soon as she had slipped into the room and shut the door.

"Ginny, this is your day, your life. I was not here— I *should not* be here. It will color everything you say and do and it's important that things proceed as before."

"Are you angry with me?" she asked, clearly confused by his tone.

Sam could not hold his tongue a minute longer. "How could you ever have been attracted to that pompous bore, Ginny?"

To his surprise, she sighed and sat on the edge of the single bed. "He's changed, Sam. Over the years, things have happened, and he is very different from the man I first met and married."

He resisted the need to point out that he had clearly married her for her money.

"When Thomas and I first met, I knew that he was attracted to me for one reason. He was an ambitious man who came from humble beginnings. My family's fortune could change things for him."

"And you saw nothing wrong with that?"

She shrugged. "He was handsome and he was very kind to me. . . ."

"*Kind?* What about loving you, desiring you? Wanting to move heaven and earth for you?"

"Sam, please try to understand that such things were not important in these times. A young woman's goal was to marry well. If love was part of the bargain, so much the better. Thomas and I . . . understood what we were getting."

Sam moved to stand next to her and cradled her head against his body. "But were you ever happy?"

"Oh, yes," Ginny assured him. "At first we were quite content. Thomas was very generous, and we shared some wonderful times."

Sam knew he had to get a grip on his own emotions and understand what this all meant for her. "Then?" he prompted.

"Thomas wanted children. He dreamed of creating his own dynasty—generations of Thorntons. I couldn't have them. My parents died, and he assumed the management of the estate. I'm not sure he had been adequately prepared for that, and it took its toll."

Sam knelt and cupped her face with both hands. "Ginny, listen to yourself. You are taking every bit of the blame for his incompetence, for his failures. Perhaps *he* could not have children. Perhaps *he* only cared about what the money would buy, not how one maintained it."

Ginny stroked his cheek. "You mustn't blame Thomas for not being as strong and capable as you are, Sam."

"Did . . . do you love him?"

"No," she replied. "I love you . . . only you."

"Then—"

"Sam, listen to me. You are my one and only true love. I have explained to you that times were different. Thomas and I are married. I have a duty to be faithful to the vows we made."

"Will you listen to yourself? *Duty?*"

She stood up. "Sam, these are different times. There are different standards. You simply have to accept that in the same way I had to accept the precepts of your time. Now please check the hallway. I must return to my guests before someone comes to find me."

Sam did as she asked and watched her hurry away from him down the hallway and back toward Thomas's booming voice.

"Ginny, are you coming? We're all ready down here."

"Coming, Thomas," she called breathlessly. "Just let me get my wrap."

Chapter 16

THE DAY FLEW by. Ginny found herself caught up in the activities, orchestrating each event, each meal, constantly attending to the needs of a house filled with guests. She barely saw Thomas except in passing as they hosted the various events of the day. As she had remembered, Thomas was in especially fine form. He was charming and funny and sober. He was tender with her and solicitous to their guests. She saw no further exchanges between him and Katherine and began to think that she may have permitted the gossip heard from Sebastian to color her view of things. She made a special effort to get close to Katherine again, feeling guilty for having thought her friend capable of deceit.

Sam did not appear at lunch, and she had no time to seek him out through the long afternoon. As the sun set and the hour approached when she would go to the library for the New Year's toast with Thomas, and then later return to the library hopefully to save his life, Ginny became more and more anxious. On the one hand, she wanted the time to pass quickly. On the other hand, she was afraid she might overlook some detail, some minor thing she had failed to notice that first time that might have made all the difference.

After Ginny left with Thomas, Sam buried himself in work. He did not want to imagine her with Thomas, laughing as they skimmed over the snow in the sleigh he had seen being readied in the stable yard. He did not want to think of her laughing with Thomas, exchanging knowing looks with Thomas, sharing the thousand and one nuances they must have shared on that day. He would not permit himself to consider what might happen if she was successful in preventing the suicide. Everything he knew about science told him that she could not change history, and yet nothing that had happened since she came into his life had made any sense at all.

As evening came and the hour of her meeting with Thomas neared, Sam found it impossible to concentrate on his work. He snapped at Boyle and then apologized. "I think I need to call it a day," he said.

Boyle nodded. "Aye. Sometimes a fresh start helps."

"Well, goodnight, then," Sam said and prepared to take his leave.

"Oh, Doc, I wonder if you might deliver a message to Mr. Thornton." Boyle dug a folded vellum envelope out of his pocket and smoothed it out before handing it to Sam. "I'm afraid I forgot all about this message. A Colonel Sutter came by the gatehouse earlier while I was helping the boys test out the sleigh. I told him not to bother ringing—knowing how busy Mr. Holt and the others were. Told him I'd be sure Mr. Thornton got the message. Do you think it's too late?"

Sam accepted the envelope and stared at it. He was holding a message from his own great-great-grandfather, written in his own hand earlier that very day. Sam turned the envelope over and opened the flap.

Dear Mr. Thornton:

  *Please accept my most humble apologies. How-
ever, I must postpone our meeting planned for this
evening at seven. I have been unavoidably called
away on urgent business of a personal nature.*

  *However, I do wish to convey once again my
genuine wish that we discuss the matter of intention to pay your debt in its entirety by deeding
your estate to me. I do not believe we need to take
such a drastic measure, and while it is true that
the debt is substantial, I am a fair man and one
who believes there must be another solution.*

  *Please do me the honor of permitting me to re-
schedule our discussion upon my return later this
evening.*

        Until then, I remain respectfully yours,

                            Cashwell Sutter

Sam reread the note and tried to digest its meaning.
If the colonel had canceled, then who had been in the
library that night? He had to find Ginny. He had to let
her know. This changed everything. He headed for the
house at a run, hoping it would not be too late.

At six-thirty Ginny poured the sherry and entered the
library. Moving as if in a dream, she saw Thomas sitting
at his desk. He was writing something in the book of
poetry and looked up the minute she entered, as if he
had been expecting her. She saw the look of surprise
cross his face as he stood and came toward her, his finger marking the page in the book of poetry.

She made her little speech about wanting to revive the
tradition of their annual toast, and he read her the
Browning poem.

She told him that the new year would bring them new
opportunities for happiness. At the last minute she took
a deep breath and said, "Thomas, I realize that there
have been some very difficult business decisions that

you have had to contend with these past few months. I just want you to know that . . ."

She had wanted to say that if he had lost Malmaison they would find a way to go on, but he would not let her finish the statement. He teased her about not being properly dressed for charades and sent her on her way. He was still holding the book of poetry when she left the room.

As she had that fateful night, Ginny climbed the stairs and got all the way to her room before she turned and started back toward the library. Somehow it seemed essential that the timing be exactly right. Nothing she would do tonight would change history as it had turned out. After all, Colonel Sutter already owned the estate. It would remain in his family. Sam's grandfather would will it to Sam. He would establish his research laboratories there. His mother would open the museum. All of that would remain unchanged. Only the fact of Thomas's untimely death would be changed, and she had already seen that this event would have no impact on the overall history of Malmaison.

She thought of all of this as she slowly retraced her steps down the grand staircase and approached the library. The door was ajar as it had been that night, and again she heard voices. Thomas's raised in anger, and the second voice, quieter, placating him. She was about to push the door open and confront Thomas and Colonel Sutter when she caught a glimpse of ice-blue fabric.

The person with Thomas was not the colonel. It was a woman. More to the point, it was Katherine. Ginny recognized the fabric of her gown, for she had been with Katherine the day she had picked it out. She edged the door open just enough to be able to hear what Katherine was saying.

"I cannot leave Tucker, Thomas," she heard Katherine say. "What you and I had is over. What we did was wrong, and if it ever comes out it will hurt two of the most decent people who ever walked the earth."

"I will decide when this is over!" Thomas raged. "I will decide, do you understand?"

"Thomas, please calm yourself. We both know that your original motive in pursuing me was less than noble." Katherine sounded weary, worn down. "You needed my fortune."

"At first, but then . . . can't you understand?" He was begging now. "I cannot exist without your help, without . . . you."

Ginny stepped back into the hallway, her breath coming in short pants as if she had run a race. She did not want to hear this, did not want to know. *Where was the colonel?*

The colonel was to come at seven. Thomas had told her that himself earlier that day. Lucas had mentioned it as well, wondering whether or not to delay dinner until the meeting ended. Confused, she glanced at her watch. It was five minutes past seven. She must be early. What she had clearly not seen that night was Katherine leaving the library just before the colonel's arrival there.

She looked around for a place to conceal herself but still keep her sights on the library door. She would not shame either Katherine or Thomas by letting them know she had overheard their conversation. She would wait somewhere nearby, and the minute the colonel appeared she would rush forward and accompany him into the library. Together they would prevent Thomas from using his gun on himself.

She glanced around and saw that the closest hiding place was the doorway that led to the butler's pantry and kitchen. She hurried along the hallway, and just as she reached the pantry door she heard the shot.

Sam came through the back entrance and paused. He had not been in this part of the house since coming back and was momentarily disoriented.

"Sir?" Lucas Holt looked up from his work. "May I be of assistance?"

"Ginny," Sam managed. "Where is Ginny?"

"I believe that Mrs. Thornton must be dressing for—"

They both heard the shot and froze. When they heard Ginny's tortured cry of, "No. No. Not again," they took off at a run.

"Go see what's happened. I'll see to Ginny," Sam ordered when they reached the pantry door and found Ginny collapsed against it.

Sam gathered her into his arms and carried her into the hallway beyond the pantry door. She was sobbing uncontrollably.

"It wasn't the colonel," she said repeatedly.

"I know," he replied. "I tried to get here. Oh, sweet Ginny, I'm so sorry." He sat on the floor and held her, rocking her until her sobs waned. "Who was there with him?"

"It was Katherine," she managed. "Katherine was the other voice. She was calling off their affair. He was upset not because he had lost Malmaison, but because he was about to lose Katherine."

"Shhh. You did everything you could. It's over. It's all over."

"I have to go in there. I have to see it through."

"No. This history you *can* change. You've seen and heard enough. It's over."

She smiled weakly. "Not quite," she replied. "Please understand that it's important for me to see this through, Sam."

He would have done anything he could have to spare her one more minute's pain, but it was not to be. Resigned to the fact that she was a woman of great strength and great principle, he helped her to her feet. "I'm coming with you," he told her. "That's nonnegotiable."

When she reached the library, the guests were all gathered. Several of them tried to prevent her from entering the room, but she pushed past them, and Sam followed close on her heels.

He watched as she started across the room, then paused. Katherine was seated in a chair near the fireplace. The chair had been turned away from the desk, and Tucker was on his knees next to her. She was sobbing hysterically.

Ginny did not approach the woman who had been her lifelong friend. Instead she approached the desk, gently pushing her way past several male guests and Lucas Holt who had gathered around Thomas's lifeless body. The room became very quiet except for the occasional shuddering sob from Katherine. Ginny stood there staring at her husband for a long moment. At last she reached over and gently touched his fingers on the book, then her knees buckled and she fainted.

Sam was the first to reach her, in spite of the fact that others surrounded her. He lifted her and carried her away from the room. Lucas Holt directed him to a small sitting room where visitors sometimes waited. "Stay with her," Sam said to Holt. Lucas nodded as he accepted the cold compress Ginny's maid, Maggie, had brought and placed it on Ginny's forehead.

Closing the door of the small sitting room to prevent curious prying eyes, Sam returned to the library. It was important that he see everything that took place. It was important that he be able to tell Ginny what he had seen, what he had heard.

Tucker Corwell had taken charge. The guests had been urged to return to the upstairs family quarters. Two other women were assisting Katherine to her room as Sam entered the library. A servant was posted at the front door to bring the police to the scene once they arrived.

"What are you doing?" Sam demanded as he saw Tucker Corwell ease the book of poetry from under Thomas's lifeless fingers.

Tucker looked up at him. His face was haggard, and

he had aged a great deal in the past few hours. "Please . . ." The single word came out in a strangled plea, and then he began to cry.

Sam wasn't sure how to react. "Mr. Corwell, you've just lost a dear friend and clearly you're upset."

Instantly Corwell's expression turned to rage. "This man was trying to seduce my wife. He was desperate to have her, and when she chose me, he only wanted to cause her more pain, more embarrassment than he already had. Look at this. . . ." He offered Sam the blood-stained book of poetry.

To my beloved Katherine—the light, the beauty, and the love of my life was written in Thomas's flowery script above the very poem he had read to Ginny. Sam's hand shook as he tried to control his own rage at what this selfish man had done.

"I don't want anyone to see that," Tucker said wearily. "You can surely understand that for this to be truly over, there can be no further evidence of scandal. It would only cause pain for Ginny, and she has been through quite enough."

Sam handed the book back to Tucker and nodded. As he watched, Tucker removed a small penknife from his jacket pocket and carefully cut away the offending pages. Then he placed the book back under Thomas's fingers. At the same moment they heard the arrival of the police. Lucas Holt was calmly filling the officers in on the details as he led them to the library.

Sam glanced toward the door, and when he looked back at Tucker, he saw that the man had slipped the pages cut from the book of poems into a thick book he had pulled from the shelving behind the desk. He reshelved the book just as the police entered the room.

"Good evening, Mr. Corwell. What happened here?" the officer said, eyeing first Tucker and then Sam.

"I'm afraid Mr. Thornton has taken his own life." Corwell stated the obvious.

The officer walked slowly around the desk, examining

the body and the surroundings with a practiced eye. "Any idea why?"

"I believe he had had several business reversals recently. Perhaps . . ."

The officer picked up the leather portfolio Thomas had left out on the desk and thumbed through it. He gave a low whistle. "I see what you mean," he murmured and closed the folder. "How's Mrs. Thornton holding up?"

"She's quite distressed, naturally. Others are with her at the moment," Tucker replied.

"And who are you?" The officer turned his full attention on Sam.

"This is Professor Sutherby, a guest in the house. I believe he only met Mr. Thornton this morning, isn't that right, Professor?"

Sam nodded. "I'm doing a bit of research," he said and saw the officer consider that statement and then decide that he was probably harmless.

"Pretty open and shut from all appearances." He picked up the folder again and studied one of the papers more closely. "Is this man Sutter in the house?"

"Colonel Sutter?" Tucker looked confused. "Why, no. I believe he was expected for a meeting along with Mr. Thornton's solicitor earlier this evening, however . . ."

There were more voices in the reception area, followed by brisk footsteps down the corridor. "Colonel Sutter is here," Lucas announced as Sam's great-great-grandfather swept through the door.

"What the devil has happened here?" he demanded.

Sam was speechless. He was about to have a conversation with his own ancestor who had died decades before Sam was even born. It was too bizarre and at the same time it was incredibly thrilling.

"Mr. Thornton here has shot himself," the officer replied. "You wouldn't know anything about that, would you, sir?"

Cashwell Sutter pulled himself to his full military height and fixed his slate-colored eyes on the police detective. "Of course I know nothing of it, Officer. I have just arrived."

"I understand you were to have a meeting with the deceased."

"Mr. Thornton and I were scheduled to meet earlier this evening. I was called away to another meeting. I stopped by the gatehouse on my way out of town and left word that I would be delayed."

"That's true, Officer," Sam said. He stepped forward and handed the detective the handwritten message. "I'm afraid the head gardener who received the message at the gatehouse forgot to deliver it. I was just on my way to do that when Mr. Thornton shot himself."

The detective fingered the page he had taken from the folder. "From the looks of this, you were about to take over the estate, Colonel."

Tucker Corwell gasped. "I had no idea things had reached such a desperate state," he murmured to no one in particular.

The colonel sighed heavily. "That's why I wanted to meet with Mr. Thornton." He stared at the body slumped over the desk. "Thomas was damnably proud and outrageously reckless with his money—or I should say, his wife's money. I warned him repeatedly against the investment, but he went to others involved in the deal, and they, of course, welcomed his participation. When it fell apart as I had told him there was a greater than fifty percent chance it would, he was in over his head. His only collateral was the estate which he had signed over in making the deal." He continued to stare at Thomas's bloody remains. "Can't we at least see to the removal of the body before Mrs. Thornton sees it?" he demanded tersely.

The detective nodded to his partner who in turn got Lucas, who was clearly waiting just outside the door. The two of them went about the work of wrapping Thomas's body in a blanket and carrying it from the library. Lucas returned shortly after that and, with a nod of approval from the detective, quietly began clearing away any evidence of the shooting.

"Officer," the colonel said, "my concern at the moment is for the living. Mrs. Thornton . . . I'm not sure what she knows of her husband's business affairs. The fortune was from her side of the family, and tonight she has not only been widowed in this tragic way, but she will shortly learn that the probable cause of her husband's actions was his squandering of her estate—including this very house."

"What are you suggesting, Colonel?"

"I am asking you to keep this business as quiet as possible. I am asking that there be no speculation to reporters from your office as to the motive behind Mr. Thornton's action. I am asking that you give me an opportunity to work out arrangements with Mrs. Thornton that will not leave her bereft of everything she has held dear in this life."

Sam wanted desperately to have Ginny hear this conversation. Would she believe him when he told her how his great-great-grandfather had been concerned only for *her* welfare?

Once again there was a commotion in the reception area. Lucas went to see who had arrived and returned with a large, burly man who swept off an opera cape, top hat, and gloves and handed them to Lucas. "I am Josiah Hudson, Mr. Thornton's attorney. I was to meet with my client and Colonel Sutter at seven. I'm afraid I was delayed." He glanced around the room. "What has happened here?"

"Thomas has killed himself," Tucker replied.

The very air seemed to seep out of the lawyer's body as his shoulders sagged. "No," he whispered. "I told him that there were recourses. I told him that—"

"It's a tragedy all right, but I'm satisfied that it was brought about by Thornton himself," the detective said, snapping shut his notebook. "I'll leave you gentlemen

to make the final arrangements. Good evening." He nodded to his partner, and they left the room.

"Gentlemen, if you will excuse me," Tucker said as
soon as the police were gone, "I need to check on my
wife. It has been a most distressing evening for everyone."

"Of course," the colonel replied, clearly taking charge
of things. "You go ahead. And you, sir, I don't believe
I've had the pleasure."

Sam found himself looking at the outstretched hand
of his own great-great-grandfather. He accepted the
handshake and managed to croak out his assumed name.

"Botanical research?" the colonel said with a glint of
interest after Sam had added his reason for being at the
estate.

"Yes, sir."

"I have a particular interest in that as well. In better
days Thomas and I often walked the estate, and while
he had little interest, I was fascinated by the variety of
the plant life, not to mention the conservatory itself."

"Gin . . . Mrs. Thornton is the one who has seen to
that part of the estate, I believe," Sam said.

"And a masterful job she has done," the colonel replied.

Hudson cleared his throat impatiently. There was
something about the man that Sam instantly disliked. He
was too focused on his own needs. Clearly he was not
happy that his evening had been interrupted.

"Ah, yes, the business at hand," the colonel said wearily. He took Sam's hand between both of his. "There is
much potential in the woodlands and the projects Mrs.
Thornton has begun here. Please assure her of my interest in exploring those projects with her in detail at a
time when she is up to it."

"I will," Sam assured him. "Thank you, sir." He took
the book where Tucker had stowed the cut pages of poetry from the shelf. "Goodnight, sir."

As he left the room he heard his great-great-grandfather say to Hudson, "Thornton was an even greater fool than I expected, but there you have it. Now, what shall we do about making certain that Mrs. Thornton does not lose her home?"

Sam waited outside the door to hear Hudson's reply.

"You'll forgive me for bringing it up, Colonel, but you are hardly the only person whose finances have been affected by the evening's events. Mr. Thornton owed me a substantial sum in fees and services—a sum I was assured I would be able to collect in full once this deal was consummated. As it is—" He was cut off in mid-sentence by the cold military command of Cashwell Sutter.

"Say not one further word, Hudson, or I will make it my personal pleasure to see that you never utter another word again. You will get your fee—your kind always does. At the moment I must reluctantly rely upon you to act as my intermediary in setting up a meeting with Mrs. Thornton as soon as possible. Do you think you can manage that?" This last was delivered in a tone that showed how seriously the colonel doubted that he could.

Sam smiled. *Way to go, Colonel!* He cheered silently and headed up the grand stairway to find Ginny.

He wanted to tell her everything that had transpired. He wanted to show her the cut pages and let her know that Tucker had removed them to save his beloved Katherine from further embarrassment. He wanted to convince her that his great-great-grandfather was a decent and caring man who had only her interests at heart.

Chapter 17

SHE HADN'T BEEN able to stop Thomas from taking his life, Ginny thought miserably as she sat in her
room and permitted Maggie to attend to her hair. She
had changed into the black mourning gown. She had
walked through her own room and Thomas's, retracing
without conscious thought the steps she had taken that
terrible night, even though now it didn't matter anymore.
She knew now that she had failed to save him because
she had misunderstood the events of that night. Perhaps
she could travel back and forth across time, but what
good was it if she wasn't permitted to change history?

Oh, Thomas, how could you? she thought miserably
as the tears rolled down her cheeks. She opened her eyes
and saw Maggie watching her in the mirror. The servant
thought that she was seeing tears of grief and would be
surprised to know that they were tears of rage.

She had played by the rules of her time. She had entered a marriage not out of passion but because Thomas
was a good man with a promising future, and together
they could build a life. Love, if it came, would be a
bonus. She had been a dutiful wife, resisting the chafing

of the constraints of her time that set limits to the possibility of bringing her dreams and fantasies to life. She had been a strong partner, excelling in her role as hostess and community benefactor. True, she had been unable to carry a child to term, but she had not yet passed her prime and she knew any number of women who had had their first child late in life—her own mother among them.

"Thank you, Maggie," she said quietly. "I must go and meet with Mr. Hudson now." Lucas had stopped by her room to let her know that the attorney was waiting for her in the library.

"Begging your pardon, ma'am, but no one would expect you to do anything more tonight. Let me ask Mr. Holt to send him away until morning and you get your rest."

"What good would that do, Maggie?" she replied softly, repeating the words she knew she had said that night. "Nothing will change with the morning." She stood up, and Maggie moved respectfully aside to let her pass.

Sam was coming toward her as she left her room. He had come up by the back stairway, and she knew that had been done to protect her from the curiosity of any guests who might not be down in the dining room where Lucas had assured her dinner was being served.

She ran to Sam's open arms and felt the strength and comfort of them enveloping her.

"It's all right," he assured her. "Everything is going to work out."

"There is nothing to work out," she replied wearily. "You were right. We cannot change the past."

"I met the colonel," he told her as he kissed the top of her head.

She looked up at him, her face alight with happiness. "Oh, Sam, how wonderful for you."

"Yeah, it was pretty awesome, to say the least. He shook my hand, and we talked. I mean, he saw me. I was an actual presence in the room, in his life." He shook his head in wonder. "Imagine that, Ginny."

She hugged him and then pushed away. "I have to go see Mr. Hudson. Shall I come to the conservatory later?"

"Too risky. Boyle might show up. Why don't I come to you once I'm sure everyone is settled for the night?"

"All right." She stood on tiptoe and kissed his lips. "I have to go."

"I know, but first you need to know some of what has transpired while you were up here." He filled her in on all of the details he had observed. He handed her the pages of poetry, watched her face as she registered the message Thomas had written and then crumpled the pages in her hand.

"I have to go," she said once again, but her voice was filled with the resignation of one who is about to act out of duty and responsibility.

He caught her for a passionate kiss. "Ginny, I know this has been a horrible night for you—in some ways worse than the first time, but you can get through this. I'm right here and I'm not going to let anything or anybody hurt you."

She smiled and stroked his cheek with her fingertips. "Thank you, Sam," she said softly and then turned to go.

"Watch out for Hudson, Ginny. I don't trust him."

"All right, but—"

"Just be careful," he warned as they heard some of the guests coming back into the downstairs reception area.

Ginny approached the library once again. The attorney was inside, pacing impatiently before the fireplace. He took out his pocket watch and looked at it, then snapped it closed and looked irritably toward the door just as she entered the room. How many small details she had missed that night, Ginny thought.

Hudson rushed to her side and began assisting her as if she were about to faint. "Mrs. Thornton, you have my deepest sympathies."

She moved away from him and strode to the desk that had been cleared of everything except the leather portfolio and some papers she had not noticed before. "Am I destitute, Mr. Hudson?" she asked without responding to his condolences.

He fingered the stack of documents that he had evidently brought with him. "There are certain financial issues that I shall be happy to handle," he began, and she realized that he was distinctly uncomfortable on a level that went beyond giving her the bad news of her financial state.

"Will I lose Malmaison?"

The attorney seemed surprised. "I thought you knew," he said, and then added almost to himself, "Of course. That is why." He sounded angry.

"Why what, Mr. Hudson? Do you know why my husband took his life?"

She saw him make a conscious effort to collect his emotions. "Mrs. Thornton, wouldn't you prefer to discuss these matters after the funeral? You must be exhausted and you've had an enormous shock and—"

"Can you explain my husband's death, sir?" She said each word slowly, distinctly, as if the man were slow or hard of hearing.

Again he busied himself shuffling the papers.

"Your husband had already disposed of the estate, I'm afraid."

Ginny delivered her next line to perfection, even though she knew now that it was a lie. "Thomas would never do that. He knows . . . knew what Malmaison means to me. He might have used the funds that my parents left me, but . . ."

She almost felt pity for the attorney, for he certainly pitied her as he looked directly at her for the first time. "Your husband had already exhausted those funds when he used the estate as collateral in a very high-risk business venture, Mrs. Thornton. I tried to advise him of the risk, as did Colonel Sutter, but he insisted. The venture collapsed, and he lost his investment."

"We can repay the losses," she said, watching carefully to judge his reaction to that thought. He came very close to laughing at the absurdity of that idea.

"I'm afraid not."

"Mr. Hudson, as you are well aware, in the recent past I lost my beloved parents. Now I have lost my husband. I cannot lose Malmaison, too," she whispered passionately.

As he had on that night, the attorney took her whispered words for grief and reached out to cover her hand with his own larger one. "It's too late. Your husband signed the papers earlier this week. Colonel Sutter came here to dissuade him, to tell him they could work out some arrangement, but Thomas was adamant. The colonel believes that Thomas was insulted by his perception that the colonel thought Thomas would default on his debts. There was no reasoning with him. You must know that these last several weeks he has not been at all himself."

"Sutter?" Ginny repeated the name as if trying to place it in her mind. She knew now that the lawyer was lying. Colonel Sutter had come later. "Sutter," she said more firmly. "He was here and did nothing?" She stood, and Hudson followed suit.

"Now, Mrs. Thornton, please—"

"You will tell Colonel Sutter that we will discuss the disposal of my home once I have buried my husband. Further, he should not assume that he will ever displace me from this property. My father built this estate. It was his pride and joy. It is and shall remain my home. This estate is all I have left, and I will not lose it. I will not."

Later that night as Sam held her and they talked about this new version of the events of that night, he gave her some startling news. "Ginny, I believe that the colonel came here tonight to make certain that Thomas did not lose Malmaison. I believe that he has every intention of returning ownership to you."

"Perhaps if I had agreed to meet with him," she said sadly. Then she touched Sam's face tenderly. "But then I would never have known you."

"I'm telling you that you can have Malmaison, Ginny."

"You said we could not change history," she reminded him.

"No, but perhaps it can be altered a bit."

She sat up and stared at him. "You were the one who—"

"I know, but what if I was wrong? You told me that you refused to meet with the colonel, that Hudson was the intermediary. Well, Hudson is only interested in himself and collecting his money. Just change one thing, Ginny. Agree to the meeting with my great-great-grandfather and see what happens."

"If I had only understood and gone into that library when I saw Katherine, this would all be over," Ginny said.

"No. I'm convinced that even if Thomas had lived, you would have lost everything. On top of that you would have been trapped in a loveless marriage with a man who would resent you for the rest of his days because you were not the woman he truly loved."

She thought about the way Thomas had pleaded with Katherine to leave Tucker and be with him and knew that Sam was right. "All right, I'll meet the colonel," she agreed.

"Good. Now, get some rest. Tomorrow is going to be another very emotional day." He pulled on his clothes.

"You're going?"

He smiled. "For now. It wouldn't do for poor Maggie to come in tomorrow morning and find you shacked up with the professor."

Over the next several days, Ginny performed the du-

ties expected of her and more. She made the arrangements for the service. She saw to every detail herself as
she thought about the meeting with the colonel and what
that might bring. If Sam was right, the possibility was
very good that Colonel Sutter was going to refuse to
accept the estate in payment of the debt. Sam thought
he might even forgive the debt altogether. In addition,
Tucker Corwell had mentioned to Sam that he felt it was
his duty to alleviate some of Ginny's debt since Thomas
no doubt had spent at least a portion of her fortune lav-
ishing gifts on Katherine.

She accepted the condolences of dozens of people
who attended the services in the family's private chapel.
She watched quietly as those same people gathered in
the large downstairs reception area to munch on cakes
and finger sandwiches as they gossiped about what had
driven poor Thomas to such disaster and whispered
about what would happen to dear Ginny now.

She walked through the gathering of mourners, aware
that Sam's eyes followed her everywhere. When she saw
Katherine, whom she had not seen since that night in
the library, she paused. Trying to analyze her feelings
as she faced the woman who had been her best friend
and her husband's lover, she realized that what would
have destroyed her then was of almost no consequence
now.

"Dear Katherine," she said as she moved across the
room and took her friend's hands in hers. She spoke
quietly so that only Katherine and Tucker heard her
words. "How are you doing? I am so very sorry that you
had to witness . . . that Thomas did that to you. Please
forgive him and know that he was not himself—not the
Thomas we both knew . . . and loved."

Katherine's eyes filled with tears. "Oh, Ginny, can
you ever forgive me?" she whispered.

"I already have," Ginny replied and drew her friend
to her shoulder so that she could release her tears.

With each passing hour, she felt a fresh dose of rage

as she remembered all the promises Thomas had made about the life they would share, the future they would enjoy together, and all the while he had been betraying her trust, selling her dreams.

It was the thirtieth of December when the attorney came to call on her for the second time. As before, she met with him in the library, sitting at the very desk where Thomas had died.

She repeated the action of pushing a heavy envelope across the table to him. "I have been able to raise some cash." This time Sam had gone with her to the pawnbroker's and had fussed and fumed about what sums the same jewels would have brought in his time. She had stated a price and held out her hand, indicating that there would be no bartering. Sam had caught her hand and demanded a higher price. The pawnbroker had grumbled, but he had paid Sam's price.

Hudson opened the envelope and counted the money. "This is impressive," he said, barely able to disguise his awe at the sum she had presented. He replaced the bills in the envelope.

"It is a first payment, Mr. Hudson. Please set up a schedule with the colonel for regular payments."

"You cannot possibly raise that kind of money on a consistent basis, Mrs. Thornton, even if you sell everything in the house and stables. On top of that, there are outstanding debts to contractors and other purveyors as yet unpaid for recent redecorating and repair projects. If you understood the documents you have read, you would see that."

Ginny stood up and placed both hands flat on the desk as she leaned toward him. "Mr. Hudson, do not insult me. I have not only read the documents, but I understand them completely. I am also aware of your personal stake in all of this." She saw his eyes flicker with surprise that he might have been too transparent. "I am simply asking you to deal with the person who cheated my husband of his property. I will attend to the other matters myself. If you cannot handle that simple request, I will retain someone who can."

Hudson raised his bushy eyebrows in surprise at her tone and pocketed the money. He took the money, she realized. *I hadn't noticed that before.* "Mrs. Thornton, you are clearly overwrought. Your husband was always concerned that you would react emotionally when the issue called for pragmatic logic. That is exactly why he insisted you know nothing of these rather complex matters. I would suggest that you meet with Colonel Sutter yourself. He is not an unreasonable man and deeply regrets your loss. He—"

Ginny came around the desk to stand directly over the attorney. "All right."

Hudson's face reddened with shock. "But I thought—"

"I changed my mind," Ginny replied with a blithe wave of her hand. Clearly the attorney had gambled on the fact that he had done such a good job of insinuating that Sutter was the villain here that he expected her to refuse to meet the man, to have him in her house.

"Set up the meeting for this afternoon here in the library. Is that clear, Mr. Hudson?"

The attorney nodded.

"And Mr. Hudson, I believe the envelope in your pocket will more than settle our account. I shall not need your services after today. Is that clear as well?"

The veins in the poor man's neck seemed ready to explode, and Ginny almost felt sorry for him. "Good day, sir," she said with a sweet smile. There. She had changed history and the world had not stopped.

Sam tried hard to stay away from Ginny during the long difficult days following Thomas's suicide. He did not want to have her distracted from performing her role. He made certain he was nearby on occasions such as the gathering of mourners following the funeral when he knew she would be seeing Katherine Corwell for the first time.

He needn't have worried. Ginny was as generous in forgiveness as she was in love. He saw that the gossip-mongers had been at work in the way every eye followed Ginny's walk across that room to face Katherine. He saw that everyone was anticipating anything other than what happened. He had never been more proud of Ginny than he was in that moment. She had defined the word "lady" for every person in that room.

At night he would slip into her room after spending long hours in the conservatory working feverishly on his experiment. Time was running out for both of them as they played out the events that had brought Ginny to him in the first place. He wasn't certain what would happen once they reached that moment in time, but he wanted to be ready. He had the unique opportunity to conduct his research using the very plants he had attempted to recreate. He was so close to a breakthrough.

They would lie together until the dark just before dawn. He would let her tell him about everything that had transpired that day, how it differed from her first memory of the same event. He would then tell her about his work, about his certainty that the peerless qualities of her malmaison dianthus might actually mean a major breakthrough in medical science.

They would sometimes make love and sometimes just lie together talking about events past and future. He would dress and leave her before dawn and as often as not he would return to the conservatory to push forward with his work. He was often exhausted and he longed for the sophisticated computerized equipment of his own time, but his certainty that he was on the verge of a real breakthrough drove him.

Wearily he walked through the palm garden, back past the cold house to the hothouse where he had set up small covered containers of solution in an effort to regenerate the polyamines of the dianthus. Every day—sometimes several times a day—he had studied them with the hope of having succeeded in his efforts to slow the senescence or aging of the carnation petals through the use of spermines obtained from the plant. A second set of containers tested the actual ability to restore vitality even after the petal had begun to wilt. So far there had been little evidence of success, and Sam was frustrated by his inability to check his data and reformulate the process if necessary with the help of computer programs.

He checked one set of containers and then the second. The first looked the same, but the second set containing the wilted petals showed a marked difference. Sam's heart hammered as he studied the results more closely. The wilted petals were soft and supple, like a newly opened flower. He ran to the first set of containers. The difference on the fresh mature petals was less noticeable but still there.

It works, he thought joyously. "It works!" he shouted and then laughed out loud as he danced around the conservatory.

"Professor?"

Boyle stood at the entrance to the hothouse and stared at him. Sam grabbed the man and began dancing around the room with him. "It works, my friend. The malmaison dianthus is not only the most beautiful flower the world has ever known, but it also has its own built-in fountain of youth."

"That's nice, Doc," Boyle said, clearly trying to humor Sam. "That's real nice."

"Nice? Mr. Boyle, this is medical history in the making here. Today marks the possibility of an antibody that could work on people as well as plants. It could prevent or even treat the onset of senescence."

Boyle gave him a quizzical look.

"Senescence!" Sam shouted. "Senility. Dotage. Feeblemindedness brought on with aging."

Boyle continued to nod and smile, but clearly didn't have a clue. "I'm real happy for you, Doc."

"Thank you," Sam replied, taking a second look at the cultures to assure himself that he hadn't been imagining things. "Now if you'll excuse me, I've got to go find Gin—Mrs. Thornton."

"I expect she'll be real pleased," Boyle assured him.

Ginny paced nervously as she awaited the arrival of Colonel Sutter. She could not help but think how her life might have changed had she accepted this meeting the first time around.

"Mrs. Thornton, Colonel Sutter has arrived." Lucas Holt stood at the library door and awaited her pleasure.

"Please show him in, Mr. Holt, and thank you."

She stood near the fireplace and watched the door.

When he entered the room, her breath caught, for there was a stunning resemblance to Sam. The colonel was shorter and broader than his great-great-grandson was, but there was something in the manner, the smile especially, that had passed through the generations. She liked him immediately.

"Colonel," she said, coming forward to greet him.

He bowed slightly. "Mrs. Thornton, please accept my deepest sympathies for your recent loss."

"Thank you. Please sit with me. I believe we have a great deal to discuss."

The colonel waited for her to be seated, then took the chair opposite hers. He sat forward, his eyes on her, waiting for her next move.

"Tell me about your family, Colonel," she said as Lucas brought the tea she had asked be delivered for the appointment.

Sutter smiled and relaxed slightly. She had caught him slightly off guard, but in a way that he clearly found pleasant. He talked about his wife with such love and obvious devotion that Ginny felt a swell of emotion rise in her throat.

"And children?" she asked as she refilled his cup and offered him another cookie.

"Four," he announced happily. "Three sons and a daughter."

She pressed him for details, already knowing the statistics from her research while acting as the curator. She wanted the stories a father might tell about them. She wanted to see what kind of father the colonel was, for that would tell her a great deal.

"Mrs. Thornton," the colonel said after permitting himself to regale her with several stories of the antics of his children, "you did not call me here to discuss my family, did you?"

"No. I believe that we have business to conduct, do we not, sir?"

The colonel set his teacup back on the silver tray and sat forward once again. "Are you up to this?"

Ginny nodded.

"Your husband made a rather unfortunate decision before his untimely death."

"Actually my husband made a number of unfortunate decisions in the latter weeks of his life, sir, but please do not judge him solely on that."

The colonel's thick eyebrows rose in surprise and respect. "One of the decisions involves your estate."

"Yes, I know. At the moment you own Malmaison. What we are here to discuss is what we can do about that."

Sutter chuckled and relaxed once again. "You are a remarkable woman, Mrs. Thornton. I had some doubts about what I am about to offer, but you have completely erased them through your candor and pragmatic way of looking at the situation at hand."

"I'm listening." Ginny held her breath. Here it was. The moment she had avoided in the first place. The moment that might change her life forever.

"I cannot afford simply to forgive the debt, Mrs. Thornton. I am going to assume that you have no recourse for meeting it other than the estate itself."

"Go on," she said, unwilling to reveal anything until he had completed his proposal.

"What I came here to offer your husband last night was a compromise, for him to continue to occupy the mansion and function as a manager for the estate. I am prepared to make that same offer to you. Please understand that any heirs you may have are not entitled to any claim on the estate and following your death, the estate—including the mansion—reverts to me and my heirs."

Ginny could not sit still. They could stay. She would not lose Malmaison. At least not entirely. In time she might even find a way to pay off the debt, too. . . .

"Mrs. Thornton?"

"I . . . This is a very generous offer, Colonel. I thank you for that. Would you be upset if I asked for some time to consider it?" *I must tell Sam.*

"Of course. Very wise on your part. Take your time." He stood up. "I'll be going now. It was a genuine pleasure to meet you. Your husband often spoke of you with something akin to awe. I can understand why now."

"Thank you for saying that, Colonel. Please let me walk out with you, and give my regards to your family. Perhaps someday we can meet."

"That would be my hope as well, my dear lady."

Ginny could hardly wait to find Sam and tell him the news. After seeing the colonel to the door, she hurried through the music room where she grabbed her shawl from the back of a side chair, then went on to the balcony doors, and down the stairs to the arbor path.

$\mathcal{C}hapter$ 18

"GINNY!" HE WAS running toward her, calling her name. "I found the formula!" he shouted.

"We can stay," she said simultaneously.

They met in the middle of the arbor where he lifted her high in his arms and swung her around.

"Oh, Ginny, sweet Ginny, I have it. Your wonderful beautiful carnations have made all the difference. I have managed to isolate the DNA clones and then replicate them. We have a polyamine that is proven to affect senescence and adaptation to environmental stress in plants, and there is every reason to believe it will also work in humans. Do you understand, Ginny?"

She had continued to smile as he poured out his flood of information. She did not understand a word of what he was telling her other than that he had succeeded. "That's wonderful, darling. I have wonderful news as well. The colonel has offered to let me continue to live in the house for the rest of my life. He will own the estate in name only. He assures me that for all practical purposes it will remain my home for the rest of my days.

Oh, Sam, your great-great-grandfather is an incredibly generous and kind man."

She hugged Sam with all her might, unable to recall when she had been quite so happy.

"Then you won't be going back," he stated quietly.

"Didn't you hear what I said, Sam? We can stay." She continued to smile but had the strangest feeling that something was terribly wrong.

"I can't stay, Ginny. This discovery is too important simply to allow it to be buried here in the past."

"But your discovery can work now just as well—better, in fact, because you have the dianthus."

"The problem it can treat is a condition of the future, Ginny. It's the result of decades of medical science that will provide the cures for various life-threatening diseases, permitting people to live longer. The one thing we will not have found a treatment for is senescence. What's the point of living a longer life if you spend those last years in senility?"

Ginny felt as if someone had come along and kicked her in the stomach at the very moment when she had thought every problem had been solved. "I understand," she said, and she did. Her head told her that his argument made perfect sense. But her heart ached.

"Come with me, Ginny," Sam urged.

How could she? The colonel had given her the time she needed to restore her family's name to the prominence and respect it deserved—to undo all of the damage Thomas had done. That's all she had ever wanted. That's what she had gone into the future to find, wasn't it?

"I can't," she said slowly. "I can't simply walk away and leave things as Thomas left them. I owe the memory of my parents more than that. I need you to understand that I have been given a second chance here to make sure that the history of Malmaison reflects the contributions of *my* family as well as yours."

His expression reflected the torture of his decision. "I have no choice, either, Ginny."

"I know," she said huskily and hugged him tight. "Must you go tonight?"

"It's the right timing—the time you came. We have the momentous event—my discovery. That might just be enough to get me back. Otherwise . . ."

She nodded. He was right, of course. This was his opportunity, as that first night had been hers. The difference was that this time they knew it. "Let me help you get ready."

Arm in arm they walked back to the greenhouse where they worked together in silence, carefully packing up his experiments and collecting a supply of the carnation plants for him hopefully to transport with him. They spoke in low tones and only about the packing of the experiment. It was as if to introduce any other topic might weaken their resolve to do the right thing.

"How will you manage it?" she asked.

He shrugged. "I'm not really certain. I think that since the conditions are right and this was your launching place, so to speak, it might just work a second time."

She loved him for not trying to dissuade her, for accepting that her cause was just as important to her as his was to him. She understood that he wanted to stay as much as she wanted to go, but each of them had a job to do. "This will always be the most special place on the estate to me," she said, brushing her fingers over the park bench.

"Ah, Ginny, I'll never love anyone the way I love you."

"You mustn't say that. You have many years left, and I want to think of you as happy and romping about with your children. Please tell me you'll take that opportunity."

He frowned. "But—"

"Promise," she repeated urgently as she hugged him hard.

He wrapped his arms around her. "All right, Ginny. I promise. But I love *you*—just so we have that straight."

She nodded, her face buried against his chest. He knew that she was crying.

"I'd better go back to the house," she said as the small clock that Boyle kept in the hothouse chimed ten o'clock. "It may not work if I'm here with you."

Sam nodded miserably, and suddenly they were in each other's arms, kissing passionately, crying softly.

"I love you for all time—across time, Ginny. Never forget that."

"I won't," she promised. "Never."

He kissed her again, and she was quite certain that if she did not leave then, she would be unable to let him go.

"I love you, Sam. Only you," she called as she ran out the door and stumbled along the path, her tears coming in great sobs now.

She had almost reached the mansion when she had to stop. Her stomach roiled, and she knew that she was going to be ill. This time Sam would not be there to wipe her brow with a cool cloth, to hold her, to make love to her. He would never be there again except in her memory. She did not make it inside the house.

Ginny was ill at least once every day for the first month after Sam left. She tried to be happy for him, tried to imagine the wonders he would work with his new discovery. As she helped him pack, he had explained the long, arduous process ahead before the experiment could actually be translated into a medicine and brought to market. There would be years of clinical trials and more research.

She tried to focus on her own goal of restoring her family's name and reputation to some semblance of respectability. In this, Tucker Corwell and Colonel Sutter were a great help. They made certain that nothing of the circumstances of Thomas's death reached the newspapers. They made it equally clear to their servants, friends, and family that anyone who repeated any of the gossip or speculation would be dismissed or cut off. As two of the wealthiest men of their time, they could demand this and expect complete compliance. Ginny now understood why there had been no news accounts in the aftermath of Thomas's suicide. What she did not understand was why there had been one newspaper account of a tea given by the colonel's wife at Malmaison in just a few weeks. Why would she give a tea at Ginny's house? Even if she did, why wouldn't the newspaper account have taken notice of that? There had been no mention of Ginny, and yet the entire guest list had been included.

The colonel and his family had extended their hospitality to Ginny on numerous occasions. They respected her period of mourning but invited her to small gatherings at their brownstone in New York City and always introduced her as Virginia Hobbs Thornton, going on at length about the good works her parents had done during their lifetime and how Ginny was following in their footsteps.

In Ginny's name, the colonel and Tucker Corwell made generous donations to various local charities. The colonel also made sure that Ginny's entire household staff was well provided for and would continue in their positions for as long as they wished. But it was the colonel's wife, Elizabeth, who gave Ginny the greatest gift of all.

Elizabeth had come to the house at Ginny's invitation for lunch. The colonel's wife had expressed a great interest in the conservatory, and Ginny had invited her and her four children for the afternoon. Ginny and Elizabeth toured the conservatory and met with the gardening staff as they prepared the estate for spring. The children were entertained by Lucas Holt in the billiard room and then taken to the kitchen for a lunch that included freshly baked cookies and milk from the estate's very own dairy herd. The Sutter children loved coming to visit Ginny at Malmaison, and Ginny found their visits a welcome respite from the interminable days without Sam.

The two women were sitting in the family dining room, lingering over their coffee, when Ginny pushed her cup aside.

"Ginny, it's none of my affair, of course, but it seems to me that your health has been quite compromised of late," Elizabeth said.

Ginny smiled. "I'm fine. Just a bit tired, and I don't seem to have much of an appetite."

"I see," Elizabeth replied. "Forgive me for saying so, but this seems to have continued well beyond what might have been expected after the shock of Thomas's death. Have you seen a doctor?"

Ginny laughed. "Heavens, no. It's nothing, really." She reached across the table and patted Elizabeth's hand. "You are a dear friend to be so concerned."

Elizabeth did not smile. "Ginny, I know precious little in this world, but with four children there are a few things I do know, and those are the signs of pregnancy. I believe that there is every possibility you may be with child."

"That's not—" The image of Sam coming to her in her room that one night flashed through her mind. They had always used protection except for that single night. Could it be possible?

"I know that this may not seem the best time for such an event," Elizabeth continued, her brow furrowed with concern. "However, in time you'll come to see it for the blessing that it is. The important thing is for you to take care of yourself and this unborn child."

Ginny tried to contain the excitement that had replaced any evidence of queasiness. "Of course, you could be right," she said. "I mean, about the pregnancy. Perhaps I should have the doctor come just to be certain."

Elizabeth nodded her approval. "I think that's the wisest course. In the meantime, I want you to go upstairs and rest for at least an hour. Mr. Boyle is quite capable of touring the conservatory with me and answering any questions I may have."

"If you really don't mind," Ginny replied, anxious to be alone so that she could digest the full magnitude of the possibility.

"Of course not. I'll ask Mr. Holt to send for the doctor on my way out to the conservatory. You go along and rest."

It was true. She was indeed pregnant. The doctor came and confirmed it and gave strict orders for her to rest as much as possible. Elizabeth and Maggie hovered over her, insisting she stay in bed for the duration of the day. As Ginny stayed in her room, she could hear the excited whispers of the servants as they went about their day. It was as if the news of the coming child had lifted the pall that had held the house in its throes since Thomas's death. Ginny listened to it all and thought about the future.

That night when the house was finally quiet, she went into Thomas's room. She wasn't sure why. It had been closed at her request since the funeral. She had been oddly unprepared to deal with his things, his memory.

Her anger had passed. After all, she, of all people, understood. If Sam had walked into her life in 1899 while Thomas was still alive, could she have resisted her attraction to him? She liked to think she could have, that she was stronger than Thomas, that she was a better person than he had been. The truth was she could not say for sure, and in knowing that she found what she needed to forgive him finally.

She walked around his room, touching his things, savoring the memories of better days and happier times. She sat at his writing desk, opened the slim center drawer, and began sorting through the papers there. It contained personal notes, for the most part—scribbled reminders to himself, letters received from friends, a blue lace handkerchief scented with Katherine's distinctive perfume.

She closed the drawer and pushed away from the desk. Something in the brass holder that sat in the center of the writing desk caught her eye. She slid the envelope from behind the ornately designed holder.

To my dear Ginny . . .

She turned the envelope over and slid her thumb under the seal. Inside was a single folded sheet of thick linen paper.

Dearest Ginny,

Tonight I will break your heart and I have the unmitigated gall to think that you might someday forgive me for that. Please do not rip this page to the shreds it deserves to become until you have read it through.

I have fallen passionately in love with another woman—with Katherine, as you will know by the time you read this. We are leaving tonight. It is the very fact that I understand—we both understand—that we are about to destroy the two dearest people we know that I pray you will understand how desperately I love this woman. I cannot live without her.

Once you and I spoke of passion and the kind of love that torments and excites. We found the idea a little silly, as I recall. Yet, once found, I assure you it is anything but absurd—insane, yes.

I don't mean to ramble. What I am writing to tell you is that this has nothing to do with you. Were I a man in control of his wits I would resist this temptation and stay faithful to the most remarkable woman God ever placed on the face of the earth. You are the dearest, most caring indi-

*vidual I know, and I am an utter fool to leave you.
Dare I hope that because of your innate goodness
you might one day find it in your heart to forgive
me?*

Dearest, dearest, Ginny. . . .

This last line trailed off the page, and she knew that
he had simply given up the effort to find words to explain what he was about to do. He had planned to run
away with Katherine. That's what they had argued
about. It occurred to Ginny that perhaps they were to
have left that night she had seen Katherine in the upstairs
hallway. In the end, it no longer mattered, for Thomas
was right. She did understand. She could forgive and
move on with her life.

"How are you feeling, my dear?" Colonel Sutter asked
as Lucas Holt escorted him into the winter garden for
the meeting Ginny had requested.

"Quite wonderful," Ginny replied.

"You certainly look radiant."

"Thank you."

There was a pause while Ginny gathered her thoughts,
and the colonel waited politely for her to state the reason
for asking him to meet with her.

"Colonel Sutter, I want first to say to you that your
kindness and generosity have been most appreciated
both by me and by my staff. As you are aware, it was
quite important to me that the events of last December
not destroy the long history of service and good works
that my family—and indeed, Thomas in his better days—
had worked so hard to achieve."

"It has been my pleasure, Ginny."

"I believe that with your help and that of my dear
friends, Tucker and Katherine, I have achieved everything I intended to set to rights following Thomas's
death. My work here is done, and it is time for me to

concern myself with my future and that of my unborn child."

The colonel frowned. "I don't understand."

"I will be leaving Malmaison, Colonel, as soon as possible."

"But, my dear Ginny, where will you go, and at a time like this, is travel really the wisest course?"

Ginny smiled. "Perhaps not, but I must go. Please understand that I have thought this through very carefully and I know I have come to the proper decision. My child and I must find our own future—a future that he or she can own, not one that has been handed to us by your generosity."

"I can see that you are determined. Is there nothing I can do to dissuade you?"

"I'm afraid not. I'm sure Tucker has probably told you that once I make my mind up about something, I am quite strong in my convictions, Colonel."

"He has alluded to a certain streak of stubbornness," Sutter admitted with a smile.

"Then it is settled. With your permission, I shall say nothing of this to anyone else. I shall leave personal letters of farewell for my servants and closest friends. If I could ask one more favor?"

"Name it."

"I will say in my notes that I have gone to make a new life in another part of the country. I will of necessity be cutting all ties to my rather painful past. I will ask everyone to understand. If you could support that, I would be deeply grateful."

"And is that the truth, Ginny?" His eyes probed hers, looking for some sign, some hidden meaning.

Ginny was tempted to tell him the truth—that she would, if at all possible, find her way back to the future where she and Sam would be together and raise their child. "If it is possible," she replied.

"And if not?" The colonel clearly was not going to let her off the hook.

"Then I shall find another life. Either way, I cannot stay in this place at this time," she said, and it was as close as she could come to telling him the whole truth.

"As you wish. You know that Elizabeth is going to be very upset with me for letting you go and not telling her."

Ginny smiled. "She'll forgive you in time. Tell her that I said I had to do this for my child." She stood up, signaling the end of the meeting.

"I insist that you permit me to fund your journey," the colonel said.

"That won't be necessary," Ginny replied.

The colonel stood as well, and then he leaned over and kissed her cheek. "You are a remarkable woman, Ginny Thornton. I hope you find what you're looking for in this world."

"Thank you, Colonel. Thank you for everything. I'll never forget you or your kindness."

The colonel hesitated for one second and then picked up his hat and left the room.

Ginny sat back down. Now all she had to do was figure out how to get to Sam. She laughed with delight as she thought of the perfect plan.

Chapter 19

SAM HAD FRANKLY had it. Freddie and Kate walked around looking like somebody died. His mother called him daily to ask if there had been any word from Ginny. Unprepared to give up entirely on the possibility that Ginny might reconsider and join him back in his time, he had told Emily that Ginny had been called away on a family emergency.

Meanwhile the work progressed—on the restoration of the house and on the advancement of his discovery. The past and the future filled his days. Longing for Ginny filled his nights. He was impatient with the work, knowing he needed to monitor both projects, but longing to be free of the responsibility. He wanted to be with Ginny, whatever the cost. Someone else could see the dianthus project through. Someone else could take the fame. All he wanted was Ginny.

"I'm going for a run," he muttered to no one in particular, and left the conservatory. He had begun to notice that his black mood was affecting his staff as well as the workers renovating the house. Everyone around him seemed glum, and they worked as if they were marking time.

Outside he paused and took a deep breath. Spring was definitely in the air. The sun was out, and the last of the snow had melted. He trudged over to the gardener's cottage and changed into his running clothes. It occurred to him that he didn't even have a picture of Ginny. There was not one thing in the cottage to say she had ever existed in his life, and yet the cottage, the house, the conservatory were all filled with her essence. *Damn*.

He took off through the woods, pounding off the strides as if the harder he ran, the less he might think of her. He reached the footbridge and noticed the brook running free. He caught a flash of color and saw that seemingly overnight the trillium and bloodroot had burst into bloom. He left the marked trail and ran the narrow path back into the deepest part of the woods until he came to the clearing where her father had built her the outdoor playhouse. Ever since she had told him the story of her special place, he had fantasized about coming here with her. He had thought of them dancing in the meadow and making love under the cover of the cedars.

Why are you torturing yourself this way? Let it go. Let her go.

He reached the foundation and walked its perimeter, careful not to disturb the delicate buds and flowers that formed its floor. He smelled the cedars as they drew him toward the place she had shown him where she would come to play or think, even in the rain.

Suddenly he felt as if something had changed. There was a presence, an aura about the place that hadn't been there before. He lifted a low branch, his heart pounding with anticipation, with a sense of joy such as he had not experienced in weeks.

"Ginny." It was a whisper. "Ginny!" It was a shout of pure jubilance.

She smiled up at him. "Hello, Sam." She held out her

hand for him to help her to her feet. She was dressed in the jeans and T-shirt and sweater she'd been wearing when he took her to New York on the day she had made the transition back to 1899. She was smiling that beautiful smile that would send his heart into overdrive for the rest of his days.

He touched her face, her hair, her shoulders as if trying to assure himself that this was no mirage. "What are you doing here?" he asked.

"Oh, well, if that's the kind of welcome we're going to get, we'll just have to go back," she teased and pretended to head back to the shelter.

"Not on your life, lady," he growled and pulled her into his arms for a kiss. "Who's 'we'?" he murmured against her hair after they had been kissing for some time and finally stopped to catch their breath.

Suddenly she became shy with him. He pressed her for information. "You said 'we'—did you bring someone with you?"

"In a manner of speaking. You see, I am . . . That is, we are going to have a child." This last came out in a rush, and then she watched for his reaction with a worried frown.

"A baby?" She might as well have told him that the world would stop turning at precisely 2:07.

She nodded. "I just thought that he or she should know you, be in your world. That's really why I came back. You don't have to marry me, of course."

"Well, that's a relief," Sam replied and saw that she could not hide her disappointment. "On the other hand, since I have thought of nothing else but marrying you since the day I got back here, maybe it wouldn't be such a terrible idea. I mean, if it's okay with you and Junior there."

"We'll discuss it and get back to you," she replied haughtily and started to walk back toward the main path.

"Hey, I'm asking you to marry me," he called as he hurried to catch up with her.

"And I'm saying that your heir and I will consider it. For now, I'm quite anxious to see Freddie and Kate and the others."

"I was kidding around," he explained. "I was kind of blown away by finding you here and then to learn there's a baby on the way. I need some time to—"

"Compute? Put this information through your microscope, perhaps? Dissect it? Why don't you go and make a nice long list of all the pros and cons of my coming back with child while I go visit with Freddie and Kate."

"What are you so steamed about?"

She whirled around to face him. "I have had a rather difficult past several weeks. I have moved heaven and earth, not to mention the possible alignment of the planets, to journey forward through time—for the *second* time—just so that you might have the pleasure of knowing your offspring. I am tired and a bit out of sorts. Deal with it," she said in a perfect imitation of the outspoken Kate's favorite phrase.

Then she wrapped her arms tightly around her stomach, gave a low moan, and dropped to her knees.

"Let's get you up to the house," Sam said as calmly as he could manage, given the fact that he was terrified of losing her, the baby, or both. He lifted her and headed for the mansion.

"Freddie? Kate?" he bellowed once inside the house.

"Omigod, she's back," Kate whooped as soon as she and Freddie appeared at the top of the stairway and saw Sam with Ginny in his arms.

"Get a doctor out here now," Sam ordered as he strode past them and went directly to Ginny's bedroom. "We're pregnant, and something's not right."

Freddie and Kate exchanged a look and quickly went into action.

The doctor came and ordered everyone, including Sam, out of the room. He was a friend of Emily's whom Freddie knew could be counted on to make a house call and be discreet about the news he discovered in making his examination.

Sam, Freddie, and Kate paced the upstairs living quarters as the clock chimed the quarter hour, the half hour, and finally the three-quarter hour.

"I'm going in there," Sam muttered and headed for the door just as the doctor left the room.

"She's sleeping now. She seems quite exhausted. I've left some prescriptions on the bedside table for prenatal vitamins and such. I'll expect to see her on a weekly basis for a few weeks and then we can establish a regular schedule once we know the babies are fine."

"Babies?" Freddie repeated. "As in, more than one?"

"I'm not positive but I'm fairly certain that I heard more than a single heartbeat. We'll get her into the office in a day or so and do an ultrasound."

"But Ginny is all right," Sam pressed.

"Yes. Quite a healthy young woman. I wouldn't recommend any traveling for the duration of the pregnancy, however. Just a precaution."

"You have my word, Doc. She's not going anywhere."

Freddie showed the doctor out, and Kate went to get the prescriptions filled. Sam sat with Ginny, watching her sleep, hardly daring to believe that she was actually here, that they were actually about to become parents.

"Ginny," he said softly as he stroked her hair away from her forehead. "I don't care what you say. I'm going to marry you, and we're going to raise our children here in *your* house, and that's that."

Without opening her eyes, she smiled and said, "Ask me nice, and I might say yes."

The wedding was held in the gardens on a balmy May evening. Emily had returned in time to take charge of everything, and the results were magnificent. The guests entered the mansion and strolled through the beautifully

restored downstairs rooms where they sampled appetizers from a variety of food stations and sipped vintage
wine.

At the appointed hour they were invited to move out
into the gardens, past the three reflecting pools and clas-
sic statuary of the formal Italian garden and into the
walled garden with its thousands of spring flowers in
full bloom. Tulips of every color vied with the trum-
peting glory of the daffodils for attention, and tucked
along each path were clusters of fragrant hyacinths and
delicate bushes of bleeding heart.

Along one side of the garden ran the arbor that connected the mansion to the conservatory, its vines inti-
mately entwined and just beginning to leaf. Kate had
created an extraordinary floral canopy for the wedding
party to stand under at the far end of the garden. A string
quartet played as the ushers escorted the guests into the
outdoor sanctuary to the strains of Chopin.

Ginny looked out the window of her bedroom at the
spectacle unfolding before her. Sam's parents had welcomed her into their family circle without hesitation.
Sam loved her, and that was all they needed to know.

"Ready, kiddo?" Kate entered the room with her usual
flair.

Ginny smoothed her gown over her slightly protrud-
ing stomach. "I just wish—"

"Oh, honey, people don't think anything of a little
pregnancy these days. They're just happy for you and
Sam. Look at you—a vision." She made a tiny adjustment to Ginny's upswept hair. "Perfect. Time to go.
Your groom awaits."

Sam stood next to his father who was also his best man.
He barely heard the music or saw the hundreds of guests.
He was only interested in seeing one person today—
Ginny. He watched as Kate appeared at the entrance to
the arbor. She was Ginny's sole attendant and was thor-

oughly enjoying the job. Sam could not help but smile as she passed him and gave him a wink.

Then Freddie, who was directing the wedding, signaled the string quartet to strike up the wedding march, and Ginny appeared at the entrance to the arbor on the arm of Sebastian Corwell. Sam knew that Ginny felt that she had completed the circle in asking Sebasian to escort her to the altar. He was the grandson of her dearest friend in that other life. For Ginny it symbolized her final peace with the past.

The play of the shadows of the entwined vines kept Sam from seeing her as well as he wanted to until she appeared at the opening of the arbor. It was worth the wait.

The setting sun played with the highlights of her upswept red hair. The gown was a delicate translucent concoction of lace and tulle that barely skimmed her shoulders with its wide square neckline but covered her arms to her delicate wrists and fell from its high waistline in a straight line to her ankles. She carried a bouquet of bright red malmaison carnations interspersed with a lacy cloud of baby's breath. She wore no veil, and her flawless skin made her emerald eyes all the more beautiful as she walked slowly toward him. He was fairly positive that this was going to be the longest evening of his life, since at the moment all he wanted was to have her all to himself without the witness of several hundred friends and family.

They repeated their vows, heard the quiet sniffling of Sam's mother and sisters and the more pronounced weeping of Kate, and it was done.

"Ladies and gentlemen," the minister announced, "it is my great pleasure to present Dr. and Mrs. Samuel Sutter."

The quartet struck up the celebratory music as they kissed and then worked their way down the aisle, stopping often to accept the good wishes of the guests and to hug members of Sam's extended family. Freddie hustled them into the conservatory where they would form a receiving line, take more pictures, and greet their guests. In the dwindling light of the day, the conservatory was alight with dozens of candles.

"It is truly the wedding of the century," Kate enthused as she sipped champagne and watched the milling crowd.

"That's a record that's going to have to stand for some time," Freddie replied with a wry smile. "After all, this is the first year of a long century."

"Nevertheless, anybody who ever thought about being anybody is here," Kate said and took off to say hello to a former client.

"It's almost time for dinner," Freddie told Ginny. "The wedding party should lead the way back to the house now."

"Pour everyone some more champagne, Freddie. I want a moment alone with my bride." Sam took Ginny's elbow and led her out a side door and into the garden. "I have a surprise for you." He handed her a small, gift-wrapped box.

"Sam, what have you done?" she asked, but he could tell that she was pleased with the gesture. She unwrapped the box and lifted the top. "A key?" She looked up at him.

"Read the inscription," he urged.

She lifted the flat silver key ring that held a single key. "Welcome to Malmaison—Ginny and Sam's Place," she read aloud, and then she wrapped her arms around his neck. "I love you so very much," she whispered.

"I'm having the west wing converted into living quarters for us and the kids," he told her. "Is that all right?"

"It's wonderful," she said as she fought against the lump of emotion that hindered her ability to speak.

Sam stood behind her with his arms around her as they looked at the mansion. "It's yours, darling. Welcome home."

"Oh, Sam, it's perfect, but are you sure? I mean, you love the cottage."

"Oh, we're keeping the cottage," he replied with a grin. "It'll be our little hideaway—strictly off limits to kids and parents."

She blushed. "Sam, what will your mother think?"

"She's frankly delighted and thinks you are some sort of miracle worker." He kissed her, meaning it to be a kiss of celebration of the moment, but knowing it would quickly become something far more intimate. "Do you think they'd miss us if we checked out the cottage now?"

She giggled. "I could always fake a fainting spell."

"Heaven forbid. My mother, my sisters, and Kate would all go into superhovering mode, and I wouldn't be able to get near you until after these kids are born."

"Then I guess we'll just have to make the best of it," she replied and bit his ear lightly before letting him go.

"Keep this in mind, lady, I've been waiting for that dress to fall off those beautiful shoulders all evening and I've already figured out a most ingenious way of making sure that it does the minute we're alone."

"You are terrible," she chastised, but she was laughing, and her eyes sparkled with delight.

"It's part of my charm."

They returned to the reception where Freddie was checking his watch, and gave a great sigh of relief. "I thought the two of you might have taken off for the nineteenth century again," he huffed.

"Not going to happen, my friend," Sam assured him. "Now, let's get this show on the road. I'm starving, and my bride needs her rest."

MALMAISON, NEW YEAR'S EVE, 2024

"Mother, sometimes you can be extraordinarily Victorian," Samantha complained in her dramatic sixteen-year-old style. "Everyone drinks champagne on New Year's Eve. *Babies* are given a taste, for heaven's sake."

"I am not everyone, and you are no baby," Ginny replied calmly. "Now, sit still and let me help you with your hair."

"I don't know why we have to have these dumb period parties every year. And this year is the worst. Roaring Twenties indeed. According to my history teacher, the country almost went under while people laughed and drank and danced the stupid Charleston."

"Don't let your auntie Kate hear you call the Charleston stupid," Ginny warned, "or you're likely to find yourself out on the dance floor learning the steps."

Samantha groaned.

"And I suppose we can count on you and Daddy doing your usual disappearing act at midnight," she said with a heavy sigh.

"Your father and I have celebrated the new year in a traditional way throughout our marriage. When you are married with a home and family of your own, then you may choose your own traditions."

Samantha grinned at her mother's image reflected in the mirror. "Are you saying that it'll be all right for me to slip away and shack up with my husband?" she teased. "You know, making wild passionate love in the old gardener's cottage smacks of Lady Chatterly and her lover."

"Samantha!"

"*Very* Victorian," Samantha repeated as she slipped away from the dressing table and headed for the door. "I'll go see if Tweedle-Dee and Tweedle-Dum are ready yet."

She had begun calling her twin brothers by the ridiculous nickname from the day she had first read *Alice in Wonderland.* Even now that one of her brothers headed one of the country's most successful Internet businesses and her other brother was at the top of his class in medical school, she continued to torment them.

Ginny checked her own image in the full-length mirror. For a woman over fifty, she didn't look half bad. For a woman who by some accounts was nearly three times that age, she looked downright remarkable. She giggled and kicked up her heel, flapper-style.

"What's so funny?" Sam asked as he entered the room and frowned. He was fumbling with the bow tie that matched his tuxedo. "Who invented these things?" he grumbled.

"Let me," Ginny said and expertly finished the job.

"You look wonderful, as always." He ran his fingers through her short hair. "When Kate told me that you'd cut your hair, I was very upset."

"That's why I sent Kate to tell you," Ginny admitted. "I wanted you to have some time to calm down before you actually saw me."

"Well, I love it. It's like seeing a whole new side of you."

"Just wait until later," she whispered.

"Don't start," he warned.

"Start what?" she asked with wide-eyed innocence.

"You know damn well what," he growled as his mouth covered hers. She felt his hands roaming over her, discovering the fact that she wore very little underneath the beaded dress. She pressed her body to his and deepened the kiss.

"Whoa, this is definitely *not* Victorian," Samantha squealed as she opened the door and stared at her parents.

Sam broke the kiss but kept Ginny plastered to his own aroused body. "Kid, one of these days you're going to learn to knock and one of these days when you're old enough, your mother is going to explain to you exactly what *Victorian* is."

"Geez," Samantha groaned as she backed out of the room and closed the door. "Well, the party's getting started and Auntie Kate and Uncle Freddie are going to go ballistic if you two aren't there," she added as she made a grand show of stomping down the hall of the west wing. "Yo, 'Dee and 'Dum, it's showtime," she added for effect as she passed the guest rooms where her brothers were staying for the holidays.

"We'd better go," Ginny said softly as she and Sam stood holding each other, their passion banked for the time being.

"One dance," he said and began to move slowly around the room with her in perfect rhythm to the music only the two of them could hear.

Author's Note

While in researching this book I came across some interesting theories and experiments that involved the use of carnations for the potential treatment of disease, the passages related to research and medicine are purely fictional. It is my personal belief that the only true fountain of youth lies in the spirit of innocence and wonder that resides in each of us, regardless of our age.

TIME PASSAGES